FINDING FRIENDS ON BEAMER STREET

SHEILA RILEY

First published in Great Britain in 2022 by Boldwood Books Ltd. This paperback edition first published in 2023.

1

Cover Design by Colin Thomas Photography

Cover Photography: Alamy

A CIP catalogue record for this book is available from the British Library. Paperback ISBN: 978-1-83518-807-1

Hardback ISBN: 978-1-80483-278-3

Ebook ISBN: 978-1-80483-276-9

Kindle ISBN: 978-1-80483-277-6

Audio CD ISBN: 978-1-80483-284-4

MP3 CD ISBN: 978-1-80483-281-3

Digital audio download ISBN: 978-1-80483-275-2

Digital audio MP3 ISBN: 978-1-80483-282-0

Large Print ISBN: 978-1-80483-279-0

Boldwood Books Ltd.

23 Bowerdean Street, London, SW6 3TN

www.boldwoodbooks.com

PROLOGUE

CASHALREE – IRELAND, JULY 1921

'Shaving on a Friday! Are you in court, Paddy?' Christie 'Red' Redfern focused on his twin brother with blurry, beer-soaked eyes and gave a mirthless laugh.

'You know your own tricks best, Red,' answered Paddy, soaping his chin. 'I am in no humour for you today.'

'For sure.' Red shrugged his shoulders and scowled, his head thumping, he could well do without Paddy's pontificating. Older by just half an hour, Paddy never failed to remind him by word or deed that he was *The Chosen One*. Ever eager to show him the error of his ways. Red thought of the trips he made to Liverpool when he could do whatever he liked away from Paddy's scrutiny and constant nagging.

'Have you fed the pigs?' Paddy's reflection glared through the rust-speckled mirror.

'It's done,' Red replied with a definite nod of his head. *Well, it will be when I get me head on straight. What a blinding night that was.*

'What time did you get in?'

Here we go again. Red sighed deeply, unable to recall the

exact time, maybe around dawn. 'Not late.' Red was desperate to put his head on the pillow and sleep. *Depending on how you look at it. I was home very early – but not on the same day I went out.* He decided not to share this information with Paddy. He looked as happy as a man going to the gallows. Still drunk, the thought made Red want to giggle. Nevertheless, Saint Paddy would not approve, so he remained as straight-faced as he could. Paddy was an eejit. Working all the hours sent. He was good for a few bob, though, when times were hard, and friends were few.

'It's about time you pulled your weight, Red, I won't always be here.'

'I don't know why you put so much work into the place, it isn't even ours.'

'No, the farm isn't *ours*. But it could be,' Paddy answered through the mirror.

'Sure, why would I be after breaking my back for such little reward?' *When I can tap a mug like you.*

'Instead of drinking every penny, you could save up, like me.'

'Well, seeing as you're so flush, could you see your way clear to—' His head bobbed like a cork on water, his hazy eyes wide and expectant.

'I'm not lending you another penny!' Paddy cut his brother's begging request mid-sentence. Ever since they were born, Red had depended on his twin's generous nature.

Red scowled, pulling down the peak of the cap he had worn from the night before, his corduroy trousers and shirt crumpled, he had missed some badly needed sleep rehearsing what he would say to Paddy, to whom, he had conveniently forgotten, he still owed money. His refusal was like a smack in the kisser, for sure!

'C'mon, Paddy, it's only for a few days.' He tried not to sound desperate as he eyed the determined jut of Paddy's jaw through the mirror.

Slowly, tantalisingly, Paddy drew a long streak of soap and stubble from the side of his face with an open razor, saying nothing, building up Red's hope.

'Sure, you'll get it back by next Friday. It's only a loan. Seven measly days.' Red tugged the cotton loops on the blue candlewick bedspread until there was a bald patch. 'I'll even pay you interest. How's that?'

'That's good of you,' Paddy said ruefully, dimming Red's hopes.

Sitting on the end of the double bed he shared with his twin brother, Red was silent as his foot impatiently tapped the bare floorboards. It would not do to rush Paddy into a decision. He liked his bit of power, and Red was usually happy to oblige. But today, he was in a hurry. He had to pay Dinny O'Mara. Although, he knew if he sounded anxious, Paddy would make him wait until the very last minute before giving him the money he so desperately needed. *The last minute is here, Paddy and you are my only chance of staying attached to my kneecaps.*

'You want to buck your ideas up.' Paddy said through a face half full of lather.

I'll keep it in mind, Father Christmas. Red's thoughts were as sour as the taste in his mouth. He did not voice his thoughts, obviously. Instead, he went for a repentant expression, nodding his head in all the right places. 'I know. You're right, Paddy. And I will.'

'You've got to get a grip of yourself, lay off the drink,' Paddy told him. 'Come in at a respectable hour, and stay away from the rebels.'

'This'll be the last time, Paddy. Honest t' God.' He wanted to knock Paddy's patronising block off so much.

'You say that every time.'

Fer Jaysus' sake! Will yer leave me with a bit of dignity! Red raked stubby fingers through thick black hair. *D'you want me to get down on bended knees? Do ya?* Red knew he had to keep his paper dry. Once he had the money, he could tell Paddy exactly what he thought, but until then, he would have to play the penitent, apologetic game.

'Well, you're out of luck this time, Red, I am sorry.'

'What!' A small explosion went off inside Red's head. He checked it. Paddy was serious. Red glared at his brother through the mirror, leaning over the washbowl. Paddy's expression was one of determined concentration. An expression that told Red he had closed the subject. It was over. Done with. Red felt the anger swell inside him, his temples throbbing. He had to sit here and listen to Paddy spouting rubbish about him saving for a future, and the bastard wasn't going to lend him the money after all!

'There's no end to it, Red,' Paddy said, waggling his razor in the water to remove the thick white suds. 'My money feels like it's on an elastic band. Back and forth, I'm losing track.'

You are loving this. Red knew he could not blow; Paddy might just change his mind. He tried another tack. 'I wouldn't ask, Pad, but you see...' Red would play on his brother's protective nature. 'I owe Dinny O'Mara, and he wants his money today.'

'Then he will have to want,' Paddy said, calm as you like, 'because I haven't got it to lend you.' He turned his cheek and slid the open razor down the other side.

'C'mon, Paddy, you know as well as I do, O'Mara's not a

man you can say no to.' Red glared at the back of his brother's head. Paddy wouldn't deny him now, surely?

'That's a pity, Red, but I have not got the money.'

'What d'you mean you haven't got it? You're loaded!' Red swallowed the volcanic anger rising inside of him. Paddy was being awkward. He wondered if he should mention what he saw his twin brother and Mary Jane Starling doing in the hayloft... He decided against it and would drop that bombshell only if matters got desperate and Paddy dug his size twelves in.

'I *was* loaded, Red, but that was before.'

'Before what?' Red's curiosity tempered the rising anger he found hard to quell.

'Before I bought a couple of boat tickets and decided to go to church.' Paddy looked smug as he continued shaving.

'I hope you'll say one for me while you're there.' If Dinny O'Mara got hold of him, he was going to need all the prayers he could get.

'I'm not going to mass; I went to the early one this morning.' Paddy's voice held a note of admonishment 'But you wouldn't know that because you weren't home.'

'So why are you going?' Red ignored the slight, but he knew confession was not until tomorrow.

'Because, brother, I'm getting married.'

So, that's what the boat tickets were for. A honeymoon!

'Mary Jane?' Her name came out like a gasp of air.

Through the looking glass, Paddy stretched his neck, pressing soapy lips together while making little upward swipes to his chin with the lethal-looking razor.

'Jaysus!' Red's voice was hang-over hoarse. He could not believe it. 'Mary Jane?' Slowly he shook his head.

'Just a quiet ceremony.'

'I'm happy for you.' *You bastard.* Mary Jane was the most

beautiful girl in all of Cashalree, if not the whole of Ireland. Did Paddy have any more grenades to throw? First the money, then Mary Jane! The girl he had set his sight on years ago. 'When are you going to marry her?'

'Half an hour,' Paddy answered succinctly. 'I want you to be my best man.'

'Are you mad?' Red could not keep the astonishment from his voice. 'Do her brothers know?' Mary Jane had three older, very protective, well-respected brothers who would not take kindly to losing the only woman of the house.

Watching Paddy finish his shave, softly whistling as he dried his cut-throat razor on the towel around his neck, Red knew Paddy was taunting him. The low, arrogant whistle told Red *he* was the loser.

However, he wouldn't be if he opened his mouth, would he? Red knew what they had been getting up to. He had followed them into the barn, and what he saw had confirmed his suspicions. Nevertheless, from that moment on, he knew no peace. Thoughts of Mary Jane tormented him day and night. In his dreams, it was not Paddy enjoying her soft silken flesh and seductive curves, Mary Jane was not making passionate love to his brother – she was with him. The dreams were driving him mad. Goading him. Tormenting him. Reminding him, he was second best. Why else would he drink strong beer and whisky every night? It was all Paddy's fault. Once again, Paddy had landed on his feet. Paddy, his father's golden boy. The chosen one. The second bloody coming of Christ!

'Too slow to get out of your own road...' Paddy's words rang in his head.

'Not like your brother, the first-born.' Dar had said, more than once. Paddy was akin to royalty in their parents' eyes.

'Have you told Dar?' This, he had to see. Their father would go berserk, his eldest son marrying on the quiet, he would want the biggest of hoolies for Paddy. Red suspected the uncontrollable rage that made grown men scatter was the only thing he would ever inherit from Dar.

'I'm not telling him.' Paddy shook his head, taking great care to straighten the grey tie over his good white shirt. A new one. 'Let's get it over with.' Paddy hoisted his charcoal-coloured jacket off the hook behind the bedroom door. When he turned to face him, Red was sure he could see doubt in his brother's eyes.

* * *

'You want me to stand for you? You won't even lend me the money to get O'Mara off my back.' Red could not believe the arrogance of his twin brother.

'Be told, will you!' Paddy flung the words over his shoulder as Red followed him. The pounding in his head was getting louder.

'Why didn't she tell her brothers about the marriage?' Red asked as they headed down a narrow path that sliced through the barley fields towards St Helen's church.

'They'd kill her... and me.' Paddy's dark eyes were hooded, and he took a deep breath. 'But she'll have nothing to fear when we move to Liverpool'.

Red stopped. They weren't coming back! The news hit him like a runaway stallion and took the wind right out of him. He couldn't breathe. Paddy was taking Mary Jane away!

'What about the farm?' he gasped. Surely Paddy wasn't expecting him to tend it.

'We'll be back in a couple of years maybe. We've got no choice.'

Red's body tightened. What a bloody fool he had been. Biding his time. Waiting for Mary Jane to tire of his workhorse of a brother. What kind of life was that for the beautiful girl *he* wanted so badly it hurt? 'And you'll all live happily ever after in Liverpool.' Red's voice was dull and flat, and he gave another scornful half-laugh.

'It's not what we planned,' Paddy answered, enraging him even more. Some men didn't know how lucky they were.

Red, walking beside Paddy, hands in pockets, resented his brother more than he had ever done. *Good-fellow-well-liked. Always doing the right thing. Always rubbing my nose in it.* The back of Red's throat curled.

'You'll have to work the farm. Stay away from the rebels,' Paddy threw the words over his shoulder, 'make something of yourself... Hurry now, we don't have much time.' His voice went on, and on, and on until the mist that gave Red his colourful sobriquet descended.

1

CASHALREE – JULY 1921

'Run, Mary Jane. Run like the wind. Don't look back!'

Twenty-one-year-old Mary Jane Starling turned instinctively, her feet moving faster. She had wings on her sturdy heels as Red pulled her from the edge of the Castletown River that flowed into Dundalk Bay on the east coast of Ireland. She had been expecting to meet Paddy. Something was wrong. Every nerve in her body screaming, instinctively knowing she should not ask. But still she asked the question. 'Red, what is it?' She kept pace with his rapid strides, her heart pounding. 'Where's Paddy?'

'We've got to get out of here before they see us,' Red gasped, dragging her further up the hill.

Mary Jane was wary, Red had not the same temperament as his mild-mannered brother. 'Who? The Black and Tans?' She knew Red liked a bit of excitement and was mixed up with people who had strong opinions and acted upon them. He was always up to something; it was only a matter of time before his antics caught up with him.

'No, not the Black and Tans!' Red spat. 'Your brothers.

They're after scull-dragging our Paddy…' His twin brother marrying Mary Jane, not even giving his predicament a second thought, had been the last straw for Red.

'Jaysus!' Mary Jane gasped. 'What did they do that for?' Her three brothers, although fiercely protective of her, were in different stages of becoming doctors like her deceased parents and were accustomed to heal, not harm. Barely able to breathe, she kept running, trying to heave air into her lungs. Everybody in the small village of Cashalree knew her highly regarded brothers, and this action was out of character for any of them. But she didn't have time to think straight, everything was moving so fast. Her heart hit her ribs like the bullets from the Vickers machine gun Red had secreted in his family's barn after coming back from the trenches.

When they reached the top of the hill, they flopped down, breathless, and Mary Jane's delicate stomach turned in disgust when she saw Red hawk thick mucus from the back of his throat and spit it onto the grass.

After a few silent minutes, her breathing calmed. There were so many questions going round in her head. She could hardly make sense of them all.

'We told nobody of our plans,' Mary Jane said eventually.

'The priest's housekeeper could have told someone,' Red sneered. 'Cashalree is a small village. It wouldn't take long for word to get out.'

Mary Jane's heart sank. Looking to her trembling hands, she knew the left one was the wrong side of a wedding ring. Paddy had her gold band in the jacket pocket of his only suit. He was going to make an honest woman of her.

Red, quiet, his eyes lowered, avoiding her questioning gaze, knew dread weighed heavily on Mary Jane's slim shoulders, and he was glad she was afraid. It would make things easier.

'Something bad has happened?' There was a quiver in her voice when she spoke. 'Tell me, Red...' Terrified, her voice rose. 'Where is he?'

Hugging his knees to his chest, Red blew out his cheeks, looking out over the patchwork fields below, choosing his words carefully, he eventually lifted his head to answer. 'They... they left him for dead, Mary Jane...' His stilted words were little more than a whisper. 'Paddy's dead.'

'No!' She bit back a scream. 'My brothers?' She watched involuntarily, as blood dribbled down his forehead to mingle with the tears running down his cheeks.

'It's not safe for you here,' Red cut in quickly. Standing up, he reached for her hand, 'I've to get you to Liverpool. They'll come after you next!'

'They attacked you, too?' Mary Jane registered the deep, open gash in his forehead.

'Never mind that. We can't stop.' He pulled her to her feet, and Mary Jane disregarded the mud that splashed her loose, pale blue coat, fastened at the hip with a single button, which she had bought specially for her wedding day. Nor did she notice the damage to her silk stockings from the gorse bushes that gouged her legs. She felt nothing but fear twisting her insides. Paddy was dead. Paddy was...!

'But how?' she gasped, holding on to her pale blue cloche hat with its white silk, eye-level daisy, her eyes darting over her shoulder, keeping a look-out for any sign of her brothers. 'Why is he dead?'

'I don't know,' Red lied, gripping her hand tighter. 'They came after him.'

'We were meeting at the church. We were to be married... Taking the night ferry...'

'Aye,' Red's tone was shaky, 'well, that's not going to

happen.' Paddy had fought well enough, but even he could not withstand a heavy cobble to the back of his head. Red flinched but could not dwell. 'C'mon now, keep up.' His voice came out in short bursts. 'They caught him on the low road.' He lied, looking back, pulling her over bracken and lumpy turf. She stumbled, but Red would not allow her to slow down. He had to get away from here, away from Dinny O'Mara, away from what he'd done.

'We must go to him!' Mary Jane's voice was urgent, her eyes wide, stark against the insipid pallor of her skin as tears ran freely down her cheeks. 'Why would you leave your twin brother on the road like that?' They were running so fast, she feared for her unborn child.

Red stopped suddenly, looking deep into her haunting pale green eyes, and said slowly, as if talking to a child, 'He's not there any more, Mary Jane. There's nothing we can do for him. O'Hanlon took him.'

'O'Hanlon? The undertaker!' Mary Jane tried to pull her hands free, but Red was too strong.

'We have to get away. We don't have long! Paddy wanted me to help you. They were his last words...'

Mary Jane fumbled in her pocket. 'I've got these,' she gasped, taking two boat tickets from her coat pocket, and handing them to Red. But something told her not to mention the money Paddy had added to her savings. The money that would set them up when they got to Liverpool. She had heard about Red's reckless reputation and was wary. Paddy was the quiet one of the Redfern brothers, gentle and kind. Whereas Red was a seditious rabble-rouser. The life and soul of the party until his money ran out. 'I'm scared!'

'C'mon,' Red's whisper had an urgency she had never heard before. 'I'll make it better.' He could not allow her to ask questions. In time, she would come to love him, the way she had loved Paddy. Until then, there was always Cissie.

'Red,' Mary Jane's voice trembled. 'I'm going to have Paddy's baby?' The silence went on forever, hanging heavy in the stillness of the hot summer air. There was not even the gentle sigh of a breeze. Nor the chirrup of birdsong. The news hit him like a kick in the guts. His brows furrowed in a tight pleat that made his head hurt and he did not trust himself to speak immediately. He recalled Paddy prattling about something, back at the farm. But he wasn't listening, his mind concentrating on getting the money he owed to Dinny O'Mara. But to hear this now, from Mary Jane... His upper lip curled.

Mary Jane's insides shrunk when she noticed the muscle in Red's jaw twitch. The disgust in his narrowed eyes plainly obvious. The same expression, she imagined, not only of her brothers, but on the face of everyone in Cashalree.

'I'm going to have a baby...' Her eyes were downcast. 'That's why the wedding had to be quiet. So my brothers didn't find out.' Her brothers were not violent men, but they were protective of her. There was no telling what they would do about her shame, but she hadn't expected them to hurt Paddy...kill him.

'Bloody eejit!' Red's lips drew back in a snarl. 'They will burn our farm to the ground for this. Then they'll come after you. Have no doubt about that. And when they do, God help you, Mary Jane.'

She let out a low, terrified whimper. She had lost her man. Her brothers would come looking for her. Mary Jane looked to Red, knowing he had always been jealous of Paddy. She shook her head, throwing off an improbable thought. They were twins, for heaven's sake. Nevertheless, she found it just as difficult to believe her brothers would do such a thing either. Her thoughts were in turmoil. She would be hunted like an animal by the men who had raised and protected her. They would not shield her now. In all her twenty-one years, she had never known terror like this. She had no choice but to leave her homeland, escape the humiliation. In Liverpool, she would be anonymous.

'That child you're carrying won't stand a chance when they catch up with you.' Red wanted her to feel the blast of shock that he had felt. He wanted to hurt her with words if nothing else. 'You'll be lucky to rear it, they'll go for you first and then the baby, you mark my words, Mary Jane, they will.'

'Oh, Red,' Mary Jane whimpered, the shock making her thoughts fly in all directions. 'I've got to get to the port of Dundalk to catch the boat. You have to help me, for Paddy's sake.'

'I'll take you to Liverpool; on the night boat, we'll make it easily,' Red said, not looking at her. 'It's my duty to my brother, and I can't fight three of yours.' He knew her brothers were feared and respected in equal measure on both sides of the Irish border. He also knew they were proud men. Men who would exact revenge for his twin brother's lust, but they were not killers.

'Your head's bleeding again, it needs stitches,' Mary Jane said, thinking how brave Red was to help her after all he had been through.

Red could not look at Mary Jane and, taking a blood-stained rag from his pocket, he dabbed his forehead. Swallowing hard, his mouth dry, he relived the walk to the church in his head...*Paddy you should have taken the rock from my hand. Slapped some sense into me. You should not have turned your back on me...*

2

LIVERPOOL – JULY 1921

'Just hold on one minute, will you!' Mary Jane held on to her cloche hat as a welcoming stiff breeze rolled off the River Mersey from the Irish Sea. Red was craning his neck in search of the man whose hooch he had been sharing all night on the journey over and Mary Jane wondered if she had made the biggest mistake of her life, allowing Red to persuade her she needed a guardian, to come to such a huge place as Liverpool. Ireland was not the safest place to raise a child right now, the clashes between the North and South of her homeland, had resulted in many deaths. And Mary Jane, unmarried by a hair's breadth, was determined she would honour Paddy's memory, by making sure she kept his baby safe.

Standing tall, her chin high and her back straight, Mary Jane held her ground as a rush of people, eager to get to their destination, barged past her as she stepped off the boat. Exhausted through lack of sleep on the trip across the Irish Sea, she was on the verge of losing her patience with Red, who had proved himself useless as a chaperone, and suspected his good deed to his brother was not entirely selfless.

'They're like these blasted bluebottles, noisy and annoying.' Red, keeping his eyes peeled for his drinking companion took off his cap. 'Jaysus, I need a drink.'

'Oh, so you can speak. I began to wonder.' Mary Jane's lips puckered in disdain. All he had done since stepping on the boat at Dundalk was huddle in whispering conversations with men he knew back home.

Standing on the quayside, Mary Jane felt an unsettling heaviness in her chest and fought hard to hold on to the meagre contents of her stomach. But it wasn't the crossing that had made her feel queasy. Her morning sickness lasted all day.

'I will get you settled, Mary Jane, it is the least I can do. You have nobody to support you except me.' Red drove the message home to her that without him she would be at the mercy of every man who looked her way. Her trusting nature – no, her stupidity – had brought her to this Her only hope of escaping her brothers was to depend on Red. She had never felt so alone, so helpless.

'Paddy has a house waiting for us in Woolton,' she said, clutching the heavy carpet bag, her only luggage, which she had packed before setting off to meet Paddy and had briefly returned to the house to get it before going to the port with Red.

'I doubt that will happen now, Mary Jane,' said Red. 'Houses in Woolton don't come cheap and Paddy would haunt me if I didn't look after you properly.'

Mary Jane opened her mouth to speak, but Red cut off her words, obviously loving the sound of his own voice.

'I know of another place. Paddy would approve.' He never took his eyes off the moving crowd. 'He was more than a brother; he was the other half of me. We started life together nine months before we entered the world, him first then me, but he trusted my judgement always.'

'Don't flatter yourself, Red,' she said. Having had a long time to think about the terrible situation she now found herself in, her tongue was sharp. 'You're as slippery as a sack of snakes – Paddy wouldn't trust you to care for a one-eyed cat.'

'I know of a place in Beamer Street,' he said, ignoring her acid retort. 'You'll love it.'

Close to tears, the heat and the crowd were already testing Mary Jane's resilience. Liverpool was supposed to be their lifeline – hers and Paddy's; set them up to give their unborn child the best life. They had dreams of owning their own business, Paddy decided she would work out of sight, while he was out front selling the delicious pies and bread she loved to bake; maybe even opening a teashop. They would do it together. For hadn't she been the best cook and baker in Cashalree. Everybody said so. But her dreams had come crashing down around her when she found out he was dead. This should have been the first day of her married life with the man she loved. How did it all go so tragically wrong?

'You've the child to think about now, Mary Jane,' Red scowled, tapping his foot, and craning his head over the large crowd. Her nostrils flared. She did not need him to tell her about her obligations. Seeming to spot someone he moved away from her.

She was determined to make a new life for herself and her child. She had given no thought to getting rid of her unborn child, nor did she consider giving it away when it was born. She took a deep breath of scorching air with a determination born from keeping three strapping brothers in line after her parents were killed on *Titanic*'s maiden voyage, knowing this was her mess and she would clean it up. While she had a tongue in her head and strength in her fingers, she would do what she and Paddy had set out to do: bake and sell pies and bread, and one day, no matter how long it took, she would have her own shop.

Realising that Red was no longer beside her, she looked around, and caught sight of him, talking to a man he had met on the boat. They had huddled together most of the way here, whispering and plotting. Mary Jane's shoulders dropped. She had no interest in what Red got up to, deciding it was better not to know, but she did not like to be cast aside like something that was of no further use. He had persuaded her he would look out for her, but when he got on the boat, he had barely spoken two words to her, playing cards and drinking with the others.

Now Mary Jane found herself standing alone in the blazing sunshine at Liverpool Docks, not knowing which way to turn. Her eyes scanned the quayside; the teashop across the way looked inviting and she longed for a little shade. The sun was high in the blue sky that matched her wedding outfit. Parched, Mary Jane knew it had been hours since she'd had a cup of tea and her mouth felt like the bottom of Marley's Well, which had dried up years ago.

The need to sit down was overwhelming as the overpowering reek of oil and smoke pervaded her senses, making her stomach lurch, homesick for that crisp, apple scent of the green patchwork fields back home. She could not help but notice the tired-looking women carrying their young on their hip, coddled in sweltering black shawls. While others flicked flies from baskets of fish, and barrows of fruit at the roadside, some were begging from people who looked as if they had little to give.

Mary Jane wanted no part of that. She had worked since

she could walk. She wasn't destitute, having her own and Paddy's savings secreted under her heel in her elegant black leather shoe, with its single bar and tapering toe after which, she was sure, her mother had named her. Mary Jane had always been a saver, beavering away every spare penny for her future, she would need to make her own way, depend on nobody except herself. And that day had come.

Red was now lost in the crowd. Nowhere to be seen as a sun-baked woman, looking older than Methuselah's mother, brushed past her and silently held out her hand. Mary Jane took two pennies from her pocket and placed them in the grubby palm of the old woman's hand.

'May God bless and keep you, Colleen,' she said. 'I can see trouble ahead for you, but the good Lord gave you strong shoulders to carry your burden. And you will be sorely tested – but listen to me when I tell you this, one day you will know the truth, and as one life ends, so your life will begin.'

'I don't believe in such things,' Mary Jane said. Her family were doctors, scientists, educated people who did not hold with such nonsense. Life was what you made it, not ruled by a chance encounter. 'All I want,' Mary Jane told the old crone, 'is a bit of peace and a sit-down.'

Paddy, the only man she had ever loved, was dead and to make matters worse Red seemed to think he was going to step into his brother's shoes. *Well*, she thought, *he could think again*. As soon as she was settled, he could take the next boat out of here. Heading towards the teashop, she stopped momentarily to look up to the magnificent clock towers of the ten-year-old Liver Building, she had read so much about from borrowed library books, wanting to know everything about what was to be their new hometown. Atop each tower were two mythical birds, which Paddy had told her about, one looking into the city to protect its people, and the other looking out to sea, to protect the sailors. Well, that may be the case, Mary Jane thought, looking through the herd of people, and still seeing no sign of Red, and she knew for certain she could rely only on herself to protect her and her unborn child.

'Look out, lady!' a deep male voice called, over the perpetual motion of the dockside, and Mary Jane jumped back, losing her hat in the process as the mass of sweaty bodies closed in. Coming from a rural village, she had never seen so many people. There were hundreds of them. All rushing around like ants in the scorching heat, determined to get to their destination.

'You need to be more careful, ma'am, you could get hurt,' he called from his lofty perch.

Shading her eyes with her hand she looked up to see a man dressed in a long, tan-coloured coat driving his horse and cart along the jetty.

'I beg your pardon, sir,' she said retrieving her hat. 'You almost ran me over!'

Paddy had persuaded her this busy port city was the place to be, explaining they could make a good living here, but she never expected to be run down for her trouble. She suspected she would have to be up before dawn and out before breakfast to keep up with this lot. She was still a little disconcerted when he raised his battered leather fedora in silent regard, and Mary Jane knew if she was ever to survive this busy dockside, she would have to be tougher than most

* * *

Cal Everdine pulled his horse's reins, barely missing the girl in the loose-fitting coat who almost walked under the hooves of his bay mare, too busy looking up to the clock of the Liver Building. In her rush to get onto the sidewalk, her hat flew off and her russet-coloured hair tumbled and glinted in the sunshine. The young woman glared at him with startling absinthe-coloured eyes, as if the near collision was his fault and he had no right to be on her road. As she bent to pick up her hat, he noticed she lost the flower, but she was so intent on giving him a look that would have slayed a lesser man, she didn't even notice. He had one last delivery to make, and he did not want to spend it in the infirmary with this young woman who could not watch where she was going. All he wanted to do was get home, have a long soak and try to cool down.

She was a feisty one, with a spirit he could not help but admire. And going by the scathing look she gave to the curly-haired man in the flat cap, Cal could see, there was no love lost on her part. He shook his head in wonder, as he saw her grip an overstuffed carpet bag and head for the teashop.

3

Mary Jane approached the teashop door, vowing she would not stay on this filthy dockside any longer than was absolutely necessary. She heard Red's familiar whistle cutting through the throng and, against her better judgement, she turned to see him pushing his flat cap to the back of his head and waited until he drew near. When he reached her, he leaned in, his words low and precise.

'Now listen, Mary Jane,' he said as if talking to a five-year-old. Not a word of apology for leaving her standing like an eejit on the jetty, she noticed. 'You go and have a nice cup of tea, and I'll be back before you even know I've gone.'

'Gone where?' Mary Jane's voice sounded calm enough, but she had no idea where she was or where she should go.

'I will fix everything,' Red replied, causing Mary Jane to raise a sceptical brow.

'That'll make a change. Because up to now, you've fixed nothing.' Her next words shot out of her mouth like a bullet from a gun, 'I can't wait to see what kind of pig's ear you'll make of anything.' Turning on her elegant heel, she made her way toward the teashop.

'I won't be long,' Red followed her, trying to make her understand. 'I'll be right back.'

'Don't give it another thought,' she said defiantly, even though she felt a million butterflies had been let loose inside her. 'I'm sure I can find my own way from here.'

'Trust me, Mary Jane.' Red took a deep breath and held onto her arm, his words hushed, like he was in holy mass. She could tell he was trying to reassure her. 'I have to meet somebody.' He was silent for a moment as if thinking. 'I cannot understand why Paddy would leave you with no money?'

'It is not your place to understand.' Mary Jane's voice held no expression. She had no intention of letting Red know she had money which Paddy had given her the last time she saw him, so he wouldn't be tempted to lend it to Red. She should never have trusted a word Red said. He had a reputation for being devious, always looking out for himself, but a woman travelling alone was an easy target. And she must protect her belongings with every weapon in her armoury. 'Who are you meeting?' Mary Jane asked. It was none of her business, of course, but she asked all the same.

'Never mind who.' Red sounded impatient, looking over his shoulder. He thrust a slip of crumpled paper into her hand. 'If I'm not back in half an hour, go and meet me here.'

Opening a crudely drawn map that showed a large X in the centre, she asked, 'Where's this?' pointing to the cross.

'The cross is the town hall,' Red explained, poking the paper. 'If I'm not back, don't forget, meet me there. Will you do that, Mary Jane?' He sounded eager for her to agree, and she reluctantly nodded her head. 'Good girl, now go and have a nice cup of tea and we'll be settled into Beamer Street before you know it.'

'I will be settled. You are not invited,' she said tersely. Then glancing in his direction, she said with a dismissive wave of her hand, 'Your head's bleeding again.'

Red dabbed his head. Giving a cursory glance to his blood-stained fingertips, he wiped them on the seat of his corduroy trousers before brushing the wound with his cuff. 'Don't forget, half an hour...' he called over his shoulder, weaving through the crowds. In seconds he was gone.

Fear of the unknown weighed heavily, and Mary took a deep breath, ignoring the curious glances of passers-by. She had to move along, standing here getting baked by the hot sun was doing her no good at all. Nor did she have any intentions of wallowing or crying her eyes out like a child who'd lost its mammy, no matter how much she longed to do that very thing. Red was a shifty reprobate, but she felt unusually vulnerable without him. He had warned her about the tricksters who cheated gullible people from their possessions. The *sharpers*, he called them, men who stole your belongings the minute you took your eye off them.

Gripping the battered carpet bag, she stepped inside the tearoom, packed with people of every shape and size, and almost ran back out again when she was met by a thick shroud of cigarette smoke. The smell of fried food mixing with the whiff of grimy travellers caused the familiar tingle at the hinge of her jaw, as her mouth filled with saliva. *Don't throw up here*, she silently pleaded, swallowing over and over, unable to turn and flee, forced into the teashop by a group of people behind her, urging her forward.

'Just tea?' the waitress asked when Mary Jane reached the front of the queue, and she nodded, watching the girl pour strong dark tea from a huge teapot along the line of six cups resting on a grid, knowing this delivery probably saved time as the queue of people behind her grew.

'No milk for me,' Mary Jane said, and the girl sighed before fetching another cup.

The tearoom was packed with travellers waiting to board their ship, but she spied an empty table by the window, praying nobody got there first. Her prayer was answered when she managed to sit down. She put her carpet bag on the table, sighed and took out the sheet of paper, which Red had given her. Mary Jane wanted to study it in detail. Not that there was much to study. The 'X' was next to an address. Forty-three, Beamer Street.

'Excuse me,' she asked a passing waitress, 'do you know where this address is, please?'

'Let me have a look,' said the young waitress, who, Mary Jane guessed, was about sixteen or seventeen, and wore her white frilled cap at a jaunty angle over raven-black shingled hair. Her dark calf-length dress was covered with a white apron. She smiled as she took the crumpled sheet of paper. The first friendly face Mary Jane had met, she didn't have long to wait for an answer. 'Beamer Street. Fancy that,' said the waitress, her smile widening, 'I'm Daisy Hayward, I live next door, number forty-five, with me mam and me brothers an' sister.' She gave no indication of where it was until she passed the paper back to Mary Jane. 'It's off the main dock road, big families, mostly Irish, friendly enough. Well, some are... but there's good and bad everywhere, I suppose.' She lowered her voice and said in a conspiratorial tone: 'The houses on our side once belonged to professionals – doctors, solicitors, bank managers, you know – the hoity-toity.' She laughed, in no hurry to move away. 'Number forty-three is a lodging house, these days. Run by Cissie Stone, for Irish navvies who come over to work on the docks. Are you taking up a position there?'

Mary Jane shook her head, and the waitress gave her another nod.

'You want to watch the landlady,' Daisy said in a friendly whisper, then stopped suddenly, a look of alarm clouding her eyes. 'She's not a relation, is she?'

'No, she's not a relation,' Mary Jane said, suppressing a smile. Daisy seemed to be one of those people who spoke first and thought later, but she didn't see any malice in the girl, in fact Mary Jane liked this girl called Daisy, whose plain speaking was refreshing after Red's cryptic instructions.

'Some of the townhouses got turned into lodgings, respectable ones, mind,' Daisy said in that friendly way of most waitresses. 'Cheap enough, but you need a letter from the Holy Ghost to get one of them. The houses on the other side of Beamer Street are smaller, groups of four, with a shop on every corner.'

'Thank you, that's good to know,' Mary Jane answered. She wondered how on earth Red had managed to bag such a sought-after place like Beamer Street, at a time when, it was rumoured, whole swathes of her fellow countrymen existed on little more than bread, dripping and sweet milky tea in cramped courts along the dock road.

Daisy was called away by a customer, 'I'm sure we'll see each other in passing.'

Mary Jane nodded. Usually, she would have been full of questions and would have loved to pass the time of day, but not today, she had too much to think about. Looking out of the window, she saw a man selling matches on the dockside. He had a chest full of medals and one sleeve pinned where his arm should have been. This country was still recovering from the impoverishing effects of the Great War, she thought, three years after it ended. She felt sorry for the brave soldier who had given up his chance of making a decent living and had put his life in danger for his country, and what did he receive in return? A chance to stand on a sun-drenched quayside hoping his matches didn't burst into flames in the heat. Jobs were scarce, but better than back home. It was obvious the man over yonder had to do what he could. Moving the carpet bag off the table and placing it on the floor beside her chair, Mary Jane knew she would have to keep an eye on her mother's clock which was inside it. It was worth a lot of money, but that wasn't the reason she had wanted it. The clock was her security. She suspected Red would leave her stranded and penniless, when the novelty of acting the hero had worn off.

Red, nowhere near as handsome as Paddy, always landed on his feet, no matter how far he dropped, Paddy had told her. There was always a gullible woman willing to pick him up believing she could change him into a hard-working, church-going man. Some hope thought Mary Jane. Red would never work if he didn't have to. He was bone-idle. Unlike Paddy... Poor Paddy. He didn't deserve... No, she couldn't think of him now. She would fall to pieces. Much better to be mad at self-centred Red than publicly cry over what she had lost. She was jolted from her thoughts and knocked over her cup of tea, when a man bent down beside her and reached for the carpet bag. Her green eyes blazing, she scraped back her chair ready to chase after him should the need arise. 'Take your hands off that, this instant, you, you *sharper*!' Mary Jane could feel herself glowing with rage as she pushed his huge hand from her belongings. 'How dare you try to rob me!'

'It was blocking the aisle,' the man said in a deep, low tone that did not carry to the other customers, and Mary Jane noticed his navy-blue gaze soften, the swarthy skin around his wide full lips crinkling in obvious amusement.

'Did I say something funny?' she asked, straightening her back, sitting tall.

'It's a good thing the tea wasn't hot,' the man said.

Mary Jane paused, looking down at the remains of her cold tea. Her freckled nose wrinkled with indignation, she placed the cup back onto the saucer and put the fallen teaspoon back in the cut-glass sugar basin similar to one they had back home. Home... She would probably never see it again.

'I haven't heard the word, *sharper*, for many years,' said Cal Everdine, surmising the angry flash in her green eyes proved his suspicion, she had spirit. Maybe it was right what they said about red-haired women, their striking beauty was matched only by a fiery temper. 'I was worried somebody might trip over it.'

'Is that so?' Mary Jane retorted. Her tone hostile as she snatched up the carpet bag and put it on the chair beside her like a naughty child.

She had an agitated air and Cal considered moving to another table. But there were no free chairs at any of the others.

'It looks heavy,' the man said as Mary Jane kept a protective hand on her bundle and wondered if all men from Liverpool were as forward. This one was as bold as you like.

Mary Jane raised a finely shaped eyebrow. 'To be sure, it's a clever man who can weigh the contents of a carpet bag with his eyes,' she said, her unwavering scrutiny defiantly matching his indigo gaze.

Struck by her eyes, he looked at her for longer than he ought. They drew him in. Stirring up feelings long buried. Just as dangerously, they spoke of hidden secrets he had no right to contemplate.

'Can I help you?' she asked, her gaze direct, unlike some women who would avert their eyes on meeting a stranger for the first time.

He nodded, indicating to the chair opposite. 'Is this seat empty?' His voice was a deep, gravelled drawl. An accent Mary Jane had not heard before. It was English, but there was a hint of something else... American, perhaps?

'Of course, the seat is empty,' she shrugged, 'can you not see that?'

'Do you mind if I sit here?' he asked placing his cup on the table, and Mary Jane wondered if she had said something amusing, because as sure as hens laid eggs, she was certain he was entertained.

'You can sit where you please,' she responded. 'It's a free country – or so they tell me.' She did not elaborate on who 'they' were as he lowered himself into the chair opposite and looked around for the waitress.

He was the man who tried to run her down, Mary Jane realised now. Taller than he first appeared and strongly built. His clothes, although well worn, were not cheapo goods. The ankle-length, tan-coloured overcoat was quality leather, open to reveal a rust-coloured waistcoat beneath, a shirt that looked far too warm for this hot weather, and hard-wearing cotton moleskin trousers. Hardly the attire of a local workman, she surmised, then she pondered for a moment. Maybe here in Liverpool, this was the attire of the working man. Although, she doubted it.

He removed his battered fedora and Mary Jane wondered if the stiff brim had been chewed by something feral. However, it was no concern of hers, and she stiffened when he smiled across the table. She had, quite unintentionally, been staring in his direction before quickly looking away.

Her attention was all over the place. She must concentrate on the here and now. But her thoughts would not behave themselves. This time yesterday she should have been making her vows. Even though she and Paddy had not been courting long, they had known each other for years. Her brothers had seemed happy she and Paddy were walking out. But they would not have been, had they known about his birthday, or the hay dance. Her hand went unconsciously to the almost imperceptible swell of her stomach. Paddy's birthday was in April. Mary Jane could feel her cheeks grow hot. His 'lovemaking' had been so quick she hardly noticed what was happening. That's when Paddy told her he had always had his eye on her. She had never been out with a boy before Paddy. Had never been kissed until that first time. A birthday kiss he called it, and she had given him the greatest gift of all. She lay with Paddy on the haycart, as the spring sun dipped down over the golden fields.. There was no hint of a breeze when Paddy took her in his arms and whispered words of love.

'You dropped this,' the man sitting opposite said, holding out the large white flower.

'Thank you,' she said sheepishly. The man was obviously being friendly, maybe wanting a conversation, which she was in no humour to indulge. She didn't want to talk. She wanted to think. That was when she saw the huge smile light up his eyes. It was a nice smile. Friendly. She looked away, suddenly aware of the heat rising to her throat. She had no business answering friendly smiles in her condition. Concentrating on the swoop and soar of birds over the glinting river Mersey, Mary Jane tried to ignore the man across the table, fascinated by a pigeon busily and unsuccessfully pecking at the cobbled sett. She had no wish to converse with a stranger who stood apart from the men in traditional garb of flat caps, corduroy trousers, and collarless shirts beneath their greasy, well-worn jackets. She felt vulnerable all of a sudden. He was too close.

'Cal Everdine,' he said.

Mary Jane felt compelled to put her hand into his, afraid he might break it, and surprised when it was so gentle. She had seen many a hard-working hand, but none like these. They were as big as shovels. Although, she thought wryly, there was nothing about him that was small. She watched as he got up and stood in the queue, head and shoulders over everybody else, and Mary Jane could not help but admire those broad shoulders and powerful frame, he certainly stood out from the crowd – in more ways than one. Whoever heard of a man going to the counter to collect his own tea?

Mary Jane hoped he did not come back to the table, he unsettled her, and she had a lot to ponder. What was to become of her if Red had run off, never to be seen again? She rummaged through the confusing thoughts in her head, trying to find a solution to her immediate plight. If Red did not come back soon, she would find the address of her lodgings. But how would she get there? Was it far?

'I got you another tea.' Cal Everdine' s voice jolted Mary Jane from her thoughts and her head shot up. 'And a little something to go with it.' He slipped the cup and saucer onto the table and put down a small side plate that held a delicious-looking custard tart.

Mary Jane was speechless. A feeling to which she was unaccustomed, and not at all comfortable with.

'Don't let your tea go cold, you look as if you need it.' He tipped his hat suspecting she had a lot to think about given her lack of conversation.

Mary Jane's heart skittered as she watched him saunter confidently to the door. He had a hint of a limp, she noted, but it did nothing to hamper his assured movements. Nor did he look back, holding open the door for a child and his mother, who smiled sweetly and thanked him in a manner so natural. He looked like a man who did not have a care in the world.

'The arrogance of him!' Mary Jane hissed under her breath, dragging her gaze from the door. But she had no right snapping at him when he was doing her a good turn. It was unkind.

She couldn't face the custard tart but lifted the cup to her lips and swallowed the warm tea before placing it back on the thick white serviceable saucer with a silent nod. The café was growing noisy and oppressive. She had to get out of here.

* * *

Cal Everdine patted the horse's nose before loading the heavy sugar-filled hessian sacks onto the cart. He squinted in the late-afternoon haze and stretched to his full six feet four inches, feeling happier than he had done in a long while. Being his own boss, he was not tied to time. Nor did he have a wife and children to rush home for. He was as free as a bird in an open cage. Distracted, he casually looked up at the clock on the Liver Building. It had just gone four. If he left now, he could deliver this load to the other end of the dock road, discouraging scallywags to take a knife to the bottom of the sacks to relieve them of their precious cargo.

His last job of the day, he thought. And his pleasure dissipated like morning mist over the Mersey. He had a long night ahead of him. As always. Back to the echoing silence. To the memories. He would not think about that terrible time. It was time to move on. But the guilt and loathing gnawed at him, eating him alive. And the voice inside his head delivered the words that had become his daily mantra.

Ellie, forgive me. Even before he'd got to her, he had suspected Ellie was dead. And when he'd lifted her weightless body into his arms, his worst fears had been confirmed. He would never forgive himself for not being there. Nor could he forget that, even in death, Ellie's lifeless eyes still had the power to accuse him. Momentarily, his thoughts were distracted by the sight of the girl coming out of the tearooms. He sighed. He could not imagine her panicking at the first sign of trouble. Ellie had been delicate. Unlike the girl in the sky-blue coat, clutching a carpet bag protectively as she crossed the cobbles, coming towards him, her head high, obviously unaware of her hypnotic rhythm. Her beauty was in her spirit, and he would wager there was not a fire on earth she could not tackle.

'I must apologise for my rude behaviour, I didn't even introduce myself,' her crisp Celtic lilt brought a moment's grateful respite from his tortured thoughts and the relief made him smile. 'I am Mary Jane Starling.'

'I think I may have surprised you.' Cal noticed her Celtic complexion flushed pink, although, he surmised this young woman was no wilting flower, and his assumption was realised when she spoke in a voice that brooked no argument.

'You did not,' she waved her hand dismissively. 'It was me. I overreacted. 'Mary Jane watched as he tossed another hessian sack onto the back of a cart as if it weighed nothing at all. *Look away, Mary Jane, you have no business here.*

'It was thoughtless of me to interrupt you.' His powerful build could be daunting, he realised, although it stood him in good stead many a time. 'I apologise. I had no right to intrude.'

'I was waiting for somebody, and they didn't turn up.'

'More fool them,' he answered, bending to pick up the last

sack. 'Can I offer you a lift?' Straightening, he noticed her eyes were not flashing like intoxicating liquor any more, they were gentle now, and dare he even think it... vulnerable. The bulky baggage looked heavy.

'No thank you,' Mary Jane said. 'I have a good pair of legs, and I am quite capable of getting from one place to another.' Her lips lifted involuntarily at the corners when she saw a spark of amusement in his eyes as he made his way to the front of the cart. Despite the limp, he hopped easily onto it. 'Thank you for the tea, it was kind of you,' she called, knowing she should never forget her manners.

'I bid you a safe night, Mary Jane,' he said, raising his hat. 'Be careful, there are some unsavoury characters around the dockyards.' Then he flicked the reins and the horse moved off as she turned to leave.

Gripping her possessions, Mary Jane made her way off the dock, away from Cal Everdine and the brooding good looks that had turned her heart into a thundering train and robbed her of the ability to breathe properly. She had no right to feel such things. Not in her condition. *You have some nerve, Mary Jane*, she told herself. *The bold bare-faced cheek of you!*

Cal shook his bewildered head, watching her flounce towards the main road. He was thirty-three years old, and for the first time in twelve years, he looked at another woman knowing, if she was his, he would never have let her fend for herself on the dockside. He flinched... How dare he think he could protect a woman.

4

Outside the main dock gate, Mary Jane stopped to catch her breath and took out the piece of paper Red had given her. It was then that she noted the instructions, which told her where she had to go next. It said:

When you get to the gate, turn left and then left again

'Bloody eejit!' Mary Jane forced the words through her teeth and jerked her head to one side. If she turned left, and then left again, she would be facing the dock wall! Trust Red to get everything wrong. He didn't have the sense he was born with.

A ragged woman rushed past and stole grain from unattended sacks loaded onto the back of a flat-backed cart. A brood of barefooted offspring followed, and they quickly scattered when a policeman gave a perfunctory chase, but soon gave up when they disappeared down a nearby alleyway.

'Are you all right, Miss?' asked the policeman as he took up his post at the dock gate once more.

'Can you tell me where this place is please?' she asked, prodding the scrap of paper.

He took it and read the address before pointing an outstretched arm down the spine of the dock road. 'Go straight down here for about three miles,' he said, 'until you see the bridge on the opposite side. Cross the main road and over the bridge you go.'

'Thank you kindly,' Mary Jane answered and headed in the direction he had told her to go. The walk would not trouble her usually. It was a good stretch of the legs. However, although late in the afternoon the sun was still blazing hot and her feet were leaden, even the gentle breeze coming in off the river did not give any relief.

An hour later, Mary Jane reached a huge soot-blackened bridge that spanned a railway and a canal. Her heart sank. According to the directions, she had to walk over this enormous humpbacked thing, to get to the town hall to meet Red.

Crossing the busy dock road took forever, as the hectic drivers of this incessant traffic had no intentions of stopping to let her cross. *This is a far cry from the sleepy roads and lanes back home*, she thought. Not one of the multitude of dock workers, carters or merchant men was inclined to say 'hello', or pass the time of day. She had never seen a place so busy!

Mary Jane managed to dodge the heavy dock road traffic, carts stacked high with bales of cotton, casks of ale, timber, coal, and all manner of merchandise that went from the docks to every part of the country. Her aching feet felt the rise and fall of every cobbled sett as she weaved her way to the other side of the road. Swallowing her rising disappointment, she recalled Paddy telling her that Liverpool was a grand place, singing the praises of the fine big houses he'd seen when he once came over. However, all she could see were back-to-back dwellings in terraced streets, linked by evil-looking alleyways that were black as the hobs of hell. In the heat her lightweight summer coat felt heavy, and she longed to remove it but knew it would be unseemly for an unescorted woman to walk the street with her coat over her arm. The smells seeping from huge warehouses lining the docks were making her feel sick. Amid the smoke-laden pong of factory chimneys, the sultry air was thick with the smell of wood from the timber yards, fish-meal – and boiled bacon! Where on earth was the boiled bacon smell coming from? Clanging chains and incessant traffic vied with the cries of gulls and pigeons, working men calling out as they unloaded ships on the dockyards, horses' hooves clip-clopping along the cobbled road, dragging carts as high as houses. The noise unsettled her, and Mary Jane doubted she would ever get used to it. Looking around, she saw not one single blade of grass and she knew, to the very depths of her soul, she could never be happy here. But what choice did she have, Paddy's persuasion that first time in April had come with unexpected and unwanted consequences. And to top it all, there was no sign of his brother.

'Just wait until I get my hands on you, Red,' she muttered. Bone-weary in the merciless heat after a sleepless night on the boat over, Mary Jane felt every tread was like wading through treacle. Her luggage growing heavier with each step. Only sheer determination prevented her from dropping everything and crying like a lost child. She stopped and looked to her left and saw the grand town hall over the way. The railings were fancy and the spires were certainly tall. Although, the whole building was completely covered in a black velvet layer of soot that draped over everything.

Dragging in a lungful of smoky air, she hoisted the carpet bag onto her hip, trudging on. The town hall looked every inch a place of importance, she thought nearing the exalted building that housed a library and a museum, now closed for the day. With the determination of one who was accustomed to fending for herself, Mary Jane knew if she wanted to see the inside of the grand place, she would go and look for herself when it opened. She had an independent streak as wide as the Irish Sea, and she needed nobody – especially Red! Her brothers had made sure she got a good education from the nuns in the convent school of St Brides. She had read the classics and could reckon up as easy as blink. But her biggest love was making the bread and pies her mother had taught her to bake from an early age, which stood her in good stead after both her parents drowned on Titanic's maiden voyage.

Mary Jane had been just twelve years old. St Brides was where she discovered she could bake better than anybody else in the convent, even Sister Maria, who baked for the cathedral. Incomparable. That is what Sister Maria called her culinary efforts. She had even gone so far as to say she showed enough culinary promise to provide pastries for the Pope, himself. Nobody in Cashalree could make the mouth-watering pies, delicious bread and fabulous cakes she found so easy to create, later selling them from the kitchen window at the farm.

Paddy would not hear of her serving in a shop! He said it was demeaning to him. However, he had no qualms about her slaving over a hot oven in a back room somewhere. Mary Jane sighed. She had had to agree if she wanted him to do the right thing by her.

And she did want to be Paddy's wife, especially when he taught her things that the nuns knew nothing about. Mary Jane dared to savour the memory of a virile man whose skin glided effortlessly over hers, and to hell with the sin. Although, she thought wearily, the nuns were right about one thing, sin brought its own troubling reward. Being exiled from her family and country was the high price she must pay. She had been stupid, believing that having babies would not apply to her. It was what happened to other girls. Flighty girls, good-time girls who had babies out of wedlock. Not her. But she was wrong. At twenty-one years, with no mother to guide her, she knew nothing of babies. Now, having had a long time to think things over, she was not so sure Paddy would have been able to trample on her dreams. She was too strong to let that happen. But life here in Liverpool, on her own, would not be easy.

She was being paid back for her pride, though. Brought down with a bump so ferocious, it would leave her bruised for the rest of her days. *Her* actions made certain her brothers would be damned for all eternity. However, she still found it impossible to believe they had committed such a terrible deed. The action went against everything they believed in.

As she had trudged through the streets, Mary Jane knew she probably looked the way she felt, bedraggled, abandoned and so deeply wretched. Slumping onto the town hall steps, she was vaguely aware a horse and cart had slowed on the road opposite. Her heartbeat quickened.

'Are you all right there?' Cal Everdine asked.

Looking up, her eyes squinted in the late afternoon sun. 'Nice to see you again Mr Everdine, but I am waiting for someone.' Mary Jane sounded cheerful, yet humiliation pumped through her veins. How could she be so stupid as to depend on Red? Everybody knew he was the most selfish, unreliable man in Cashalree. However, she must not allow her humiliation to show. She had her pride – and she was keeping it! 'He will be here very soon.'

'Please, for the love of God, let me help you. This is no time or place for a woman who doesn't know the area to be hanging around alone.'

Mary Jane avoided eye contact with Cal, struggling to prevent her lip trembling, his concern allowing the vulnerability she had kept hidden for so long to emerge. But she was reluctant to reveal something so private as the helplessness she felt to define her. Silently, she counted to three.

'Could you tell me where Beamer Street is from here, please?'

When Cal heard the subtle catch in her voice, his heart lurched and his hands tightened around the reins. A naturally gentle man, Cal Everdine wanted to strike her absent companion with such force it would knock him into the middle of next week!

'I can take you there,' he said, watching her shield her hauntingly beautiful green eyes from the glaring sun.

'Would you do that?' Mary Jane's relief was expressed in her tone.

'I'm going that way.' His deep drawl had a reassuring sound. 'I live on that street. What number are you looking for?'

'Thank you, that is so kind of you. It is number forty-three.' Red might never show up, while Cal Everdine had offered her nothing but help and support. That is what she must go by, not the word of that good-for-nothing Redfern, who had filled her head with nonsense. *Sharpers indeed*! 'I would be grateful for the lift. If it's no trouble,' she said, reaching the edge of the pavement.

'It's no trouble. I live opposite over an empty shop.' He could see her clearly now, close up, and she looked scared. 'I suspect you've never been to a place like Liverpool before?' With its warren of back streets and throngs of people going about their business. People too busy to notice a beautiful young woman who, likely as not, needed a friend.

'No, you're right,' she managed, strangely moved by his concern. She swallowed the lump in her throat that prevented her from saying any more. *Please don't be kind*, she thought, knowing if he were to show her any sympathy, she would lose the last gossamer thread of courage, which, once released, would drown her in a sea of tears.

Jumping down from the cart, Cal came round to her side, holding out his hand to help her up onto the wooden bench. Once steady, she was glad of the high sacks of sugar which shaded her from the sun.

'Settled?' he asked when he returned to his seat, gently flipping the reins.

'It's very kind of you.' Mary Jane didn't have a clue where Beamer Street was, relieved that this man obviously knew his way around.

'I'm on my way home,' he said. He lifted a flask of cold water and offered it to her while keeping his eyes on the road. 'You can use the cup, if you prefer, I never do.'

'Thank you,' Mary Jane said, gratefully unscrewing the cup from the army-issue flask. He stopped at the kerb, while she poured water into the tin cup. Then, after handing back the flask, she eagerly slaked her thirst. Moments later, they were on the move again, and she was glad he did not talk much, like Red, who loved the sound of his own voice. Cal's quiet strength soothed her frazzled nerves.

'Look,' he said with a hint of hesitation, 'I am not one to pry, and please tell me to mind my own business if I overstep the mark...'

'I will,' she answered, not wanting to go into the whys and

wherefores of her visit. Or the shame she left behind. She waited for him to continue.

'I'm looking for a cleaner,' he said abruptly, and Mary Jane's head swivelled around quickly, taken by surprise.

'Is that so?' she asked, her breath hitching in her throat. She could not have been more shocked if he had slapped her across the face. A servant! Is that who he thought she was? Someone so desperate she would be grateful to fetch and carry for him. 'Well, if I find a willing skivvy, I'll send her straight to you.' *The cheek of him*, she thought. 'You wanted *me* to come and clean for *you*?' Mary Jane could not hide the incredulity from her voice. 'Are you out of your mind! Do I look so desperate I will cook and clean for a pittance?' Then, looking down at her torn stockings and grazed legs, she tried to be civil when she added: 'I am going into business.'

She would have to start slowly, sell from a basket at the roadside. Then, after selling enough pies and saving hard, she would open a place where she could make her pies and bread and cakes and sell them on site. Cleaning for a man – apart from her brothers – had never entered her head.

'I am sorry if I have offended you, I didn't mean—'

'You didn't mean to show me exactly what you thought.' Mary Jane's tone became tighter. 'You think I am just another ignorant Irish peasant who will drop at your feet and kiss the ground you walk on, showing my gratitude for allowing me to clear up after you!'

'That's not what I meant.' Cal's eyebrows shot up; he intended only to offer her help, not treat her as a servant. God alone knows why he ever offered her a job in the first place. He was rarely home. Had little in the way of belongings and a cleaner would be hard pressed to fill a day's work let alone a week. There was nobody to look after except himself and he liked his solitary lifestyle.

'I know full well what you meant, Mr Everdine.' Mary Jane's head jerked from side to side with every word. 'You thought you would take advantage of a poor woman on her uppers – well, let me tell you something.' Her hackles were well and truly up now. 'I have my own plans, thank you very much, and they do not include fetching and carrying for any man.'

'Not even that disappearing husband of yours?' Cal asked, noting the ring on the third finger of her left hand, which she quickly hid beneath the carpet bag. Now why would she want to do that? he wondered.

5

Cal saw Red hurrying towards them as he turned into Beamer street. He pulled on the reins and the cart came to a stop.

'Mary Jane. Thank God!' Red was breathless and his voice sounded full of relief when he reached the cart. 'I went to the town hall, and you weren't there!'

'No, you eejit! I was half dead with the heat. Mr. Everdine offered me a lift.'

Red studied the man sitting next to her for a moment. His dark eyes hostile, obviously he did not share her gratitude and Mary Jane's suspicions were confirmed when Red said in clipped tones, 'I'll see to her now.' He held up his hand to aid her descent from the cart, and Mary Jane felt her face redden with embarrassment at his rudeness.

'I can do it myself!' She slapped his hand away. 'I managed to get this far without your help, I'm sure I can get down from a cart without it, too.'

Cal considered the wiry Irishman who was hopping impatiently from one leg to the other, his eyes everywhere but on his wife. He did not need to be a genius to conclude this drunken

Irishman was, indeed, *an eejit* and disliked him on sight. The cheapskate had obviously spared every expense to get her here. Cal did not fail to notice the shoddy copper band that had turned her wedding finger green; a trick used by some of the old tails haunting the dockside bars.

'Thank you very much for all your help, Mr. Everdine,' Mary Jane's tone held a quiet reprimand for Red, who, with a drunken leer, moved his hand to her waist. Outraged, she shrugged his arm away and spoke to her rescuer, 'It was very kind of you to bring me here.'

'To be sure,' Red mumbled, a surly expression clouding his features. 'She'll not be there again.' Barely touching the peak of his flat cap, he turned back to her, his voice full of barely suppressed anger, and Cal longed to interject, but knew that to interfere between man and wife was frowned upon. However, given the disrespectful behaviour of this ignorant man who had left this beautiful woman alone, stranded in a new country where she knew nobody, was unforgiveable.

But, thought Cal, who was he to dictate how a man should treat his wife? Hadn't he done the same thing, all those years ago! He nodded, gently flicking the reins, and moved off as the Irishman held Mary Jane's arm possessively.

* * *

'What on earth were you thinking of? Taking lifts off strange men.' Red did not lower his voice as he gripped Mary Jane's elbow and led her away.

Humiliation burned inside her, but she refused to make a scene in the street, and far from being thankful to Mr Everdine for helping her, Red showed nothing but irritation, because she had not waited for him at the Town Hall. 'Don't you dare speak to me like that, Red!' Mary Jane hissed. Nobody but her brothers chastised her, and she wasn't going to let this jumped-up little rebel do it now! Watching the cart roll along the opposite side of the road, Mary Jane turned to Red. 'Where the hell have you been? You smell like a brewery!'

'Never mind all that,' Red said impatiently. 'It didn't take you long to get acquainted, I see.' He loosened the neckerchief in the sultry heat, which even at this hour was still too hot. The newspapers were given cause to lament that 'day after day of the "African conditions" were proving a severe strain on the "English constitution"' and the public were urged to limit their use of water as the country was in the grip of a prolonged drought. Judging by the smell of Red, he was following the advice with determination with disregard for soap as well as water.

'I'm surprised you bothered to come looking for me, at all!' Mary Jane's voice quivered with indignant rage, after all, Red had offered to take care of her and all he had done so far was bag a free crossing to Liverpool and drink himself into a state. Now he was dishevelled, slurring his words and hardly able to walk a straight line, and Mary Jane surmised he had barely given her a second thought!

'Sure, I suppose 'twas a good thing himself happened along, to offer a stricken maiden a lift.' His words were laced with scorn. 'The big man saved you from a long walk. Although it is no surprise.' Red's eyes slowly skimmed her slim, shapely body that did not yet show signs of her forthcoming motherhood and Mary Jane longed to slap the lascivious grin from his face, but common sense told her that would be the worst thing she could do. She was in a strange place and knew nobody. She would bide her time, until she managed to get her bearings, hopefully then he would have gone back to Ireland.

'When will you be going home?' she asked. Surely, he wanted to see justice for his brother.

'Not for a while, at least.' His arrogance dissipated and was replaced with something she could not fathom. Scorn perhaps? 'I have to save for my ticket, and I can't expect you to pay for it. You have other things to worry about.'

Having no intention of supporting him like Paddy had done, Mary Jane knew this was not the first time Red referred to her shame, begotten on the wrong side of a wedding ring. On the boat over, he had the impudence to draw attention to her condition while introducing her as his wife who was expecting their first-born. She had been about to open her mouth and protest at the suggestion she would ever marry a man like him, when she'd realised that to do so would vilify her.

'You may have escaped the wrath of your family and the village, Mary Jane,' Red had said later, 'but a damaged reputation will last a lifetime, even over here.'

Mary Jane was unable to deny the destructive, often hypocritical loathing that pursued fallen women.

'Don't forget I am the one who is doing you a good turn, by helping you escape your murdering brothers.' The disgust in Red's eyes was plain for Mary Jane to see.

'But why would you do that?' she asked, puzzled as to why he would stand by her when her own flesh and blood had slain his twin brother. It didn't make sense.

Red turned her toward him. 'Look Mary Jane,' his voice, although taut, told her the drink had obviously given him courage, 'I could give your child the name he deserves.'

'I beg your pardon?' She was unable to believe what she was hearing. Not five minutes ago, he had looked at her like she was dog dirt on his shoe. Now he was asking her to marry him, and his brother not yet two days dead!

'You won't get a better offer. No decent man will give you a second glance, in your condition. You are soiled goods.' There was a moment's silence before his tone took on a pleading note. 'Can't you see I am offering you respectability, and a name for your child—'

'My child may get the right name,' Mary Jane countered, so angry her blood almost reaching boiling point. 'But it most certainly would not get the right father.' She pulled her arm free and moved away. Coming to this godforsaken place was one thing, she thought, but marrying Red was something else. That was one sacrifice too many! She would rather pull every single hair out of her head and wear a sign saying *unclean* than be beholden to Red. However, she must hold her tongue, which was in danger of running away with itself.

'I'd die a humiliated spinster, before I ever considered your offer,' Mary Jane whispered, holding on to as much dignity as possible, while wanting to rattle every tooth in his head. 'I can't let you take on responsibility for me and my child,' she said a little louder, refusing to become his doormat. Because she knew, without a shadow of a doubt, this conniving, shiftless leech of a man would suck the marrow from her bones while she fetched and carried for him.

'I'm not good enough for you, is that it?' Red sneered. 'Well, let me tell you this, Mary Jane, the golden son is gone – and he's not coming back.' He paused for a moment, and when she did not respond, he leaned forward, his words spiky, his breath sour. 'You might want to ponder on that. Life for a woman on her own, with a child to raise, is the road to penury.'

Mary Jane leaned forward too, looking him in the eye, clear in the knowledge she was strong enough to tackle anything life threw at her. 'I will not depend on any man to keep me,' she said defiantly. 'I have the wherewithal to make my own way, thank you very much.'

Red did not respond immediately. Digesting her words. Eventually, he said slowly and clearly, 'So, you do have Paddy's money?'

Mary Jane had to think quickly. Red must never find out about the money squirreled away, because, although it was quite enough to keep her going until she began to make money of her own, he would make short work of it in the alehouses and gambling dens along the dock road, even though she had contributed as much as Paddy.

'I have a talent at my fingertips,' she said. 'Everybody says so, I will always make my own way, selling my bakes until I have saved enough to open my own business.' She watched the light that had shone so brightly in Red's eyes dim. He had not expected her to be so forthright. Nor did she feel the need for false modesty. She would get nowhere by being coy about her skills.

'You know what they say about pride, Mary Jane.' Red's voice held a veiled threat, she was sure, but she had no intentions of letting him think he had got the better of her.

'It's a chance I'll have to take, Red. If I fall, it will be on my terms.' She began to walk away checking the house numbers as she went. But it was Red's next words that stopped her in her tracks.

'Well, I wasn't going to tell you this, but you forced it out of me. Paddy didn't want to marry you. He told me yesterday morning, before we left for the wedding, he had made a big mistake. He was standing by you for the sake of the child – he didn't love you.'

'You're lying.' Mary Jane could feel tears brimming her

eyes, her words choked. 'He told me all the time. He said he never felt for any girl the love he felt for me.'

'Words are cheap. If you use the right ones, they will buy you anything.' Red was goading her, she could tell. And she could see was the badness that drove him on.

'Such as the ticket that brought you here?' she asked, her spirits rising when she saw him flinch. 'And as for you helping me. I doubt that. You were too busy spending what money you had on being sociable. And where, exactly, did you get the money to buy so much drink?'

She waited, but all he said was, 'I don't have to save your name, Mary Jane...' Red would never admit to selling the wedding ring Paddy had bought for her, replacing it with a copper washer bought cheaply from a chandler's shop. 'Just remember that.'

Not for the first time, Mary Jane wished she'd had a mother, or a sister. Somebody she could have talked to. However, it was not to be. Her mammy had died when she needed her most, the only girl in a family of three protective older brothers, who hadn't a clue about *women's troubles.* And if they did, they certainly didn't connect them to her. 'I already have a name,' she said, 'my brothers'—'

'The same brothers who killed *my* brother?' Red sneered. 'They don't scare me.'

'They didn't scare Paddy either.' There was no mistaking Mary Jane's insinuation, and she felt small for saying it, but Red needed to be put in his place.

'They will come looking for you – if they haven't already been arrested.' Red told her, raking his thick black hair with stubby fingers. In his mind, what happened to his brother had nothing to do with him. He did everything in his power to erase the memory of picking up the large slab of stone and, with every ounce of force he could muster, hammering Paddy's scull 'til he heard it crack.

* * *

Cal Everdine pulled up the cotton blind, looking down to the sun-baked street, watching the children play while their mothers sat on front steps, knitting, sewing, or fanning their face and neck with a newspaper to try to cool themselves. The heatwave had lasted for months. Cal decided to take only one daily bath, instead of his usual morning and night. Standpipes had already been put at each end of the street of bay-windowed, three-up-three-down terraced houses on this side. And families, on the opposite side, who lived in the four-story Georgian town houses that his father had bought when he was just a boy, were doing likewise.

His attention was drawn to the Irish girl he had given a lift to. She was walking next to the drunken ignoramus as they made their way from where he had dropped her off and, for the life of him, Cal could not see what possessed her to have anything to do with him. She seemed such a headstrong woman who did not suffer fools, yet she would have to go a long way to find one such as Redfern, who, it was rumoured, was paid to take information back and forth to his countrymen. Cal had heard of the wiry Irishman who came to Liverpool, stayed a few weeks at a time before returning home but never worked. The pattern was always the same. And while he was here, the only thing he worked hard at was feeding his drinking and gambling habit. What Mary Jane saw in such a rogue, Cal could not fathom. All he did know was that if he were ever fortunate enough to have a woman like her, she would want for nothing. Nothing at all.

6

Red was sure his brother would not have come over here empty-handed. Yet, when he had checked Paddy's pockets, all he could find was the gold wedding ring for Mary Jane. After selling the ring which he had replaced with the copper band, he had used the rest of the money to have a good time on the ferry. He would have to bide his time. Wait until her guard was down. Find the money and get the hell out of here before her brothers turned up, knowing it wouldn't take long for the Starling brothers to find out where she was. Nor the local Garda.

As they walked along the street, Mary Jane eyed the scrubbed steps leading to polished front doors, just a stone's throw from the river estuary. The houses looked clean and well cared for, and she wondered how Red knew of such a prosperous-looking place. The proud women of Beamer Street kept their houses spick and span, he had told her, and mentioned they even used the water they boiled their potatoes in to wash their front step.

'Sure, you know an awful lot about the place in the short amount of time you've been here,' she said.

'Cissie Stone is a friend of my aunt, we used to come here when we were younger.' He had no intentions of telling her why he knew so much, or why he came over to Liverpool so frequently. Cissie Stone's house was well known in certain circles as a safe house for fellow countrymen. He had heard that even the great Michael Collins himself had stayed over, on his way to America. 'Rich merchants built the villas near the docks to be close to their work,' Red told her. 'Though, their families weren't so keen on living here.'

'Maybe the smell of oil, grease, and smoke doesn't agree with everyone,' Mary Jane answered. She had seen for herself the overcrowded courts off Scotland Road, and the warren of jerry-built houses along the dock road, located north of the city centre bounded by Kirkdale in the north and Everton to the east, with the River Mersey running along the west side. However, accommodation was not like that in this long row of Georgian mansions. Across the cobbled road, the houses were different again, smaller, but well kept. At the end of each row of three-up-three-down bay-windowed houses stood a corner shop. A butchers on one corner, a dairy on the other and an empty shop under an unlit flat.

'This whole street is owned by one man. Can you believe that? Mary Jane.'

'I hope it stays fine for him, whoever he is.' Mary Jane was unimpressed. 'Money does not bring happiness.' She could not imagine ever being happy again.

'I wouldn't turn my nose up. These houses must be worth a fortune,' Red said, admiring the large houses with four floors, from the cellar to the attic. The heels of her shoes clipped the pavement and all heads turned. Children stopped playing, while mothers ceased their talk to watch her long strides devour the cobbles. She suddenly felt as if every woman in the street could see inside her soul, making her feel vulnerable in a way she never had before, as shame licked at her like the flames of hell.

'Would you look at the cut of this one, Philomena,' a woman with a pinched face and a brood of children hovering about her skirt said loud enough for Mary Jane to hear.

'Those stockings have seen better days, Ina,' said Philomena in agreement as Mary Jane recalled the gorse bushes catching at her legs.

'Well, if she's anything to do with that Red fella,' Ina crowed, 'she hasn't got much going for her. He'd rob the eyes from your head.'

'He would so, Ina,' Philomena answered at her neighbour's observation.

Mary Jane felt every eye was on her. Nevertheless, she would not cower. She owed these people nothing. She nodded, smiling to the gawping women as she approached them. Her manner poised, shoulders down, head high, her back was poker straight. Not one of them returned the smile.

'Do you think she owns the *whole* street?' Ina, with her snatched-back hair and Donegal accent, asked her neighbour in a voice that carried on the still air.

Mary Jane raised her chin, her stomach a tangle of trepidation, and swept along with an air of one who had the world at her feet in an area renowned for Irish inhabitants who had come over before, during and after the famine. *So, this is 'Little Ireland.'*

'Take no notice of Ina King,' Red tried to soothe her, but Mary Jane paid no heed. Nor did she have the inclination to ask how he knew the woman's name. 'The ring will shut them up,' Red told her

Mary Jane looked at it. It was cheap and ugly. In the short

space of time she had worn it, the washer had turned her finger green. But it would have to do for now.

Mary Jane was surprised when she saw Cal Everdine' s horse standing outside the empty corner shop on the opposite side of the street, its whitewashed windows preventing prying eyes from seeing inside. She stood gazing at the whole building and as her eyes travelled to the upper story, she saw Cal Everdine at the window.

Crossing the cobbles, she approached the enormous Clydesdale, running her hand along its shining chestnut-coloured flank, as she had done back home with her brothers' horses, and her father's before he died. The horse lowered its head, nudging her arm as if in greeting. Gently, Mary Jane scratched his broad forehead, and he nuzzled her shoulder, his nostrils flaring with pleasure.

'Hurry up,' Red called from the other side of the street, and she patted the horse before crossing back to where Red stood waiting.

'Is this it?' she asked, looking up and resting her hand momentarily on the fleur-de-lys railings that sat on top of the eighteen-inch red-brick wall. The house was three storeys high and below pavement level was a cellar. Above her, stone steps led to Doric columns that sat neatly either side of the front door. Hardly the type of residence either of them was used to.

'It is,' Red said in a voice that told Mary Jane he was feeling very proud of himself.

The house had a panelled, pillar-box-red front door, not the usual forest green or chestnut brown of the other houses. This one, like all the others, looked tidy and well-cared-for. Not run-down and neglected, with sagging curtains hanging from the long sash windows, like some she had passed along the dock road. Unlike the other houses in the street, this front door was tightly shut. Red was just about to knock when the door was quickly opened and he dragged her into the spacious lobby.

'Jaysus, you wouldn't go to her unless you were desperate for money,' said a woman with a broad Belfast inflection and frizzy corrugated hair who was coming out of the house.

The smell of smoked haddock wafted behind her, causing Mary Jane's stomach to turn again as they headed into the vestibule while the woman pulled a couple of children onto the step.

'Her interest rate alone could fund the national debt.' The woman loudly voicing her disgust did not look at Mary Jane as she pinched the running nose of a squalling baby on her hip with a handkerchief, five children running around her. The swarming children, alerted to the fact a stranger was in the vicinity, hushed their noise and eyed Mary Jane with suspicion, staring with naked curiosity. Although they quickly lost interest when their mother flounced down the stone steps, leaving the door ajar.

'Shut that bloody door!' a female voice yelled.

Mary Jane quickly found the snip, closing the front door immediately.

'She has the voice of a banshee,' she whispered to Red, who put his forefinger to his lips and made a shushing sound.

'She'll hear you,' he said. 'That's Cissie, the landlady.'

Mary Jane's eyes became accustomed to the gloom and noted that the outside lavishness did not extend to the interior, which was grim, to say the least. 'By the look of that paintwork, I'd say she was in desperate need of a cleaner.'

'Don't come over all hoity-toity, Mary Jane,' Red said through his teeth, 'just remember why we're here.'

'I know why I'm here, Red,' she said with determination, 'but I'm not so sure about you.'

'I've come to take care of you,' his voice suddenly softened. 'I've a duty to Paddy.'

'Don't let that be a bother to you,' she answered, fed up with having him around her already. 'I can make my own way from here.' Left to her own devices, she was sure she could manage.

'Cissie's a good woman – if you stay on the right side of her,' Red said, trying to change the subject as he made his way down the long lobby. 'You'll have to be civil.

'I'll see for myself, then I'll decide if I need to be civil,' Mary Jane parried. Brought up in a house full of men, subservience was not an option. She had to be able to look after herself. And she had no intentions of cowering to a woman whose dirty skirting boards were in complete contrast to the outside show of clean front windows. 'I don't trust a house where the front door is always shut tight.'

With a sweep of her eyes, Mary Jane took in the grubby wood panelling that covered the bottom of the vestibule wall. Outside splendour and inside filth were the sign of a devious mind, as far as she was concerned. Growing up in a doctor's house, she had always been clean.

'Will yer be standing out there all night?' a raucous voice came from the front room, and Mary Jane raised a questioning eyebrow.

'Yes, that's definitely the screech of a banshee.' She realised that not only did she have to live in this mausoleum, but she had to pay for the privilege.

Red pulled her towards the parlour door halfway down the passage. 'Don't make a scene, Mary Jane,' he pleaded, his tone urgent. She was surprised when he guided her into the parlour, his attitude changing out of all recognition. 'Cissie, there you are,' he said as if addressing a long-lost friend. His voice was not the usual lazy grunt, but loud and over-bright. Mary Jane watched him cross the room like a playful puppy, pushing his flat cap to the back of his curly dark hair once more and putting his arm around the well-upholstered shoulders of the landlady. 'Well, Cissie, here she is.' The corners of his mouth twitched into a familiar grin. 'Didn't I tell you my wife was a fine-looking woman?'

Mary Jane just about managed to suppress the astonished gasp that threatened to contradict his enthusiastic declaration. She had no idea Red was going to introduce her in this manner, and so help him, when she had a word with him later. Because she was going to have to use every ounce of willpower not to choke the lying weasel with her bare hands!

A strained hush descended, as the two women observed each other. Mary Jane's eyes narrowed, her brows pleating. How dare this large woman with jet black hair and matching eyes look her up and down like she was a plucked chicken hanging in the butcher's window.

Cissie said not one word as she scrutinised Mary Jane. Then, a moment later she spoke. 'So,' dark eyes glinted, and crimson lips puckered, making Mary Jane feel even more uncomfortable., 'You're Red's wife?'

'She is!' Red cut in quickly, moving towards Mary Jane and putting a bold hand around her slim waist. She glared at him, causing him to fidget, then remove his hand as if her body were scalding hot. He rolled his hat through his fingers.

'Does she not have a tongue in her head?' Cissie asked.

'She does,' Mary Jane, standing taller, answered stiffly, glaring at Red, 'and she is not afraid to use it when she gets the chance.'

'You remember the man we met on the boat?' Red explained giving an apologetic half-shrug while jerking his thumb over a dropped shoulder, in the direction of the docks. 'Well, he's Cissie's husband, he told me she had a room going spare...' He rubbed the back of his neck with the other hand. A sure sign to Mary Jane that he felt trapped.

'That's my business.' Cissie gave Red a warning look. 'Suffice to say, she needs my help... and that's *all* she needs to know.'

'I could have come to Liverpool on my own,' Mary Jane said, refusing to be silenced. 'I do not need help.'

'And why would you travel alone,' asked Cissie Stone, a brazen hussy of a woman dressed in a tight-fitting blouse that failed to confine her overflowing bosom, 'when you've a husband to take care of.

'I don't need a man to protect me.' Mary Jane realised she must be cautious. Suddenly overcome with fear her brothers would catch up with her, Mary Jane realised having Red as her chaperone, may not have been one of her better ideas. But she was stuck with him by the look of it. Quickly she covered her hand when she caught Cissie glaring at the brass ring on the green third finger.

'Ahh... The ring.' Red, always quick off the mark, also noticed Cissie looking. 'We had to pawn her gold wedding ring for her fare.' He put his arm round her, the weight of his forearm pressing into Mary Jane's slim shoulder.

Summoning every ounce of her steely willpower, she decided not to shrug him off. After all, she was carrying his brother's baby. Her reputation was the only precious thing she had – apart from the clock – and she wanted to keep it at all costs.

'Sure, don't we all have to pay our way?' Cissie purred,

making Mary Jane wonder why her every utterance was a question. 'Will you be seeking work on the dock, Christie?'

'Monday, I've a start on Monday,' Red told her, as Mary Jane's eyes lowered to her shoes. She said nothing for the time being. However, for as long as she had known Paddy, she had never known Red to get out of bed for a job, let alone his country!

'Isn't that delightful,' Cissie's tone lacked conviction, 'especially when there are so many men out of work in *this* country.'

'Ahh, you can't keep a good man down, Ciss.' Red was a stranger to hard work, Mary Jane knew, and shied away from it every chance he got. Earning only enough to get him through the door of the nearest alehouse. Paddy told her his brother was an expert at sitting on an inch of beer all night, biding his time until some innocent mug bought him another. He was so bad for business; the landlord gave him the price of a pint to go and drink in another pub. The request included an order never to darken his door again!

'You will pay the rent every Friday. A fortnight in advance,' Cissie said, interrupting her thoughts. 'The room is at the top of the house.' She extended her left hand, palm up, and Mary Jane opened her mouth to tell the landlady she only needed a single room, but Red nudged her and gave the merest shake of his head, a silent warning to say nothing.

She would have to pay his share too, it seemed, and Mary Jane made a mental note to find alternative lodgings as soon as possible. Turning her back on both of them, she took money from her purse, placing the precise amount in Cissie's hand, watching the older woman push it down the front of her blouse.

'The top floor has only got one room, so you will not be interrupted.' Cissie's natural lilt was tempered by the smoke and grime of the dockside. 'You have to share bathing facilities and make your own toilet arrangements.'

'You have a bathroom!' Mary Jane's spirits rose as fleeting thoughts of a good soak in a relaxing bath erased the simmering anger she felt towards Red.

'There's a tin bath hanging on a six-inch nail on the back wall.' Cissie was unflinching in her candour. 'And the lavatory is at the bottom of the yard. Take your own candle.'

'I see.' Mary Jane's intense disappointment was apparent in the sound of her voice. She could only imagine what it would be like to sink into a cooling bath and ease her aching bones. She daren't try to imagine how she would manage to carry a tin bath up all those flights of stairs to the attic, and then lug jugs of hot water to fill it.

'I'll have no cooking after seven o'clock, and I expect you to keep the room spotless.'

'If it is in the same state as the rest of the house,' Mary Jane whispered to Red, 'I'd have to scrub the room before I could keep it clean.'

'I want the stairs brushed and mopped every day.'

'I hope it stays fine for you, missus, but I haven't come here for a job,' Mary Jane replied sharply. She'd had enough of this one's rules and regulations and was taking no more from a painted jezebel who was obviously a stranger to soap, hot water and a floorcloth. Mary Jane thrust her determined chin forward. 'I am nobody's servant, and I answer to no one.' Red's silent pleading made it obvious he wanted her to keep quiet, but she ignored it. He was not the one who had just paid the rent. 'This house is crying out for a good cleaning, but I have absolutely no intentions of being anybody's skivvy.'

Cissie Stone's nostrils flared, and her eyes were stark. 'You come over here thinking you can have it all. But you're wrong, let me tell you. This is not a place for women who think they are above their neighbours.'

'Is it not?' Mary Jane parried, noting a face prematurely lined through a constant scowl and alcohol, which she could smell even though Cissie was on the other side of the room. 'Well, let me tell you, I can be tougher than the rest, I've had a lifetime's training.' Mary Jane was so angry she could spit.

'You'll be leaving here sooner than you think, if you don't watch that lip of yours,' Cissie said, but Mary Jane was able for her.

'I shall,' she retorted. 'Just as soon as I find cleaner accommodation.'

'Mary Jane!' Red's eyes widened and his lips curled into a snarl. 'Remember yourself.'

'Oh, I haven't forgotten,' she said, too tired, hungry and harassed to care overmuch. 'But I won't put a morsel to my mouth until I am sure to be eating off clean crockery.' With that she turned on her heel and left the room, knowing Red was holding Cissie Stone back, trying to calm her.

'It's her condition, Cissie, you must make allowances...' Red's pleading voice came clearly through the half-open door, and Mary Jane only just managed to stop herself from going back into the room and giving both of them a piece of her mind. How dare he make excuses for her, she seethed. If there was any excusing to be done, she would do it herself, but not to the likes of Cissie Stone.

'Is she saying my house is dirty?' Cissie asked Red. 'Because she won't find better!'

Mary Jane's eyes took in the elaborate parquet flooring, caked in street grime. If this was the best there was, she thought, then God help her. The curved cornicing that matched the extravagant scrolled corbels proved an ideal place for the spiders. She noted the multitude of woven webs that hung from the intricate plaster roses around the gas lights. Mary Jane ran her fingers along the wooden rail above the cabbage-coloured tiles where decades of built-up dust and nicotine made her fingertip yellow. This house would come up a treat with a bit of loving care, she pondered. Deep in thought, she imagined what it must have been like, to own a place as grand as this once was. She imagined the ship owners and the businessmen who once lived roundabout, but not any more. In the hands of Cissie Stone this lovely residence was in danger of being ruined by neglect. Scraping her fingernail along the acorn shaped newel post, Mary Jane removed a sticky, brown ribbon of grime. It would take more than hot water to get this lot clean, she thought, itching to get her hands on a scrubbing brush. She crossed the lobby to the parlour door and her hand stilled on the round brass doorknob. There was not a sound within, and the door was closed tight.

'Red,' she called, rapping the door with her knuckles, 'is there any hope of me seeing this heavenly room?'

There was a long silence. Then she heard him.

'I'm coming, Mary Jane!' His strangled voice sounded strange, and she had a good idea he wasn't saying his prayers in there. Moments later, he opened the parlour door, 'I was just saying to Cissie—'

'I'm not interested.' Mary Jane noticed one of the buttons had popped open on Cissie's blouse before she turned away and she had an idea that Cissy was the reason she had ended up here instead of the more select area of Woolton. 'I want to see this room before I have to set to and clean it.'

'Cheeky madam,' Cissie said, 'you'll be out on the street before you know it.'

'You might be doing me a favour, missus!' Mary Jane

retorted, her disgust obvious as Red gripped her arm and steered her towards the stairs.

'This way,' he said, pushing her none too gently. 'You should see the view, Mary Jane. You can see the river from the window.'

'A delight, I'm sure.' Mary Jane slowed to a more dignified pace, not trusting herself to trip on the darkened stairs.

'It's all she has for now.' There was a nervous inflection to Red's forced laughter and Mary Jane knew the reason as soon as she walked into the room. The unmade double bed, covered in grubby sheets and threadbare blankets, was placed under the sloping ceiling. The air was humid, and the heat was overpowering. She had to squint her eyes as the sun was setting and Red hurried forward, lighting two candle stubs.

Dripping a little candlewax onto the end of the mantle over the unlit fireplace, he stuck them down, and although the flame was not very illuminating, it added to the sweltering atmosphere.

'Is this it?' She had been led to believe this was a progressive country. A land fit for heroes coming back from the trenches, but up to now she had seen no evidence to support that theory.

'Cissie's a good woman,' Red's tone was pathetic in his attempt to pacify her. 'And you won't find better for the price she's asking... It won't be for long, Mary Jane, a few weeks should do the trick.'

'Oh, I'll be out of here long before that, Red.' Her eyes took in the smoke-blackened walls and the shedding wallpaper where previous damp patches couldn't hold it. The musty stench proved that any clothes left hanging in this room would not be fit to wear at the end of the day. 'And what's the idea of telling that woman I was your wife?' Hand on hips,

Mary Jane had not yet taken off her coat, unsure she was going to stay.

'I had to save your reputation, Mary Jane. What would it look like, you an unmarried woman, in your condition and us sharing a room—?'

'Woah!' she said as if holding back a horse in full flight. 'You just catch yourself on a minute!' She almost choked on the words. The very thought of it. 'What do you take me for?' Her eyes were wide. 'I might be carrying your brother's child, but that does not give you the right to take his place. If you think I'm going to let you sleep in the same room as me, you are very much mistaken.'

'But we've got to make it look like we're man and wife.' Red paced the meagre room, his hands dug firmly in his pockets. 'I've sorted it out with Cissie.'

'Then you can go and un-sort it!' *The audacity of the man.* 'Who, in God's good name, do you think you are, and more to the point who do you think I am?'

'I know who you are, Mary Jane.' Red's voice took on a sinister tone, low and cold in the high temperature of the room as he moved towards her. 'I know exactly who you are.' He took her chin between his fingers and thumb, squeezing lightly, not enough to hurt her, but to let her know he could overpower her if he wanted to. 'But do you know who I am?' He forced her to look him in the eyes, so like Paddy's, yet not at all. Paddy's eyes had never chilled her blood like Red's were doing now, and quickly, she jerked her head from his grasp, refusing to let him see her acute fear.

'Don't you ever do that again!' she said, her determination born of that fear.

Quiet now, Red pushed up the sash window, but the cord was damaged, and it would not stay open. Busying himself, he looked for something with which to wedge it and, as it would not be needed for the foreseeable time, he jammed it open with the poker.

'I'm sorry, Mary Jane,' he said a short while later, turning to face her, now the affable man she knew – and a shiver ran down her spine, chilled at the speed his personality changed. One minute he was terrifying, and the next he was calm and easy-going. That was not normal, surely? Mary Jane looked through long lashes, she had no intentions of being confined to a small room like this with Red.

7

Red, in one of his black moods, was restless. But Mary Jane had no intention of giving in to his constant pestering for her money. He had no plan to go home, he said, not even for Paddy's funeral, and she wondered if he had feelings for anybody except himself. His eyes followed every move she made, making her skin crawl with his intensity. That first night, Mary Jane slept in the bed with the bread knife under her pillow, while Red slept fitfully on the only fireside chair. The first thing she would do tomorrow was to scrub every inch with hot water and gloopy Aunt Sally disinfectant until the floor was clean enough to eat her dinner from. Only then would her mother's clock take pride of place on the mantlepiece. All through the sleepless night, questions were racing through her head. Even now she could not make sense of her brothers killing Paddy, they were church-going, peace-loving men. And although he had put her in the family way, Paddy was going to stand by her. How did they know Paddy was on his way to the church? They would gain nothing from killing the man who promised to marry her, and everything to lose.

'I will pay you back every penny when I get my first week's wages,' Red said the next day, pulling out his empty pockets, he held his arms open wide, 'I haven't a meg to me name.'

'You must have had something!' she said, noting the half-empty beer jug on the table.

'Cissie bought it,' Red said pathetically 'She said it was a welcome back drink.'

'Paddy would be appalled you have brought me to this,' her voice dipped, and Red had the good grace to look ashamed.

'I'll make it up to you Mary Jane?' He turned his back to her, looking out of the thin sash window, overlooking the back yard that had once housed fine stables but were now filled with junk.

Then a sudden thought struck her. 'You've never once mentioned him,' she said and noticed Red wince. 'Your own twin brother. The closest person to you. How can that be? It's as if Paddy never existed.'

'Leave it, Mary Jane, I can't talk about him now.' Red quickly changed the subject and there was something in his manner that made her suspicious. Was there more to Paddy's death than Red was prepared to tell her? 'Who told my brothers about me and Paddy?' There was an urgency in her voice.

'Just leave it, Mary Jane.' Red moved away from the window and lit the stump of a cigarette. His hands were shaking.

'Somebody must have tipped them off about us running away! But who knew?' She didn't want to ask the question, but it was past her lips before she could stop it.

'I did,' Red whispered after a moment's silence, 'but I didn't mean to, I didn't know they would kill him!' He was unable to meet her demanding gaze. So innocent. So trusting. If she knew what really happened, she would run a knife between his ribs, for sure. He had to tell her something. 'We were on our way to the church when they came round the hill...'

'How did you get the cut above your eye?' she asked, spreading her hands on the table, leaning towards him. If it was the last thing she did, she was going to get Red to tell her everything.

'One of them swung out and caught me,' he said.

'That'll be Colm, he couldn't knock the skin off a rice pudding.'

Red was grateful beyond words when she presumed it was her youngest brother who had fought him. He could not tell her the real reason her husband-to-be met his maker. Paddy had the money *he* owed Dinny O'Mara. But Paddy wouldn't lend it to him. He had it all, did Paddy. The money. The girl. The freedom... Red took in a long deep breath of air. 'They got to him before I could. By the time I got there, Paddy was already dead...' Red's voice was barely a whisper.

'Are you sure it was my brothers who killed him?' Mary Jane paced the floor, rubbing the backs of her arms. She shivered, cold to the bone in the stifling heat.

'I'm certain,' he said. 'Your brothers are hard men. You can't cross them.'

'But they are not killers! They are healers – they took the Hippocratic oath.'

'They will come after you next,' Red said, 'and God help you.' He had to put enough doubt in her mind, so she didn't dare go back home. If she went back to Ireland, she would discover the truth. Red could feel the noose tighten around his neck even now.

'What about Cissie? Does she know why we are here?' Mary Jane asked. There were plenty of people who lived in these parts who knew people back home. It would not take long for word to get back.

'Cissie has had many a runaway here, this is a safe house.'

'Rebels?' Mary Jane asked, inadvertently giving him the answer. 'You run errands for the republicans?' Red looked to the floor, his hands in his empty pockets. He dare not tell her he was on the run from Dinny O'Mara after not paying back a loan. It was better if she thought he was in with the Republicans. That meant she would be in no hurry to flee back home, and he need not accept culpability.

'I'm so sorry, Mary Jane.' He had lusted after her from the moment Paddy had brought her home. She was full of life and deserved a man who could show her a good time. The best house. The richest food. She didn't deserve this rundown attic in a lodging house by the Liverpool dockside. She deserved green fields and fresh air to raise the child.

'You said Paddy didn't want to marry me?' Mary Jane could scarcely get the words out.

'He didn't want to leave the farm... He was saving you from the shame.' The lies tripped over each other in their haste to leave his mouth. He could not let Mary Jane know the truth. How could he tell a pregnant woman he had killed her sweetheart? His own brother!

'It doesn't matter,' Mary Jane whispered, knowing she had been naïve; Paddy's persuasive talk had made her reckless. She did not love him in the way she had dreamed she would love her husband, not truly. She didn't feel the way a new bride should feel. Excited? Fervent? Emotional? None of those things. She was marrying Paddy to give her baby a name and the respectability her family had always enjoyed. Red was right. Paddy was only marrying her because he had to. They both knew her brothers, no matter how caring and respectable, would march him to the church to marry her. So why on earth would they kill him? 'You knew Paddy and I were coming here?' She watched Red, slump in the straight-backed chair, his elbows resting on the table while his fingers raked his bowed head. He attracted trouble like a magnet.

'I'm sorry,' Red's voice was low and dry, 'if it could have been any other way...'

'You should be sorry,' Mary Jane, suddenly angry, spat the words, in no humour to placate Red. 'You should never have told my brothers – you should have protected him. Gone to get help.' But she should not blame him for what had happened to Paddy. She had lain with Paddy so she was guilty too.

'You won't say anything... about Paddy?' Red looked nervous. '...To Cissie, I mean.'

'Why would I? It has nothing to do with her.' Mary Jane felt the bile rise to her throat. It was becoming obvious why Red had been so eager to accompany her here. He was scared her brothers would do the same to him as they had done to Paddy.

'Cissie is a fine woman, once you get to know her.'

'She is no concern of mine,' Mary Jane told him and the more she thought about why she was here, the more she felt cheated. This was not the place she and Paddy were supposed to be. This was a place Red had chosen. The husband was conspicuous by his absence. No wonder Red had wanted to come here. 'She's a trollop of the lowest order, and you're no better than an alley cat! You suit each other perfectly.'

Red breathed a sigh of relief, Mary Jane may not believe every word he told her, but at least she wasn't asking awkward questions. 'I can see you're tired,' he tried to placate her. 'I managed to get some bread and cheese, have a bite to eat.' When he opened the grubby beef cloth to reveal the brittle, sweaty cheese and stale bread, Mary Jane baulked. The food was only fit for pigs.

'You have it,' she said.

'I'll put the kettle on.'

'Where do you intend to put a kettle?' she asked, looking around the sparsely furnished room, with no fire in the grate, and certainly no stove.

'There is a gas stove on the landing,' Red told her. 'We share it with the people downstairs.'

'I won't bother, thanks all the same.' Mary Jane had seen the filthy stove on the way up here and she doubted she could eat anything cooked on it. 'If I'm to stay – and that is a big 'if' – I will not live in a pigsty.' She and her unborn child deserved better.

8

LIVERPOOL - AUGUST 1921

Determined to get away from this lodging house, Mary Jane knew the only way to earn more money was to ask Cissie for the use of her kitchen and oven, although she had to steel herself to pluck up the courage to ask Cissie for the use of her facilities and ventured down to the parlour to put her case forward. The thought of last night's humiliation adding strength to her backbone, which she sorely needed. 'I will pay extra for the use of kitchen facilities,' she told Cissie, who could refuse anything bar temptation. And she was always tempted by money.

'Of course,' Cissie gave her a look that said she wouldn't have it any other way. 'I'll not give kitchen space away buckshee.'

Even though the price was more than Mary Jane had bargained for, she knew she had no choice.

'It's down here.' Cissie led her to the half stained-glass door at the end of the wide lobby and down three stone steps.

When she saw the kitchen, Mary Jane's heart sank. She was

going to have her work cut out getting this lot cleaned up before she could start baking.

'That cooker is manky,' she said, her stomach turning when she saw the grease-covered stove laden with an unidentifiable black crust that may once have been food. The tiled floor was so dirty, she had no idea what colour it was supposed to be. 'How the hell nobody has died of food poisoning is beyond me.'

After a long day on her knees, with a scrubbing brush, hot water, and Aunt Sally disinfectant to hand, the kitchen was clean enough to cook in. But Mary Jane responded when Cissie had the temerity to come and inspect her work.

'I want a lock on the pantry door,' she said, knowing her ingredients would not last long if they were within easy reach.

'You brazen hussy, you come into *my* house and tell *me* you want locks on *my* cupboard doors!' said Cissie. 'Well, let *me* tell *you*, there will be no such thing.'

'In that case, I'll not be leaving my stores here.' Mary Jane would have to haul her ingredients up and down three flights of stairs, twice a day, if she was to be sure her quality ingredients were not exchanged for shoddy goods.

* * *

The weather still showed no sign of producing any rain, and Mary Jane could feel her clothes growing tighter as she queued in the butcher's shop, dismayed when she saw Ina King, the woman who had remarked on her torn stockings that first night. Edging nearer to the counter, Mary Jane studied the meat on offer, knowing she had to be particular about what she bought. There would be no scrag ends or cheap cuts in her pies. Only the best she could afford would go into them. She had to make an impression quickly if she was to save for her own business. Quality was obviously of no importance to Ina, buying the cheapest minced meat, which Mary Jane would not feed to a dog. She watched the portly butcher carefully. In his blood-stained, navy-blue striped apron and straw hat, he had a cheery word and a compliment for every customer. Buttering them up before they even reached the counter. Keeping his customers occupied with his blarney, he dropped the meat into the brass pan, and Mary Jane noticed his little finger pushing down the scales. As Ina was being blithely flattered by his easy wit, he was giving her less meat.

'I think you need to add a few more ounces to that pan,' said Mary Jane, nodding to the scales. The easy-going chatter suddenly stopped, and Ina turned, giving her a quizzical albeit admonishing look.

Mary Jane said, loud enough for all to hear: 'You probably didn't notice his little finger pressing on the scales, when you were having such a good laugh.'

'You might be right there, missus,' said the butcher brightly. 'I will check the weight again.' Mary Jane could not be certain, but she was sure he muttered something under his breath. A moment later, he looked Mary Jane in the eye and said with forced joviality, 'Mrs Redfern is right, ladies. You lot were so busy entertaining me; I didn't realise.'

'She has her eyes to business, does Mrs Redfern,' Ina King scornfully quipped, even though the observation was in her favour. Then in a lower voice just loud enough to be overheard, she said, 'Mind, if I had a husband like hers, I'd have my eyes out on stalks, because he's not above diddling people out of a few bob neither.'

'How long has that beef been hung?' Mary Jane ignored the slight when she finally got to the front of the queue. She was in no humour to fight Red's battles, and she knew Ina spoke the truth. It was just a pity her good character was being brought into question by association.

'Long enough,' the butcher said icily, letting out a long, impatient sigh.

'Your tone could be a blessing on a hot day like this,' Mary Jane said, eyeing the best cuts of meat in the window. The butcher glared, which, to a meeker shopper might have proved intimidating, but not to Mary Jane who matched his stony frown. 'That meat does not look dark enough to me,' she persisted, 'I'm sure a good vet could have it on its feet in no time.'

'You'll not get better around here,' said the butcher with a lofty air. A challenge, to which Mary Jane rose magnificently.

'To be sure? In that case, I expect to receive every morsel of meat my money can buy. I don't want bone or gristle, nor do I expect fourteen ounces of meat and two ounces of fat when I ask for a pound of best beef.'

'I beg your pardon!' His neck turned a mottled red, she noticed, as his eyes quickly skimmed the line of customers. No doubt weighing up how much of an argument he could risk, and his ready smile quickly returned when he saw the line of women watching the floor show. 'I think you may have drawn the wrong conclusion, when you saw me steady the pan,' he said in a more affable tone, knowing she had obviously clocked his little deception, but he did not wish to come into direct conflict and lose a sale. Becoming friendlier, he addressed the women in the queue: 'An eagle-eyed woman obviously knows good meat when she sees it.' He gave a theatrical bow and encouraged the other women in the queue to applaud Mary Jane.

'I am not here to buy half a pound of scrag ends, Mr,' she

said, lifting her chin in confident defiance. 'I've been around enough farms and butchered more animals than I care to remember.' She stretched the truth just a little. She had helped Paddy to carve a small lamb. Once. 'I want the best, and lots of it. I am prepared to pay good money on the nose, but if you cannot supply me, then—'

'Now, now,' he said, catching her elbow, 'let's not be hasty.' Not one to let a good sale go, he stretched his moustachioed lips. 'I'm sure I can tempt you with something.'

There was no mistaking the lascivious tone in his voice and Mary Jane gave him a look that could wither a horse. 'I doubt that.' She stiffened, this fella would try it on if she let him, and there was as much chance of that as there was of her dancing down Beamer Street with a pan on her head. 'I've seen better.' Her eyes skimmed the trays in the window. 'I could braise some of that beef in a slow oven for a week and still be able to sole my shoes with it.'

'Not this lot, you won't,' he said, pointing to the next tray, aware they had a captive, highly inquisitive audience. Mary Jane eyed the meat, it was pricier, but still within her budget, although she wasn't going to let him off easily.

'It's filling I'm after, not padding.' She would start as she meant to go on, with the best. There was no point in selling shoddy goods. That was not the way to run a business and certainly would not keep her customers at the market or help her to get new ones. Her child's welfare depended upon it.

After a bit of arguing and a fair bit of haggling, Mary Jane got what she wanted at a price that would give a good return.

'If we work together,' she said in a low voice, which did not carry to the other customers, 'we can both make on the deal.' As she left the shop, carrying a half-full wicker basket, her back was straight and her head held high. The butcher shook his head in bewilderment. He had never met anybody quite like Mary Jane before.

Reliving the scene in her head, pleased at her own audacity, Mary Jane did not see Mr. Everdine coming round the corner, until she walked slap-bang into him and dropped the basket of provisions. The roots of her russet-coloured hair tingled, as the blood rushed warmly up her neck to her scalp, and Mary Jane silently scolded herself for being so clumsy.

Not one to admit, not even to herself, that Cal Everdine unnerved her somewhat, she could not determine the tangle of emotions that robbed her of her voice. So close, she detected the clean smell of soap, mingled with something she had only met once before, when she and her brothers went to the courthouse to have the deeds of their house signed over, after their parents died. The official had been smoking a big fat cigar, which had fascinated Mary Jane. She had never experienced the aroma before, and she liked it. Even though her brothers were practicing doctors, who had a bit of money put by, they smoked only clay pipes, unlike the men of wealth and importance who afforded themselves the luxury of fine cigars. Yet, Mr. Everdine was a working man, a carter who worked from dawn 'til dusk.

'Please accept my apologies,' he said, taking her elbow to steady her, his indigo- coloured eyes holding her gaze longer than they ought.

'It... It was all my fault,' Mary Jane stammered, about to retrieve the meat from the pavement. However, before she could, he was gripping the floppy red cuts of beef between fingers and thumb. When he straightened, he seemed at a loss to know what to do with it. 'Here, give it to me.' Mary Jane was annoyed with herself for acting like a first-class eejit. 'It was my fault.' Quickly, she wrapped the meat back in the newspaper and shoved it in her basket.

'You're not going to cook that, are you?' he asked in surprise. 'It's been on the dusty pavement.'

'That's not the only place it's been,' Mary Jane answered logically. 'The abattoir is not noted for its marbled floors.' It had taken a fair bit of haggling to get the meat she wanted at the price she was willing to pay.

'Yes, but...' he paused and, smiling, shook his head. 'Of course, you are right,' he acceded to her womanly knowledge. 'Who am I to know such things?'

Mary Jane was impressed by his warmth, but more so by his genial compliance. The men she had known were not noted for their sensitivity. 'A bit of a wash under the tap,' she said practically, 'it will be as good as new. After all, it is going to be cooked.'

'I can get you some more,' he said apologetically, and Mary Jane looked at him with something akin to suspicion. Why would he do such a thing when she had told him a good wash would suffice?

'There is no need,' she said a little primly. 'It's very kind of you to offer, but I can manage from here!' She bid him good day, leaving him watching her proud departure. If she was going to make a go of earning her own living, she had to be sure she was starting the same way as she meant to go on. That meant being independent, not letting any man be a drain on her.

9

'You can't have lost your wallet?' Mary Jane's irritation silenced Red's muttering as he dragged a mismatched cushion off the brown leather chair, knowing this was not the first time he said he had lost money. 'Where could you have lost it? Think now, Red. Retrace your steps. Remember where you've been, who you've been with...' *Which alehouse or bookies runner have you visited?*

'Shh, Mary Jane, can't you see I'm thinking.' He moved about the room, scraping back his thick dark hair with one hand and lighting the stump of a cigarette with the other. 'I visited St Augustine's church... To light a candle and give thanks for our good fortune.' His gaze never met hers and he took a deep draw of smoke into his lungs, giving himself plenty of time to get the lie straight in his head. After a short while, he coughed, thumped his chest, and continued, 'Then I came upon himself – the flower seller with a barrow on Stanley Road.' He nodded to the milk bottle displaying a few limp violas, 'So I got you some.'

'Losing your wallet is easily done, I suppose,' she said,

eyeing the paltry flowers that were insufficient to call a bunch. 'Is the barrow next door to the pub by any chance?' Mary Jane knew he could embroider a tale until it was unrecognisable. His eyes hooded, avoiding her gaze.

'I can't say I noticed, but I told Cissie I'd be straight back down with the rent. She's going to town this afternoon and is waiting on the money.'

She watched him throw the cushion on the floor with such force, it skidded across the room. Plunging his hand down the back of the chair, he continued scattering horsehair stuffing onto the floorboards. His eyes fixed on the cracked ceiling as his hand slid back and forth.

When he told her, he had been taken on at the docks, Mary Jane was delighted. Each day she would give him his carry-out of fresh, thickly cut bread and cheese, not forgetting his *baccy* money so he could have a smoke at breaktime and a few coppers to whet his whistle at the end of a day's toil. She enjoyed having the room to herself. The solitude gave her a chance to come to terms with her impending motherhood. Knowing she was carrying a part of Paddy with her was little reward for his loss, but she was comforted by the thought, nevertheless.

Straightening up, Red shook his head and sighed, with nothing except a mouldy crust of bread and a tram ticket to show for his endeavours.

'It had the rent money in it.' His face was a mask of disappointment, which Mary Jane would have believed had she not seen him practise the expression many times. However, something in his manner told her he was genuinely upset this time. He had been so pleased when he came in from the docks last night with his wage packet. Red was in high spirits, waving it above his head, informing her they would live like kings on the proceeds. He had even suggested she stop selling her bakes in the local market, telling her, if her brothers came looking, that would be the first place they would go. But Mary Jane had paid no heed, wondering why on earth they would think of coming to Liverpool looking for her. There was no forwarding address with the note she had left for them. She had written:

Don't worry, or look for me, I am safe with Paddy. We are going to be married today. M.J. xx

When Red told her he had to work a week in hand, she thought the idea was ridiculous. Suspecting he was lying, she refused to give up her own work. Mary Jane knew people around the docks lived hand to mouth, day by day, they could not afford to wait two weeks for money. There would be an uproar. However, she had nobody whom she could ask. The local women turned their back when she walked down the street and continued their conversation in whispers.

'Was there anything in it to lose?' she said, unable to keep her thoughts to herself. Eyeing the stony look in his eyes, she did not trust his volcanic temper to remain dormant.

'Are you doubting me?' His words were little more than a whisper, causing a beat of apprehension to flutter in the pit of her stomach. 'After all I've done for you!' Since he started on the docks, he had become even more high-handed than usual. Even going so far as to take on the attitudes of real husbands, telling her what time his tea should be ready, expecting her to fetch and carry for him – even though he had not yet handed over a penny. It was only the proceeds of the pies sold in the market, and her own secret stash of money that kept them from the poorhouse.

'All I'm saying is—'

'Accusing me of lying? I've pulled my tripe out on that dock – and I won't have you doubt me.' Red's voice grew louder, overpowering her words and Mary Jane knew that to argue was futile. Instinct told her something wasn't right as she busied herself collecting his plate and putting it into the galvanised bowl, for washing. That was when it happened again.

She felt the first stirrings of motherhood, like a butterfly's wing fluttering inside her, and she stopped what she was doing, to ensure she had not imagined it. But there it was again, and Mary Jane's hand went quickly to her stomach, her heart so full, it brought tears to her eyes. With renewed determination, she vowed she would do all she could for this child. As she pounded the boiled potatoes into mash, her eyes filled with tears. Exhausted, Mary Jane had been up since four this morning, baking her pies and tarts, then she hawked them in the market before trundling back in the suffocating, arid heat of the afternoon to make their evening meal.

'I've been good to you, Mary Jane,' Red's tone softened when he saw her tears, 'bringing you over to this country, making sure you are safe from your brothers...'

'Is that a fact?' Mary Jane wiped her eyes and took a deep breath. She had heard enough of his blather.

'I'll tell you a fact.' Red's tone was spare, tight. 'If it wasn't for me, your brothers would have found you already. But remember this. You're no better than those women who parade along the dock road looking for unsuspecting men to fleece.'

'What did you say?' Mary Jane slowly turned to look at him, her voice deceptively calm as a cyclone of fury rose within her. How dare he! She had kept him fed and housed; from the minute they stepped foot in this forsaken place. Her eyes glowered with rage as she sliced the bread she had baked earlier. Her hand holding the bread knife rose swiftly, and he caught her wrist. Gripping it hard, she dropped the knife as he possessively pulled her close so her hand splayed across his chest. She could not move. If she was a man, she would knock him to the ground. But she wasn't, she was a pregnant woman, defenceless against his strength.

As he brought his face so close their lips were almost touching, he said: 'I persuaded Cissie to take us in, knowing she doesn't take pregnant women.' He sneered, his stale beer breath enveloping her, as her knee met his groin with incredible force. Red doubled up, gasping as Mary Jane pulled free from his grip, rubbing her wrist. The action allowing her long enough to quell the desire to pick up the knife again and use it.

'May God forgive me for stooping to your level.' If the truth came out that she and Red were not man and wife, she would make herself homeless in this portside town and endanger the life of her unborn child. However, Mary Jane knew her maternal instinct to protect her young would dictate her actions from now on. Taking in a long stream of steady, unhurried air she leaned forward, her eyes full of danger, her words low. 'Don't ever call me that again,' she said, her eyes unflinching as they met his, 'or so help me, Red, I will summon my brothers, and they will go for you, before they go for me.' Her voice was determined, silencing his obvious retort with its intensity. She knew he was wary of anything or anybody relating to authority. Edging towards him, just a little, Mary Jane said in a voice that sent a chill through him, 'Until then, Christie Redfern, you'd better sleep with one eye open...' She bent and picked up the knife, leaving the threat hanging in the air.

'I'm sorry, Mary Jane,' he said when he recovered enough to speak, 'my mouth runs away with itself sometimes. I didn't mean it. You know I would never hurt you.' He looked sheepish and his mouth turned up into a lazy grin. 'You wouldn't attack me in my sleep?'

'Don't tempt me, Red.' She noticed his temper died as quickly as it flared.

'I don't know what came over me,' he said, his eyes now soft and round like Paddy's.

'You will if you ever say it again.' Mary Jane eyed the chamber pot under the bed, and knew she would have no compunction about using it as a weapon if need be. Nevertheless, she was tired of the fight. Tired of the isolation. Tired of the fact, she was paying him to protect her, when she was far stronger than he was. Mary Jane suppressed a sigh that would let him know she had calmed completely and was now thinking rationally. She had to get out of this house, away from his skulduggery that was dragging her down. Away from the vinegary landlady who took Red to her bed when her husband was away, who looked Mary Jane up and down, but never in the eye. Red slammed out of the room and hurried down the stairs without a word.

Placing the galvanised bowl onto the table to collect the dishes, ready to take down to the scullery, her eyes were drawn to the chair. Red had been quick to say his wallet was not down there. Maybe she should have a look. Scraping the back of her hand along the hardwood frame, Mary Jane dug into the nooks and creases. Then her fingers brushed against something cold and soft. 'Yes!' Mary Jane cried, managing to pinch the cheap leather wallet with finger and thumb. After a bit of tugging, she prised it free. Moments later, she had it in her hand. Delighted, she hugged it to her bosom. He could pay the rent! Red told her he had kept the rent money separate. Opening the flap, she poked her fingers into one of the two pockets, searching, then the other. Nothing. Both were empty, save for a few bits of paper.

She took out the folded papers and gasped with dismay when she read them. One was a paid invoice from the landlord of the Jolly Jack Tar along the street and one from the Tram Tavern over the bridge. Another contained the bogus name of a well-known local bookie!

Then she discovered a small brown square. Unfolding it, she found his first, *and* second, week's pay packets. He *had* lied all along. How could she be so gullible? Red was now earning his own money, and by the look of things he intended to keep it for himself. Mary Jane realised with a certainty born of experience, she was no longer of any use to him.

She flung the wallet with such force across the room that it bounced off the wall and hit the window. Red had every intention of paying his debts, it seemed, but only to the creditors who would subsidise him in the coming week.

'I kept you from the day we stepped foot in this place,' she cried. 'Well not any more!' He had taken her for a fool for the very last time. Did he think he could spend every penny he earned enjoying himself, and expect her to fund his wasteful lifestyle? Red could go to hell!

Looking around the clean but austere room with its peeling wallpaper and musty smell, the yearning to be anywhere but this tiny attic room, with a man she could not bear to look at, could not be quelled. She had to get out of here. Closing the attic door, she went quietly along the landing and stood at the window.

Outside, the street was quiet, and Mary Jane opened the stiff sash window a little, allowing the feeble breeze to enter the stuffy confines of the house. Letting out a long uneasy sigh, she needed to work out what to do next.

The distant sound of singing voices, and the plink-plonk of an upright piano came from the public house further down the street, invading her troubled thoughts, wondering what it was that attracted men through the opaque doors of the tavern, like moths to a flame. Although she would never know. Carrying a child out of wedlock may be the most shameful thing she had ever done, but walking into a crowded bar full of drunken men was unthinkable. Looking across to Beamer Terrace and the bay-windowed houses that went right down to the docks, her gaze, as usual travelled to the river, towards her home across the sea. Lost in thought and homesickness, she heard the clip-clop of horse's hooves and could not bring herself to move. Watching Mr. Everdine padlock the huge double gates before stopping to also gaze down towards the river, she wondered if he was dreaming of far-off lands, as she had been doing, or if he just wanted to go for a swim in this suffocating heat. Turning, he pushed his key into the brass lock of his front door and stepped inside the dark interior, closing out the world behind him. What was his story? she wondered. She could see his broad outline moving about, through the upstairs window, her curiosity growing. He lit the gas mantle, and Mary Jane watched him blow out the match. The flare at the end of the thin stick wavered, as his lips formed a gentle 'o', seeming reluctant to be extinguished. Another breath, stronger this time, put out the flame and he threw it out of the open sash window. As he was about to close the window, his hands were momentarily still. He looked up with unswerving intensity in her direction but did not acknowledge her. She should look away. But something in his gaze held her fast.

Mary Jane gave a small bow of her head, admitting she had seen him, and he did the same. She should feel ashamed, but she didn't feel any such thing. She was just being neighbourly. So why should she feel she was doing something wrong?

A long-lost memory came back to her. Legs akimbo, aged about nine or ten, she had freewheeled down Mulligan's Steep on an old boneshaker bicycle her brothers had made for her. The two-wheeler had no brakes, and the rapid decline was sharp, even more thrilling for the danger it promised. The same feeling, she experienced when she saw Cal Everdine.

Her eyes fixed on the man in the window, whose hand stilled on the bottom sash before closing it securely for the night. If she had any sense, she would heed the voice inside her head that told her to beware, but Mary Jane was headstrong and didn't listen to this particular piece of common sense. One thing she did know, however, was that she had no right to feel this way. No right at all.

10

Mary Jane could stand the suffocating attic air no longer and decided to go downstairs and sit on the front step awhile, as she would have done back home.

'Davey Haywood put that girl down, this minute! And you, Ruby Stone, get yourself away home!' There was a pause as two young people, no more than fourteen or fifteen, separated, and ran laughing into their respective houses, her landlady's daughter passing her in a flash, dressed in the latest fashion of a dropped waist, navy blue sailor dress complete with white collar of navy-blue edging. 'She's always up for a lark with the boys that one,' she said to Mary Jane when she saw her watching. It was the girl from the teashop who wore her dark hair in a shingled bob. 'She's a little harem-scarem, but harmless enough. Carrying on like a pair of hooligans.' Daisy gave a half-hearted clout to her brother that did not connect, and he grinned as he went whistling up the lobby. 'It's the heat,' she went on.' Ma says it brings out animal urges. I think she's right, because my brother acts like a chimpanzee when that girl shows her face. Our Davey ought to have more sense now he's in long trousers!'

Mary Jane was taken aback at Daisy's friendliness. Even when she waved to the neighbours or said *how 'r ya*, her greeting was ignored.

Daisy tilted her head to Cissie Stone's house, and whispered, 'That girl is always egging the lads on. She'll be getting herself talked about one of these fine days.'

Mary Jane knew Cissie's girl was getting herself talked about already, especially by some of the male boarders, who did nothing to hide their admiration of her pubescent attributes. Although, having a mother like hers, was it any wonder? Cissie Stone gave board and lodgings to men who had little regard for authority, stayed up singing and drinking until the wee small hours, without a single rebuke from the landlady. To Mary Jane's way of thinking, it was little wonder the daughter looked elsewhere for attention when her own mother was loath to give her any. However, she didn't know if her observation would vex or please her neighbour, so she remained silent.

'How are you settling in?' asked Daisy and Mary Jane buried her troubles, not wanting to divulge anything about her past

'I'm managing,' Mary Jane answered, giving nothing away.. 'You're Daisy, if I remember right enough,' she said with a ready smile.

'Daisy May Hayward, but everybody calls me Daisy. You looked a bit lost when I first saw you if you don't mind my saying.'

'I remember,' Mary Jane answered. She liked the girl's frankness; it made a nice change from being ignored by the rest of the street, especially Ina King who seemed to have taken an instant dislike to her for some reason. A woman of indeterminate age came out to see what all the fuss was about, and Daisy moved over for her to stand on the step.

'This is my ma, Molly Hayward, she's a widow,' Daisy told Mary Jane, who smiled and nodded a greeting to the girl's mother, who was pulling her shawl around her ample but well-upholstered frame.

'As you may have gathered,' said Molly with an easy smile and an outstretched hand, 'my daughter is like the *Daily Post* – always first with any news.'

'Sorry, Ma, you know my tongue runs away with itself,' Daisy answered, and Molly gave her a motherly nudge with her elbow.

'I'm Mary Jane Star— Redfern,' she quickly corrected herself, almost giving the game away, and once more she wished that Red had not told everybody she was his wife.

'I see your husband come and go,' Molly said with the same frankness as her daughter, 'like quicksilver – there and gone in a flash.'

'He is so,' Mary Jane answered in a low voice; she wanted to tell her neighbour a lot more but feared that if she did, she would forget to stop.

'How are you? I see you going out each morning with your basket full of bread and pies,' said Molly. And the concern in her voice brought an unexpected, and unfamiliar, lump to Mary Jane's throat. Not usually given to bouts of self-pity, she straightened her back and took a deep breath of humid evening air, ignoring the sting at the back of her eyes.

'Have you settled in then?' Molly asked, and Mary Jane nodded, not trusting herself to mention the snub from the other women in the street, which hurt more than she would admit. 'I wouldn't have imagined a nice girl like you lodging at Cissie Stone's house.'

'It's a roof over my head,' Mary Jane answered simply. She surmised that Molly had been a neighbour of Cissie Stone for many a year, given the familiar way Daisy had spoken. So, it was wise to keep her own counsel, until she got to know everyone better.

'Well, I'll have to get my lot in for their supper,' said Molly. 'Don't be a stranger, I always have the kettle on the boil.' They headed indoors but didn't close the front door and she sat a while longer.

Mary Jane could tell Molly was the motherly type. The kind of woman she expected her own mother might have been, had she lived longer. Standing, she turned to go back inside, about to step into the passage when she saw Cal Everdine crossing the street. He was headings toward her, and she waited until he reached the gatepost.

'I was wondering,' he said in that familiar drawl that was not from around these parts, 'I have seen you go out in the mornings with a heavy-looking basket.'

'You have,' Mary Jane did not like enquiries into her private dealings.

He pushed his battered fedora to the back of his head, revealing indigo-coloured eyes set against a mahogany complexion, and Mary Jane was surprised at how much younger and more handsome he looked. 'Please, tell me to mind my own business...' he paused, 'Although I am sure you will. I have a barrow that you might like to use, it's not huge, but...' He cleared his throat, 'I mean, it's yours if you want it, you are very welcome to have it.' Cal knew he was making a right hash of this. He had watched her struggling to carry the weighty basket, realising she was with child, and that fool of a husband allowed her to do so. That was when he had hit on the idea, a barrow would help with her walk to and from the market. 'I can bring it over now if you like.'

'That's very kind of you, Mr Everdine,' Mary Jane's heart felt like a runaway train, 'but you see—'

'I've overstepped the mark,' he interrupted. He had intended to come over yesterday to offer the handy-sized barrow he had made specially for her – although he would keep that part to himself.

Mary Jane hastened to enlighten him, her words coming out in a rush. 'No, honestly, it's not that...' She lowered her voice. 'You see, my landlady would say I had the cheek of the divil himself, parking a barrow outside her house.' Nobody had been so kind as Mr Everdine, and she must not throw his generosity back in his face. 'Even though a barrow would be a godsend to me, Cissie would throw me out on the street.'

'It's a pity about her.' Cal Everdine's words showed contempt, and Mary Jane could not help but like him even more. Nor could she believe her good fortune. First, Molly had invited her in for a cuppa, and once again, Cal had been her Good Samaritan. 'Here,' he said, fishing in his waistcoat pocket, 'this is the spare key to my yard, let yourself in any time you please, so Lady Muck doesn't have to insult her eyes by seeing a barrow outside this house.' He was quiet for a moment, as if weighing something up in his head, then he said to Mary Jane, 'I have a gas oven you can use to bake your pies and bread, and it would do until you get fixed up. You could prepare your bakes in your lodgings and cook them in my kitchen...' He stopped at the sight of her stunned expression and wondered if he had said the wrong thing, knowing how independent she was.

'You would do that for me?' Mary Jane could not believe he would put himself out like this. Cissy Stone had taken full advantage of her baking, since she had been renting her oven, and had no compunction whatsoever about slipping a pie or two into her cupboard when Mary Jane's back was turned.

'Well, I'm not home most of the day,' Cal explained, 'it's no use having it sitting there going to waste. You might as well get some use out of it.' A ghost of a smile shone from his eyes, and if she wasn't supposed to be a respectable married woman, Mary Jane would have flung her arms around his neck and kissed him.

'I don't know what to say... Thank you so much, Mr Everdine!'

'Cal,' he said firmly. 'My father was Mr Everdine, I'm Cal. And it is my pleasure.' He could hardly believe how pleased he felt that she had taken him up on his offer, and straightening his hat, he turned and headed back across the street. 'Call in anytime.'

Mary Jane hugged herself. Life had suddenly got better.

11

LIVERPOOL – SEPTEMBER 1921

The arrangement with Cal changed Mary Jane's fortune. She spent most of her day out of Cissie's lodgings, which left her feeling stronger and more independent than ever, much to Red's annoyance.

Although one thing had not changed. She could feel Red's lingering eyes stripping the clothes from her body, making her feel dirty, as the thrum of her own heartbeat pulsated inside her head. Keeping her eyes low, so as not to meet his lascivious gaze, her stomach tightened as she cleared away the breakfast dishes, keeping herself busy with mundane chores before taking her uncooked pies and bread for baking. Red knew she needed the table cleared, yet he had no intention of moving, waiting for her to ask him to shift himself so he could start an argument. She nearly had enough money to move out of this house and out of his reach.

The night before had been humid, and she must have kicked off the bedclothes in her sleep, when she was woken by something moving up her bare leg. Startled, she had lain there, too scared to breathe, let alone move. But it didn't take long to realise the thing that had disturbed her sleep was Red's hand stroking her inner thigh. Suddenly wide awake, she had realised he had climbed into her bed, lying next to her. Her fear had quickly turned to anger, and she had gathered every ounce of strength she could to thrust her elbow into his stomach. Red had let out an uncontrolled groan and landed in an untidy heap on the floorboards. Yet, just as quickly, he had been back on his feet, hovering over her. Mary Jane knew she was not having a terrible dream and had used the only weapon in her armoury, threatening to scream the house down if he came one step nearer. His tread was light as he slunk out of the room, and she had breathed a trembling sigh of relief. Pushing a straight-backed chair under the handle of the door, she had felt safer. But for how long?

* * *

'I received a letter from home, telling me about your brother's accident,' Cissie Stone told Red a few evenings later. Mary Jane was passing the parlour door on her way to the stairs, with her ingredients for tomorrow's bakes. The words stopped her in her tracks. An accident? Is that what was being said back home?

'I believe it happened while I was travelling over here.' Red answered in a convincing tone, that proved to Mary Jane how easy it was for him to lie. Red knew Paddy had been murdered. On his wedding day. By her brothers, he had said. Paddy was dead before they even headed for the boat.

'His death must have come as a shock?' Cissie said, her voice softer than usual.

'I didn't go back, for the funeral, to me he is not dead,' Red had a conscience that could be stretched like elastic if he chose to ignore something it wasn't happening. 'I mean, he is still alive to me, looking after the farm.' There was a moment's silence in the room behind the half-closed parlour door. 'I couldn't ask Mary Jane for the boat fare,' he continued, 'she is the only one earning since work dried up at the docks.'

What work would that be? Mary Jane wondered. Red had only done enough to pay his bar bill since he got here. Fighting the urge to go and tell the landlady the truth, Mary Jane hurried upstairs with her box of ingredients, and closed the attic door with the heel of her shoe. But she couldn't keep still. After locking away her ingredients in the small cupboard she had bought cheaply from the market and lugged back here on the handcart, she made her way down the stairs and outside to the front step where the air was cooler.

Molly was putting out her empty milk bottles on the step next door. They had got into many a conversation at this time of the evening when Molly's children were settled inside after a day's play and Mary Jane, glad of Molly's friendship, had finished her day's work, selling baked goods. After a catch-up, Molly went inside and Mary Jane moved to go back to the attic, catching sight of Cal locking the large double gates leading to the stable, and her heartbeat quickened. As he did most of these unusually warm late summer nights, he stood with his back to her, his hands in the pockets, gazing down to the river, lingering for a while before turning to go indoors. Mary Jane suspected that underneath his quiet exterior, Cal Everdine's feelings were as deep as the River Mersey. In the time she had been using his oven – free of charge – he was polite, never failing to greet her with a smile and the nod of his head, or the light touch of his fingertips to the brim of his battered hat. If they met in the street he greeted her like an old friend. Yet, in an unguarded moment, he seemed deep in thought, and didn't say much, apart from good morning or good evening – but why would he? He owed her no conversation, although he did acknowledge her presence, unlike the women of Beamer Street, who pointedly ignored her when she walked along the street. She watched Cal turn, pause a moment to give her a goodnight nod, and disappear through the door and stairs that led to his flat above the empty shop. Mary Jane had become accustomed to living in Beamer Street, thanks to the friendship of Molly and Cal Everdine. Her savings were growing nicely, and very soon she hoped to have enough money to make an offer to rent the empty shop across the road.

* * *

Cal looked down to the quiet street towards the river, the gateway to the Americas, to Canada, where he spent so many of his formative years. After his nightly bath, he retired to his bedroom down the hall. The full moon giving enough light to see the sparsely furnished bedroom that contained only a queen-sized bed, a chest of drawers he had made while recuperating from his war wounds and a table, with a single chair he had made to go with it. The room was far from cosy, but there was no point in furnishing a flat that was rarely used except to sleep in. This place was serviceable for his needs. Not lavish, as would be expected from a man of his means. But what good was money when he had nobody to share it with. He worked to fill the hours in his day, not to earn. But the more he worked, the more the money piled up. He could have anything his heart desired, except the one thing he wanted most. Looking across the street, his eyes raised to the empty attic window. Mary Jane had made him realise how much he missed the company of a woman.

12

When she got back to the lodgings the following day, Red was in Cissie's parlour as usual. Mary Jane crept past the door and up the stairs, giving her a chance to take the money she had earned that day and hide it somewhere safe, knowing Red would think nothing of going through her purse if he thought there was money to be had.

Separating the rent money, she had enough to replenish her stock. Mary Jane had an idea. Opening the door, she went out onto the gloomy landing and headed towards the small window at the far end. The pelmet was deep enough to hold a tangle of dusty fern and, climbing onto a rickety chair, she lifted the plant from the pot, secreting a roll of pound notes under the withered house plant, so neglected she doubted it had seen water since the beginning of the drought. Satisfied her money would be safe, she climbed down and went back into the attic room as Red was coming up the stairs.

'How're you fixed for a few coppers?' he asked in that pathetic tone which grated on her nerves like fingernails scraping a brick wall.

'Money doesn't grow on trees, Red. I can't just conjure it out of thin air,' she said. She was working so hard to pay rent, keep her and Red in food and fuel, and buy her ingredients, determined she was one day going to manage her own bakery and teashop. But that didn't matter to Red as long as he got his ale money. Mary Jane was tired of his dark moods dragging every bit of spirit from her. He was nothing but a sponge, soaking up everything she could offer and giving nothing in return. She refused to bow to his begging, his insistence their straitened situation was all her fault.

'I would not be in this position if it wasn't for—' She stopped suddenly, reluctant to blame Paddy, yet unable to put her shame into words.

'If it wasn't for what, Mary Jane?' Red's hostile glare was proof she deserved to be punished, with words if nothing else. 'You need to bring down that proud tilt of your head, because, as we both know,' he glared at the expanding swell of her stomach, 'you have nothing at all to be proud of.' The return quip she had ready, dissipated like morning dew in daylight. 'You wonder why none of the local women will speak to you.' Red was itching for that feisty spark that made her eyes flash. 'They can see you for what you are, Mary Jane.'

'And what am I, Red?' Mary Jane leaned forward. She had put up with enough of his stinging comments. 'Nobody knows the truth except you and me.'

'You hold your head so high, you will drown when it rains.' He was going to make her feel small if it was the last thing he did.

'Well, I'm a long time waiting – it hasn't rained for months – and as for that lot out there, I don't care what they think,' Mary Jane answered defiantly. But she did care. She cared deeply. Her good name was everything to her, never having had cause to hang her head in shame before she picked up with the Redfern brothers. She silently berated herself for thinking badly of the man she had intended to marry. The man who promised to stand by her, and she realised that Red's poison whispers, regarding Paddy only marrying her because he had to, and not because he loved her, had begun to take a toll. She was in no position to be stuck-up. All she wanted to do, was bake, sell her pies, and bread, and save enough money for a better future. Unconsciously, placing a protective hand on her abdomen, she knew her child deserved the best she could give it.

'I would not have taken advantage of you, as Paddy did.' Red's rasping tone was calmer now, yet it broke the silence so abruptly, she almost jumped. 'Did you know he laced your lemonade with poteen at the dance?' Red watched her reaction closely, satisfied he had knocked the wind right out of her when her jaw dropped and her eyes opened wide. But just as quickly she recovered.

'Paddy didn't bring my drinks, after the first. You did!' She always suspected Red would sink lower than a snail's belly if it got him what he wanted. 'You have always been jealous of Paddy. Even in death, you strive to tarnish his name.'

'Believe what you like, but how would I know such things if he hadn't told me,' he asked, before going on to described the intimate lovemaking between her and Paddy.

Mary Jane shuddered. The way he was telling it made their love sound sordid. Shattering the beautiful memory.

'How could I possibly know all of that if he hadn't spouted every detail?' Red sounded triumphant, not revealing he had watched from the dark depths of the hayloft.

Mary Jane's fingers gripped the flat iron as she fought to stay in control. 'I'll tell you what I think, shall I?' Red pulled himself up straight in the chair. 'If it wasn't for me saying I was your husband, you'd have been driven out, and not just from Beamer Street either; the women around here are more particular than they are given credit for.'

'You could have told Cissie I was a widow.' Mary Jane wished he had, because saying he was her husband had caused her nothing but heartache. 'You have never offered so much as a penny towards the rent. You work only enough hours to serve yourself.' Red was silent for a time, his belligerent glare taking in every inch of her.

'You and your fancy ideas about having your own business. Well, d'you know what I think?' he snarled like a feral animal. 'I think you are heading for a fall you will never recover from.'

Mary Jane said nothing. She had learned that to react invited an onslaught of Red's volcanic outrage. Yet, her silence seemed to unnerve him and caused him to slam out of the door and head for the ale house, giving her a few hours of solitary cogitation.

Save for the gentle tick of her mother's clock, silence hung heavy in the small triangular attic room. As soon as she could afford to, she would be out of here. She had quite a bit saved, but she would find a new place, before her baby was born in January.

13

'Do you want some tea?' Mary Jane asked Red, after a day's work. The situation was not ideal and was getting more unbearable each day. Even though she didn't look in his direction as she filled the kettle from the single brass tap, she felt Red's eyes boring into her back, watching her every move.

'Don't put yourself out on my account.' His surly answer told her he was still simmering because, for the second time, she had refused to give him her hard-earned money for beer. They were both silent and only the sound of Mary Jane peeling potatoes broke the leaden stillness.

'Could you not see your way clear to letting me have the price of one gill,' Red pleaded, 'just to get me through the door?'

Mary Jane shook her head, not daring to look at him. 'You'll get no more from me until you've paid what you owe me.' There was a determined edge to her voice that Red had not heard before. Watching her move from the single brass tap to the fireplace, her movements graceful even in the fifth month of her pregnancy, Red wondered why she had chosen his quiet workhorse of a brother, instead of him. Why hadn't he plied Paddy with the booze, the night of the haymaking, then it might have been him who took her to the hayloft? He knew he could entertain her in ways that his brother never could. That gnawing itch, which he could not scratch, tormented him ever more. His dark thoughts leaving nothing out, imagining her body beneath him.

When she placed the shepherd's pie on the table, he could not look at her in case she saw the longing in his eyes. When she picked up his plate, he put up his hand and shook his head. He could not eat a morsel. He was too full of yearning. Mary Jane didn't have a clue what she did to him.

'Don't flick your cigarette ash all over the floor, I have to clean it!' she snapped, her abrupt command destroying his craving. 'And find something to do. You're getting under my feet!' Straightening, she unconsciously smoothed down the coarse calico apron she wore over her skirt to try to disguise her expanding waistline. Aware of Red's feelings toward her, Mary Jane did nothing to encourage him, and everything to distract him from unsavoury thoughts that made his breathing faster. Her hands trembled as she reached for the cups and saucers. Filling the room with their clatter, she took a deep breath. *Easy does it*, she thought, trying to act naturally, feeling Red's hungry eyes take in every inch from the top of her aching head to the tapered tip of her shoes. Pulling a colourful shawl, she had knitted, around her tired body, she was determined not to let him see he was unnerving her.

'I don't know why you're not going down the docks, queuing with the other men,' she said, pouring the tea into his cup. 'Offering your services for a day's work.' Mary Jane knew his wrath was preferable to lustful glances.

'I'll tell you why I don't go down there, shall I?' Red's words were forced through his teeth. 'Because my face doesn't fit, that's why!' He slammed a rolled-up newspaper on the table. 'I could stand there for a month of Sundays and I wouldn't get a start.'

'There are plenty of Irish men on the docks – in fact, most of the docks were built by Erin's sons.'

'I've heard things,' he told her, his tone petulant, 'in the bar, I've heard what they say– Paddy need not apply!'

'Go tell it to the priest, Red!' Mary Jane did not believe a word of it. 'The docks are swarming with Irish men offering their labour for a day's pay.'

'Met them all, have you?' There was no mistaking the accusation in his belligerent tone.

'No, I have not! And well you know it!' Mary Jane felt a rare tightening of her throat, and the fizz of unshed tears to her eyes, knowing Red took every opportunity to make her feel small. Keeping busy, she removed the boiling kettle from the coals, pouring hot water into the white tin bowl to wash the dishes, and replacing the kettle in the grate with the flat iron.

'I shouldn't even be here,' he said. 'I should be home tending my own farm – but I can't do that, can I?' He was goading her again, something he did when he could not get what he wanted.

'Did Cissie mention another room?' Mary Jane did not want a repeat of that night, not so long ago.

'I haven't the money for another room,' Red answered, taking his cup so roughly, he slopped tea onto the tablecloth, 'and well you know it!'

'You have no intentions of getting any work, by the look of it,' she said in a low voice, frustrated by his lethargy for earning anything resembling an honest bob. She felt she had got herself into something she had no control over, and the feeling did not sit comfortably. Mary Jane had always been independent, free to do as she pleased. However, that autonomy was being eroded day by day.

'What's so wrong with marrying me?' Red asked abruptly. 'I could bring up my brother's child as my own, I would provide for you both.'

'You wouldn't, Red, we both know that much.' Mary Jane was well aware that raising Paddy's child was the last thing on his mind. And marrying him was the last thing she wanted either. She took the flat iron off the fire and spat. Watching a ball of saliva bounce across it, she spread the cotton pillowcase on the table, opposite his shepherd's pie, and resting the iron on an upturned saucer she waited for it to cool a little. There wasn't much to iron, but she had to keep busy. Keep moving.

'You could do worse than me,' he sneered. 'Better than being terrified the truth will come out.'

'I'll take my chances where I can.' She was under no illusion that Red saw himself as her saviour. Well, he could think again! She would take shame before she took Red for a husband.

14

'I'm going to America,' Red said as he slumped onto the rickety straight-backed chair.

'I hope it stays fine for you,' Mary Jane answered with a hint of mockery, wondering who in their right mind would lend him the fare given his terrible reputation. When she refused to subsidise his drinking habits, Red had quickly found someone who would treat him to a few jars in the alehouse, even though he felt no inclination to pass any money over to pay for food, light, or rent. Without another word, he did what he always did, got up and left.

'I won't be late.' His words sailed up to the room from the stairwell as he headed out.

'Be as late as you like,' Mary Jane leaned over the banister and yelled down the stairs, listening to the heavy tread of his boots as he descended them and Mary Jane heard no more until much later when his voice was loud and clear. His sociable stories were a signal to Mary Jane that he intended to stay up half the night with Cissie Stone and her other Irish lodgers, long after the alehouse had shut! Mary Jane had been invited only the once to Cissie Stone's get-togethers, and she vowed never to attend another when the inevitable singsong was terminated with fisticuffs.

'Low, lie the fields of Athenry,' Red's resonant voice sailed through two ceilings, ensuring little sleep for those not present at the late-night *hooley*. And before long, the nostalgic, sometimes mournful, songs brought lonely tears to Mary Jane's tired eyes.

'Don't go on about it, Mary Jane.' Red cupped his hands around the brown clay pot, to see if there was any hot tea left. There wasn't. It was almost noon when he had managed to drag himself off Cissie's sofa after passing out at God-only-knows what time. Mary Jane did not believe he had slept on their landlady's sofa all night and wondered if Cissy was funding his passage to America? Not that she cared, as long as he was out from under her feet. He had said more than once he intended to leave, yet he never had.

'I'll just borrow this,' he said swiping the money she had earned that morning, and had been foolish enough to leave on the mantlepiece, 'I just need a livener from the Tram Tavern, to get rid of this fuzzy headache.'

Mary Jane was left open-mouthed at his audacity. *I can't carry on like this.*, she thought, fighting the urge to cry. *He'll have me in the poorhouse.* No doubt, he would then move onto the next meal ticket. It's what he did. He was renowned for it.

Looking around the room, she took in the trail of devastation, he had left for her to clean up. A cracked saucer overflowing with the wrinkled remains of foul-smelling dog-ends, too small to hold except with a pin. Alongside the saucer lay a soap-filled shaving brush and a cut-throat razor. She removed a white enamel cup from the mantelpiece and felt queasy when she saw a layer of black hair splinters floating on the scummy surface. Even her brothers cleared up their own mess, she thought, as she gathered the shaving tackle. They would never expect her to clean away this lot.

She gave a small sigh. Her brothers would never dream of washing a plate or making a pot of tea, mind. Women's work, they called it. She wondered how they were managing without her. Had they been picked up after she left? Paddy would be well buried by now. What happened to the farm? Was it still standing? If so, would his father keep it on? What would he live off if he couldn't? Why didn't Red ever talk about it? Mary Jane knew Cissy received regular letters from home, yet, neither she nor Red gave her any news. Maybe he had heard something from home that would force him to move to America? Questions danced in her head, a captive to the isolation in this house and the unanswered questions that repeated. Mary Jane needed to get out, and she remembered the apple pie she had promised Molly. Making her way downstairs she decided to take the barrow back to Cal's yard across the street first. Once she and Molly started talking there was no telling how long she would be, and she didn't want Cissie complaining about the handcart in front of her front door.

Unlocking one of the huge double gates, Mary Jane manoeuvred the handcart into the neat yard, which although there had been no rain for weeks was cleaner than many dusty places she had seen. There was a place for everything, and everything was in its place, but Mary Jane silently berating herself for not opening both gates to get the barrow through easier.

'Here, let me...' Cal Everdine's voice, like balm to an open wound, was quiet, assured and so close behind her, Mary Jane could swear she heard his heart beating.

'Thank you,' she answered allowing him to take the handles of the cart and push it to the covered section of the yard he had built specially. She wondered if she should stay a while and chat, but Cal Everdine did not seem to be a chatting kind of man. Mary Jane felt that he only spoke when he needed to and didn't waste words on idle gossip.

'The cart has been a great help,' she said, unable to drum up the courage to ask him if he knew the address of the landlord so she could make enquiries about the empty shop downstairs, and he nodded, smiling, his dark blue eyes crinkling at the corner. He must smile a lot she thought distractedly, given the tanned crevices at the outer corner of his eyes.

'I am glad to hear that,' he said and there was a moment when neither of them spoke. Yet there was no awkwardness in the silence between them, just a stillness, as if the world was having a rest and they were the only two people awake. Maybe when Red went off to America, she would ask Cal the landlord's address.

'I must be off,' Mary Jane said, moving towards the gate, 'I promised Molly a fruit pie.'

'And sumptuous it looks too,' his eyes twinkled as Mary Jane felt the heat spread from her neck to her cheeks. What a first-class eejit she had been. Not leaving Cal a pie – and he had been so kind lending her his handcart!

'I'll save you one, tomorrow,' she said by way of apology, 'I didn't think you would be interested…' her words trailed.

'I shall look forward to it,' he answered, his genuine smile reaching the twinkle in his dark eyes that held her gaze.

Mary Jane thanked him, her heart swelling, in reaction to his kindness. If only every man could be like Cal, she thought.

There was no tension in the softness of his expression as he faced her, standing easy.

'I erm... I should go... Have a nice pie...' Mary Jane gasped when she realised, she had said the wrong thing. *Have a nice pie! Talk about rubbing salt into the wound!* She had meant to tell Cal to have a nice *day*, something he always said to her – and she had messed it up good and proper. Her face was so hot Mary Jane was sure she could fry an egg on it.

Turning quickly, she bumped into the side of the open gate and scrabbled to grab hold of it before it closed, and she hurried outside. As the gate closed behind her Mary Jane took a deep breath to try and restore a modicum of dignity when she heard the muffled sound of laughter on the other side. Well! She pressed her lips together, isn't it a good thing he can see the funny side.

Crossing the cobbled street, which was alive with children playing hopscotch and football, Mary Jane headed over to Molly's house, her splaying fingers drawing back wisps of unruly damp curls. As she neared the stone steps leading to Molly's front door her lips stretched into an easy smile. Cal must think she was an eejit who had mislaid her marbles. Have a nice pie indeed!

* * *

The interaction of the holy trinity, food, health *and* money rarely visited the streets off the dock road together. At any given time, there was a lack of one or the other, if not all, and Mary Jane was determined she was not going to end up the same way. She ached at the scrawny bodies of some children, saying a special prayer for them at eight o'clock mass on Sundays, wishing she could afford to feed each and every one who would gaze longingly at her bakes from the home-made barrow in the market along the dock road. At least one of those poor mites received a free pie each day, she made sure she kept at least one back, and on the rare occasion she had anything left over, she shared them among the children who waited eagerly to see what was left. Although, she noticed, the Haywood children who were drawing on the step with a broken slate, were a good size, and adequately dressed in good clothing, nothing fancy, but clean, and serviceable and none looked as if they went without a hearty meal.

After her early start and long walk from the market this morning, her legs were heavy, and Mary Jane longed to sit for a while.

'You look beat,' Molly said, and Mary Jane raised a tired smile.

'That's what happens when you are up before the lark and working while most people are still dreaming.'

'Maybe you need permanent premises to work and sell from,' the older woman said, and Mary Jane looked to the empty shop across the road and had already thought it was a wonderful idea – if only she had the wherewithal to do so. After a welcome cup of tea, Mary Jane knew she couldn't linger, no matter how much she longed to.

* * *

'I've brought you a fruit pie,' Mary Jane told Cal the following day and his eyes sparkled with gratitude.

'There is nothing like home-baked pie,' he said carefully taking it from her. 'Can I cut you a piece? You look all pink and flustered.' His eyes danced with unasked questions, and Mary Jane wished she could tell him everything, but that would sever their friendship for sure. What person in their right mind wanted to befriend a harlot like her.

'It's so warm,' Mary Jane said as casually as possible. Word of her delicious bakes was spreading, and business was brisk. No sooner had she parked her barrow in the market than she had a crowd gathered around her, all pushing money in her direction for meat pies, fruit pies and crusty bread.'

'Why don't you put your feet up for an hour or so,' Cal asked, and Mary Jane gave him a wan smile. 'What time did you get up this morning?'

'Same as every morning,' Mary Jane answered. 'I had my first batch of uncooked pies in your oven by five.' Red had not returned the night before. Her pleading with him to contribute fell on deaf ears. If anything, he was even more selfish now than he had ever been. He had not tipped up so much as a farthing since she had been taking her bakes to market, telling her every day he would be gone soon and needed every penny for his boat fare.

'I don't know what I'd have done without you and Molly,' she told Cal whose eyes softened.

'You do too much,' he said, worried in case she was putting herself and her baby at risk.

'And you fuss too much,' she laughed, enjoying his concern while trying to ignore his worried expression. 'Anyway, I have to go.' Mary Jane said reluctant to get back to the attic.

Climbing the stairs, she heard an unfamiliar noise, and as she reached the landing she saw Red, head down, mooching through her carpet bag. He took out the picture of a country scene she had torn from a disused newspaper. The village was identical to Cashalree, and Mary Jane felt her anger rise when he tossed the picture without a thought, onto the bare floorboards. *He's going through my private belongings*. The words rang through her head like a clash of cymbals. His back to her, he threw her clean flannel drawers over the banister, rooting for her market money, no doubt. Having secreted her pie money inside the leg of her drawers, she had tucked them at the bottom of the carpet bag, believing no decent man would dare go near a woman's undergarments uninvited. The money she and Paddy had saved was still in the plant pot on the pelmet over the attic window, and she intended to use it for rent on the empty shop when Red eventually went off on his travels to America. If he got wind that she had enough money to open a shop, he would bleed her dry without a doubt.

Red was so busy trying to find her money, he obviously had not heard her coming up the stairs. Mary Jane said nothing. She couldn't. The words would stick in her throat. He knew how important that money was to her child's future. Suddenly Red looked up, his face devoid of culpability. The heavy silence mushrooming, filling every nook. The tension stretching into forever. She stayed silent, not daring herself to speak, waiting for the obvious lies. When Red pushed past her and stood by the table, he opened his mouth a few times like a new-caught fish.

'Mary Jane, I...' He said eventually and, lifting her chin, Mary Jane stretched her back, standing tall, unyielding, as her unwavering glare passed between them. She had put up with a lot from Christie Redfern, because his brother was the father of her child. The love she thought she felt for Paddy was based on the need to give her child a name, a decent upbringing, and now she knew without a shadow of doubt, what she felt for Paddy was not love, but gratitude. The same feeling, she had when Molly spoke to her that first time. It was relief that he was going to do the right thing by her. As if she had got into this precarious situation all by herself. Staring at the open carpet bag in his grubby hands, Mary Jane knew Red had gone too far this time, as he made a grab for something at the bottom. She noticed the assortment of coins in his hand. Without a word, he began stuffing *his* belongings into the bag. His Sunday shirt, the shoes, and trousers he wore for mass. Her eyes darkened.

'So, you're finally going then?' Sharp barbs formed on her angry words. He had taken her for a fool. She should have shown him the door that first night when they arrived in Liverpool. He was a waster, a gambler, and now he was proving himself a thief.

'I told you I'm going to America.' His voice was urgent, his head dipped, not looking at her. Cissie had told him there were men coming over from Cashalree. She told him everybody back home knew Mary Jane's brothers had not murdered Paddy, and Dinny O'Mara wanted to ask Red some questions.

'America, you say?' Mary Jane raised an eyebrow and felt the rage growing inside her when she saw him slip her money into his pocket. Taking in a lungful of dusty air, she paused from telling him he was lower than a worm's belly as a thought struck her. If he was going to America, then she would no longer have to hide her money, feed him, or clean up after him. Maybe he was doing her a favour after all.

'Well, the country's welcome to you, and good riddance.' Her tone was emphatic. 'But you'll not take the wages I walked the streets of Liverpool for. I worked hard for that money. And you'll not have it.' She nodded to his clenched fist that held her savings, and the angry bile burned her throat.

'I was going to leave you a note.' His eyes were as round as two side plates, as if the idea had just entered his head.

'I'll be glad to see the back of you.' Mary Jane picked up her straw boater and took the lethal-looking pin from her hatband.

He watched her every move, the nervous pulse at his temple pumping, and she felt braver. 'You have brought me nothing but heartache and worry since the day we stepped foot in this place.'

Keeping his distance, and an eye on the hatpin, Red reached over to put some of the money he had stolen onto the table, but Mary Jane's anger had grown to such a pitch, she was unable to control it as she slapped every coin from his hand, livid as a hellcat when she saw that all of the money was not there.

'No doubt you relieved the bulk of the money in some alehouse,' she said, pushing the words through clenched teeth, watching the scattering coins pirouetting like prima ballerinas before rolling across the floor. Red fell to his knees, scrambling for every penny. Seeing him crawl over the bare floorboards caused Mary Jane's lip to curl in disgust.

'I hope you and America get along,' she said, 'but my biggest wish is that I never have to set eyes on you, ever again!' She flung a pair of leather braces, which he had missed, into the bag, hitting him in the face. 'If I was a man, I would beat the living daylights out of you. But I'm a woman who can look out for herself. God alone knows, I've been doing it since I got here. And I don't need you to tell me I've done something really bad, something unholy.' She put her hands flat on the table and leaned forward. 'Because I must have done, to deserve a saviour as bad as you.'

'You lay with my brother. Women who have unholy alliances on the wrong side of the blanket should expect what's coming to them. I wouldn't have you if you were the last woman on earth,' he snarled. 'I know you for what you are.'

'You don't intimidate me, Red,' she said with a toss of her head.

'The truth will come out one day, Mary Jane,' he countered, 'and it will show you for the harlot you are.' He stuffed the money into his pockets, glaring at her, silently daring her to retaliate. 'Back home, you would have been scorned as a woman of easy virtue, ripe for the picking, but Paddy carried your secret to his grave.' Red's tone, laced with venom, goaded her, but she had heard enough.

'I shall have to live with it,' she said defiantly, watching him take a step nearer to the door. 'But know this, I never asked for *your* help.' The memory of him catching her arm, running her to the ferry so fast she stumbled at every turn, taking her away from everything she had held sacred, was still clear in her head. 'I had no time to think straight. You were the one who made me feel unclean, nobody else,' she said.

'You did that to yourself, thinking you were better than everybody else,' he sneered. 'Nobody was good enough for you. And won't the women roundabout be justified when the truth is aired. That you were living in sin with one man, while carrying his dead brother's bastard.'

Red's razor-sharp words sliced through her, piercing her heart, but she recovered quickly.

'And why would a man help a woman who was the cause of his brother's demise? Tell me.'

'Paddy said I must help you.'

'I doubt it. You strung me along with your promises and threats, but not any more. Those days are over,' she said. 'I would have managed.' Angry tears welled traitorously in her eyes, and she swept them away with the pad of her hand. 'I would have made my own way.'

'I was coming to Liverpool anyway, all I needed was the fare to get over here,' Red looked determined. 'My brother's death did me a big favour.' He waved a bunch of papers in front of her face. 'I have Paddy's birth certificate and his army papers.'

Mary Jane gasped, watching Red stuff them into the inside pocket of his herringbone jacket. 'How did you get hold of those?'

'He was carrying them in his pocket on the day he was murdered,' Red replied quickly, his thick dark eyebrows drawing together as if she was some kind of idiot not to know that.

'So, you stole the identity of a dead man?' Mary Jane was horrified. 'How could you!' Mary Jane shook with rage and disgust, knowing without a shred of doubt this man must be in league with Old Nick himself.

'I wouldn't have taken the papers – or your money – but I'm desperate,' Red sounded contrite, but Mary Jane didn't believe a word, appalled at the depths to which he would stoop to ease his own greedy desires. His eyes were pleading, and she knew she would have given him the benefit of the doubt at one time, but not any more. Gone were the days when she felt sorry for him, believing he was misunderstood, a soul crying out for redemption.

'I believed every word that came out of your mouth at one time, because you were Paddy's brother, but lies trip off your tongue quicker than butter off a hot knife!' He had betrayed her trust once too often. And now she had actually caught him stealing her money. If she had not walked in, he would be long gone, and as far as *he* knew, leaving her penniless – a selfish, heartless man who had no moral compass – leaving her and his own twin brother's child potentially destitute. 'You're devious, Red, and you are an expert at hiding it behind a smile.' She slammed her hand down on the table. 'And you will be back with your tail between your legs, when you are on your uppers with nobody else to bail you out.'

'If you remember, I slotted in here much easier than you did. You don't have a friend in the world except me.'

That was what he would like to think. He was leaving her with nobody to depend upon, but she had Molly and Daisy and even Cal Everdine who had helped her more than Red would ever know. Taking a long, steadying breath of air, Mary Jane fought the fury rising up inside her. 'Leave the money and get out.'

'I'll just have the lend of it until I get settled. I will send it all back to you, every penny.'

'I would like to believe there is some good in you, but I can't.' Her words were softly spoken, deceptively so, for she felt far from calm. 'Leave the money and go.' Her words were like ice despite the heat of the room.

'You'd see me with nothing, when I have been so good to you, bringing you here and finding you a place to live?'

As much as she would like to leave her mark to match the scar above his right eye, she did not go for him as he deserved. She must protect her unborn child. Mary Jane did some quick calculations in her head. She still had the money hidden under the plant on the landing, which would see her through. And if all else failed, she had her mother's clock.

'Take the money and get out, don't send it back to me, I never want to see or hear from you, again.' Mary Jane stepped aside, and Red did not hang around long enough to hear any more. Slinging the carpet bag over his shoulder, he left quickly, slamming the door behind him, while every nerve in her body screamed.

Light-headed, Mary Jane slumped onto the nearest chair, her hand gripping the edge of the table near a basket of untouched fruit and vegetables. When she was no longer able to hear his tread on the stairs, she tried to let her body relax, intent on calming her pounding heartbeat. Closing her eyes, Mary Jane concentrated. Her head felt like it was full of buzzing bees. What man in his right mind would reduce a pregnant woman to this, she wondered. Feeling nauseous Mary Jane knew that, had it not been for her 'condition', she would never have let him get away with the trouble he had caused her, but, if truth be told, she thought, had it not been for her 'condition', she would never have come here in the first place. Looking around the depressing room, with unblinking eyes, to the sloping ceiling and narrow sash window that let in little natural light to see the smoke-stained, peeling wallpaper, Mary Jane suspected, if she stayed in here for one moment longer, she might never go out again. Taking her shawl from the hook behind the door, she hurried down the narrow passage to the window.

She lifted the flowerpot and removed the fern, feeling around with the tips of her fingers. Then she grabbed the pot and emptied the plant on the floor. There was nothing there. Red had found that money too! Mary Jane sat on the bare floorboards, and for the first time since she had been told the news of Paddy's death, she sobbed. What was she going to do? She could not buy supplies or pay the butcher without money. Visions of being shamefully thrown onto the street filled her head. Pride before a fall, had never been so apt.

15

The pitying looks told Mary Jane that most people in Beamer Street knew Red had scarpered. She realised that he had stolen more than just her money, he had stolen her freedom, her friendly, outgoing nature and he had made her suspicious. That was the feeling she loathed most of all. She felt relieved when Molly invited her in for a cup of tea.

'You look a bit lost, girl, if you don't mind me saying,' Molly said.

'I'm fine,' Mary Jane said, offering a weak smile as if to cement her words.

'You don't look fine,' Molly said. 'In fact, I'd say you look a bit washed out.'

Please don't be nice to me! Mary Jane tried to swallow the words stuck painfully in her throat.

'I know what it is,' said Molly, 'you're homesick, am I right?'

Mary Jane gave a little nod of her head, knowing that wasn't her only worry. She was quiet for a while, giving nothing away, or so she thought.

After a moment, Molly said in a tentative tone, 'It's not you they've got no time for, you know,' as if reading Mary Jane's thoughts. 'No, it's not you at all, it's himself. They know you are a fine girl, but him... Well, he's something else altogether.' Then, after another pause, she sighed and said, 'You'll notice one thing about me, I speak as I find.' She hoisted a well-developed bosom with crossed forearms, her manner straightforward. 'I don't believe in beating about the bush, so I'll tell you – it's your 'usband what gets their goat, they see him as a no-good waster, and if the truth be told, they feel sorry for you, having to go down the dock road and the market selling your pies and pasties in your condition.'

Mary Jane pulled her shawl across her swelling stomach. She knew Red was no good, having spent his days cadging money and nights propping up the bar along the street. He was the one who had suggested an illegal game of pitch and toss down the back alley, and the one who ran with the money when the bobbies turned up with their whistles and their truncheons.

'You don't have to say anything, we've got eyes in our heads,' Molly offered. 'We can see him for what he is – and how he got you, lass, I'll never know.'

Mary Jane lowered her eyes, she had not long met this woman, but how she longed to tell Molly the truth, that Red was nothing to her. She had been as angry with his scrounging ways as they were. Still, she could not do that. Red made sure of it when he created the myth as soon as they arrived not wasting a moment to tell everybody about his long-suffering wife, Mary Jane. The last part was always said on a laugh as he pronounced himself the luckiest man in Liverpool.

Mary Jane knew if she told the truth she would condemn herself. The women of Beamer Street would not put up with a loose woman living amongst them. Back home in Ireland, she would be run out of the village, the town and even the country. Even now, thinking about it, her shame burned hotter than the fires of hell. But as her pregnancy became more obvious, she could not possibly admit Red was not her husband.

'So, you'll be staying, then?' Molly asked without preamble.

'I don't have much choice in the matter.' Mary Jane could not contain the words and she saw the older woman's interest pique.

'And why's that?' Molly asked, pushing back a strand of prematurely greying hair, and, at close quarters, Mary Jane could see she was not as old as she first suspected. 'Are you in trouble?'

Mary Jane shrugged helplessly, knowing she certainly was in trouble. Red made sure she was penniless before he took off. The flour and yeast she needed to bake her bread had all but gone, and she was about to be evicted and forced to roam the streets. She should have got away from Red when she had the money, she knew that now. But knowing it did not make the situation any easier.

'I'm not one for poking my nose in people's business,' Mary Jane said primly, thinking it was about time she went back.

'Are you not?' Molly looked so surprised, her eyes widened. 'Well, you'll soon get over that.' She did not appear to take umbrage to Mary Jane's sharp retort, brought on by worry and disappointment. 'You can't blow your nose in this street without someone knowing about it. My Albert used to say my nose would never rust through lack of use. I can't keep it out of anyone's business.' With that, Molly's face contorted, and an explosion of laughter burst forth. Throwing back her head, Molly filled the air with a burst of untethered joviality and Mary Jane could not help but admire the woman's honesty. Many would have kept their mouths shut about wanting to know their neighbour's private goings-on. But not Molly. She seemed proud of the fact, and Mary Jane found herself beginning to laugh too. It was a strange sound that she had not heard for a long while.

'Take no notice of me, Mary Jane, I have these funny moments,' Molly said, drying her eyes, suddenly surrounded by children of varying sizes who had come to find out what was making their mother laugh so much. 'These two are mine, Freddy and Bridie,' Molly said, patting each of their heads, before addressing Daisy. 'Daisy's me eldest, as you know. Then there's our Davy.'

'I'll see to the little ones,' said Daisy, ushering the smaller children into the front room.

'She's a nice girl,' Mary Jane said, and Molly gave a small jerk of her head.

'My Daisy's a blessing, I don't know what I'd do without her,' she sighed. 'Since my Albert were taken on the Somme, she's been a godsend to me,' she sniffed and leaned forward. 'She makes little fancy cakes for the customers.'

'I met her in the teashop, when I came to Liverpool,' Mary Jane said, relaxing now. 'It was the same day I saw Mr Everdine...' She stopped talking suddenly, his very name made her cheeks hot, but at least she hadn't called him Cal, as he had invited her to do.

'Ahh, Mr Everdine,' Molly said, 'he keeps to himself.' She gave a small inquisitive shrug of her shoulders. 'I see you have a barrow and keep it in his yard.'

'He gave me the loan of it when he saw me struggling with the basket,' Mary Jane said. 'It was very kind of him to help me.' She drained her cup of tea and finished a slice of fruit cake that Daisy had made.

'That cake was delicious,' Mary Jane said to Molly, omitting to tell her it was a bit on the stodgy side, however with a bit of training she suspected Daisy would make a first-class baker. 'But I must get on, I'm keeping you from your chores.'

Mary Jane stood up to leave. Molly had a friendly, albeit inquisitive manner about her, and if Mary Jane stayed any longer, she would tell the older woman everything, which was a chance she dare not take.

As they reached the front door, Mary Jane was about to descend the steps when Molly tilted her head towards Cissie Stone's house. 'You must be in God's pocket, he talks to you a lot,' she said in a low voice, 'even her next door can't get Mr Everdine to hold a conversation and she's... well...' Molly pulled her shawl tighter and wrinkled her pudgy nose. 'She's got a very persuasive nature, if you take my meaning.'

Mary Jane nodded, surmising she knew what Molly meant. 'It's a pity she couldn't persuade herself to clean up a bit now and then!' Mary Jane said primly and looked to Molly as they both laughed. 'I'm not one to talk about people, but that place was filthy before I took a scrubbing brush to it.'

'At last,' Molly sounded relieved, 'someone who's not afraid to speak her mind.'

Mary Jane shrugged. To hell with being discreet, she thought, it had only caused her isolation and heartache. 'All I know is, I couldn't eat a morsel until I had scrubbed the place clean. I could smell the house before I saw it, old cooking fat and tobacco fumes do not make for a pleasant atmosphere. I could not put my head down until I'd scalded the pillowslips.'

'Another reason the women are not speaking to you.' Molly lowered her voice, so her words did not carry. 'It's where you live and *her* carry-on. Strangers coming and going at all hours, in and out like a fiddler's elbow. It must get you down?'

'It does.' Mary Jane sighed. 'But there is nothing I can do

about it. I have nowhere else to go, he made sure of that before he left for America. I know nobody – except you and Daisy and Mr Everdine.'

'He's gone!' Molly's eyes widened in horror. 'Well that just goes to show how low he could sink.'

'But America!' Molly said, surprised when Mary Jane's staccato explanation convinced her that Red was probably not coming back. 'Where did he get the money for the ticket? Come on let's go back inside and have another cuppa and you can tell me all about it.'

Mary Jane gave a miserable shrug. plucking the skin on her fingers, twisting the cheap copper ring on her left hand, which now irritated the hell out of her.

'He could have found himself a job on board a Cunard ship going to New York, I suppose,' Molly said as they went back inside.

'It's more likely he'll stow away until he gets there rather than pay for a ticket,' Mary Jane answered, She tried to lighten the conversation with a bit of levity, not comfortable with bearing her soul, seeing it as a drain Molly could well do without. Even though she did insist it was not a problem. 'Good riddance to him.'

'That's the spirit,' Molly said, placing the two refilled green cups onto mismatched saucers. 'For the shock,' she said. It didn't take long for the two women to indulge in deep conversation.

'I've given the children their supper and tucked them all up in bed,' Daisy said sometime later, and Mary Jane felt that Molly's friendship was like manna from heaven.

'What am I like, keeping you here so long,' Molly laughed. 'The nights are getting darker, cooler, and I heard tell that it was going to rain, any day now.'

'Thank goodness for that,' Mary Jane answered, happy for the first time in weeks.

'Come in tomorrow and have a cup of tea, there's always one on the go in here. I'll tell you all about my Albert's people, you might know them. The O'Maras – they lived near Cashalree!'

Mary Jane stifled a small gasp. 'Would that be Dinny O'Mara's family?'

Molly nodded.

Mary Jane wondered what she was going to tell Molly when she asked why she had come to Liverpool? She would not be able to mention Paddy's demise. She could not tell Molly the truth. Some things were better left unsaid. But then, she thought, she may not be here much longer. With no money, she would be evicted for sure. There was only one thing she could do – pawn her mother's clock.

16

Taking the meagre provisions from her wicker basket the following day, Mary Jane placed them on the table and her heart sank. Maybe if she made her pies a bit smaller, she could earn more, but that wasn't her style. She was noted for giving value for money, and what little band of regular customers she did have came back time and again because they could rely on her. There had to be another way. She managed to get six good-sized plate pies from her ingredients, and twenty-four bread rolls. It wasn't much and wouldn't earn her enough to buy more ingredients, but she had an idea. She would scour the country lanes, looking for windblown apples, pears, and berries for jams and jellies. It was going to be a struggle in her condition, but she didn't have any choice.

'Damn you, Red!' Mary Jane swiped angry, frustrated tears from her cheeks, knowing she could not go into Molly's house in this state. She would upset the children. Picking up the pie she had promised Cal, she left the attic and closed the door behind her. 'Deep breath, Mary Jane,' she whispered as she descended the stairs, 'it's no use crying now. This was never going to be easy, so you'd better get used to it.'

Cal accepted the plate apple pie from Mary Jane with a look of appreciation.

'Maybe we could share it,' Cal said. 'I could make you a cup of tea.'

'Thank you,' said Mary Jane, 'another time, I have to get on.'

'Yes,' said Cal, 'of course. Maybe later.' Unbeknown to Cal, she had a five-mile walk ahead of her to collect the fruit, and a five-mile walk back.

* * *

The country air reminded Mary Jane of home, and although she did not stop long to ponder, she was swept up in the beauty of the English countryside in rare, late September sunshine. Bramley apple trees where burgeoning with plump green apples, and she decided she would only pick the ones that had fallen from the tree, she was no thief. The fallen ones, as far as she was concerned, were the Good Lord's gift. The branches of blackberry bushes arched under the weight of plump luscious fruit, and she picked them to add to the apples she had foraged. Nuts, rosehips and plums were all gathered to be made into jams and tinctures and pies and crumbles. Mary Jane filled her basket, which had begun to weigh heavy, glad she had brought Cal's barrow to help her. It was dark when she got back to Beamer Street, weary and in desperate need of a cup of tea. Molly was standing, as usual, at her doorstep, her eyes widening when she saw Mary Jane pushing her barrow along the street.

'You look done in,' Molly said in her usual, pragmatic way,

and Mary Jane gave her as wide a smile as she could manage, too exhausted to try to think of an excuse as to why she had been gone most of the day. 'Come and have a cup of tea and tell your old friend about it.'

'I'll just go and put this lot inside,' she said, nodding towards her load. When she got inside the house, Cissie Stone was waiting in the hallway, arms folded, her lips tightly puckered.

'You owe me for the gas you used baking your pies and bread, before you slunk off to him across the road, missus.' Cissie put the flat of her hand on the door frame and her other hand on her hip. 'I am not giving free gas so you can make your fortune.'

Some fortune thought Mary Jane as the full realisation hit her. If she had to pay Cissy more money for gas,, then she would not be able to pay her rent. She would be homeless at the most vulnerable time of her life.

'I paid what you asked and I'll pay no more,' Mary Jane told Cissy Stone before she slammed out of the front door. She needed one person on her side at least. Hurrying up Molly's steps, she rapped with bare knuckles on the front door. She was going to have to rethink her situation. What she should do is move away. But did she have the strength or the time when she felt so physically and mentally drained, struggling while Red had blithely drunk every penny he earned, and saw no wrong in so doing, had taken its toll. Believing she owed him, if only for allowing her to use his name and having no choice in the matter, she had let him go with every penny she possessed. And for what? She had nothing to show for the effort she had put into keeping him fed and housed in the hope he would not reveal her humiliation. But now she wondered if she had done the right thing after all. Maybe she would have been better off going it alone. In fact, she was sure she would.

'You're a kind woman, Molly,' Mary Jane said, feeling a little awkward sitting at her next-door neighbour's table, stirring tea. 'I don't know what I'd have done without you.'

'Think nothing of it,' Molly answered, plucking chicken feathers from the good-sized bird lolling in the sink. 'If you can't help a neighbour in distress, then who can you help?'

'I might not be a neighbour for much longer,' Mary Jane's voice cracked with pent-up emotion. She wasn't usually one to give in. She was a fighter, always had been, always would be. Yet, her shame grew malignantly inside her. How could she tell Molly she had been the most stupid of stupid fools, who trusted Paddy when he said he would make it better in Liverpool. Red had only looked out for himself too, not for her.

'It can't be so banjaxed that it can't be fixed?' Molly said.

'Oh Molly,' Mary Jane said eventually, drying her eyes with the clean tea towel Molly offered, 'Red took every penny I had saved, all of it!'

'He left you with nothing – in your condition?' Molly said in the same motherly tone she used with her own kids.

'I'm sorry, this is my problem,' said Mary Jane. 'I'm being silly, after all, my woes are nothing compared to bringing up four children, like you have done.'

'Never mind about me,' Molly said, 'I've got plenty to be happy about.' Molly put a slice of walnut cake on two side plates. As she put one beside Mary-Jane, she said in a voice laced with pride, 'This is one of our Daisy's.'

'I'm sure it is delicious,' Mary Jane said, 'but I couldn't eat a thing right now.' She watched Molly's eyes fill with motherly concern and a smidgeon of curiosity.

'Well, as you know, I'm not one of those women who will

tell you it's none of my business, because the curiosity is eating me up inside.' Molly pulled her straight-backed chair closer to the table, 'I want to know everything – every last detail, leave nothing out!'

Mary Jane looked up through watery eyes, and her trembling smile turned into a rib-aching laugh she did not know she was still capable of. 'What would I do if I didn't have you to talk to, Molly.' However, she was going to have to play it by ear. She wasn't sure just how much truth to tell Molly just yet.

'One thing I will tell you, hand on heart, I am no Ina King. I will never give away any secrets you trust me with.'

'I like people,' Mary Jane began, 'but it came as a shock when I got here and nobody spoke to me, not even when I went out of my way, they turned their backs on me... I tried, Molly, really, I did, but they ignored me time and again.' Mary Jane shook her head. 'I never thought I would find a friend in this street and then you...' Her voice faltered, and Molly made gentle shushing noises. 'I should have said good riddance to him months ago,' Mary Jane swallowed her tears, 'because now I only have myself to look out for.' She gave a wobbly smile, but still the tears flowed treacherously down her cheeks. 'It's my condition, take no notice, I'll be fine in a minute.' She gave a small, almost scornful laugh and rolled her eyes. 'This baby makes me so emotional.'

'Come on, tell me the real reason,' Molly said in a firm but gentle voice, after getting up from her chair opposite and giving Mary Jane a motherly hug. Then the dam burst, and Mary Jane had nothing left but tears, knowing it was no good being proud, when you had so little to be proud of.

'I have no idea where I'm going to get the rent money,' Mary Jane had not intended to tell Molly everything, and especially not like this, but as soon as her friend gave her a kind word, she allowed everything Red said or threatened to burst from her lips like water through paper. 'There's nothing left.' Her voice sounded desolate even to her own ears. 'He's gone through my savings, the lot. The rent is due tomorrow and now Cissie Stone wants to charge me for more gas, even though Cal... Mr Everdine has let me use his oven for weeks. If I pay her for the gas, I can't pay my rent and she will throw me onto the street for sure now that Red has gone.' Swallowing tears of frustrated anger, she looked across the table at Molly, who was sympathetically shaking her head. 'She told me that very thing.'

'Oh, did she now?' Molly rose from her chair and headed towards the kitchen door when Mary Jane stopped her. 'This would never have happened if your husband had been here.'

'You might be right,' said Mary Jane, careful not to divulge the fact she was not married to Red, or anybody else for that matter. 'Cissie had her eye on Red from the minute she saw him – she made no secret of the fact; said I wasn't good enough to polish his shoes.' Managing to halt the bitter laugh that rose to her throat, Mary Jane shook her head. Red had sewn her up good and proper with that lie, hadn't he? Although Molly was a fine and decent woman who had battled her own problems, Mary Jane didn't know Molly well enough to confide the fact she was an unmarried mother-to-be.

'You said he fought at The Front,' Molly said, and Mary Jane nodded.

'They all came back different after the war,' Mary Jane said. She had told Molly enough for today.

'When Lloyd-George said it was a war to end all wars, he probably meant it,' Molly said, heaving a great sigh, 'but it wasn't the end of our battle – the women's. We had to carry on with no men and little money. We were promised a better life after the war, but it never came... Still hasn't if I'm honest.' 'You have done a wonderful job with your children,' Mary Jane said, and she meant every word. If she was half the mother Molly was, she would be happy. 'I'll make you a blackberry pie for tea.'

'That's very kind of you, Love,' Molly said. 'Food never goes to waste in this house, so I won't say no. But don't worry, we'll sort something out,' Molly said, sitting down opposite. She patted Mary Jane's hand. 'D'you think she'll let you pay late, give you time to get the money together?'

'I doubt it very much, and even if she did, she would add interest, which would only make a bad situation even worse.'

'You said Cal Everdine lets you use his oven?' Molly ventured, she had seen Mary Jane coming and going with the handcart but didn't know she had an arrangement to use his oven. 'That's very good of him.'

'I think he felt sorry for me.' Mary Jane felt her neck and face grow hot and given the prolonged silence from Molly, she felt obliged to explain about Cal offering her a job that first day she came to Liverpool, and how she rebuked his offer.

'I should not have been so proud,' she said with a wry smile. 'Anything is better than nothing and baking my pies in his kitchen gets me out of that garret every day.' She gently blew cooling air into her tea, not looking up to see Molly's reaction.

'I didn't see him as the kind of man who would allow anybody over his threshold; he is so private. And he certainly doesn't look like a man who can afford to employ a cleaner.'

'Well,' said Mary Jane, 'I won't be imposing on him much longer, I can't expect him to pay the gas bill for my baking, if I have nothing to offer in return.'

'I suppose you could always bake his bread, or make an evening meal,' said Molly, obviously not as scandalised as

Cissie Stone had been when she found out Mary Jane was baking her goods elsewhere. Mary Jane did not she tell Molly she was already making Cal the occasional pie.

'There's always my mother's clock,' said Mary Jane, although she did not want to part with it.

Molly, although suitably sympathetic, said in a quiet voice, 'You don't want to be beholden to the pawnshop.' The older woman's kindly voice was low, subdued with concern and Mary Jane knew that she might not have a choice.

'I wouldn't get a penny for the wedding ring,' she answered. 'It's only a brass washer, not worth anything. Something will turn up, I'm sure.' Ever the optimist, Mary Jane believed you only sank so low before you bounced back up again. Nevertheless, if she sank any more, she felt she was now in danger of disappearing altogether. Since Red had bolted with her money, Mary Jane was left without enough to buy basic necessities, never mind luxuries like meat for her savouries. A thought struck her! She still had Mr Brook, the butcher, to pay for her last order of meat, and although he was a genial entertainer to the housewives of the surrounding dockside, he was a shrewd businessman who gave little away for nothing.

'You could always bake Mr Brook one of your lovely pies,' Molly smiled.

'Wssht,' Mary Jane dismissed Molly's compliment with the wave of her hand, 'anybody can make a pie or a loaf of bread, there's nothing to it.'

'Huh! That's easy for you to say, but there are some around here who could reinforce their walls with their baked offerings.'

'I've baked since I was that high,' Mary Jane said, pointing to her knee.

'You'll have the butcher eating out of your hand,' Molly insisted.

Mary Jane suddenly felt as if she had outstayed her welcome, even though Molly protested and said she had done no such thing. All the same, Mary Jane got up from the table and made to go.

'You come in any time you like,' Molly said walking her to the front door.

'That's very kind of you.' As they got to the front door, Molly stopped and, turning to Mary Jane, she said in that no-nonsense way of hers, 'You don't want to be stuck in that piddling little room all day, it'll drive you scatty. Call in any time.'

'Do you mean it, Molly? Are you sure I wouldn't be in the way?' She didn't want to intrude or add to her friend's burden, but spending time in that den of iniquity next door didn't bear thinking about.

'You won't be in the way, I've told you umpteen times, though you might want to run fast after spending a few hours with my squabbling brood.' Molly laughed.

'I think they're a delight,' Mary Jane said, giving Molly a hug and closing the door firmly behind her. However, her joy soon turned to outrage when she saw her belongings strewn about the front step – all except her mother's clock.

17

'The thieving harlot!' Mary Jane cried, as she flew down Molly's steps and stormed up next doors. She gave a swift nod to Daisy who was just returning from a long day's work at the dockside café. 'She's not getting away with this,' she told Daisy, giving little thought to her actions as she banged on Cissie Stone's door. When there was no reply, she pushed the letter box open and yelled inside, her voice echoing along the dingy lobby.

'Come out of there, you dirty slut!' Mary Jane was past being friendly or refined, this woman had tried her patience once too often, and if Cissie Stone thought she was going to get away with stealing her mother's clock, then she could think again.

'Mam, come and see this!' Daisy called. Worrying about Mary Jane's uncontrolled rage, she scurried up the lobby. 'I think there's going to be trouble.'

Molly and Daisy reached their front step just in time to see Mary Jane kick the front door, which was swiftly opened by a red-faced Cissie Stone, who looked a little worse for wear, with her hair all mussed up, and her blouse buttons done up wrong – and there was a distinct smell of gin wafting about her as she spoke to anybody who was passing.

'This trollop owes me a week's rent! Who can blame me for letting the room to those that pay on the nail?'

Mary Jane could hardly believe what she was hearing. A man in a cotton undershirt, his braces dangling, now stood in the doorway, and tried to entice Cissie back into the lodging house, but Cissie was insistent she was going to have her say.

'A week's rent she owes, and I want it now, or you won't see your precious clock again!'

'I owe you nothing, I am paid up until the end of today, Saturday, as you well know,' Mary Jane protested, moving forward, her rage catching in her throat, making her voice crack indignantly.

'Don't you dare put a foot over my threshold,' said Cissie Stone, blocking the doorway with her whole body as a crowd gathered to watch.

'You're deluded, if you think you're getting a week's rent out of me until tomorrow.' Mary Jane had gone through so much she was ready to do battle.

Cissie, hands on her hips, leaned forward from the door-frame of the house and for a short while Mary Jane thought she might topple down the stone steps as she rocked from side to side under the influence.

'You owe me, don't try to deny it.' Cissie was foaming at the corners of her mouth and Mary Jane knew she had to keep a clear head, otherwise the battle could be lost. 'You're a week in arrears,' Cissie spat the words and Mary Jane wondered if Red had anything to do with this. But she knew she had handed the money over, and it was written in her rent book and signed by Cissie herself.

'I most certainly am not, I paid you every penny last Sunday!' It was Mary Jane's turn to be outraged.

'Himself borrowed it back off me,' she was referring to Red, obviously.

'In that case,' said Mary Jane, 'take it up with *himself*.'

'You'll pay me a week's rent and the gas money you owe as well.' Cissie put her hand out, palm up, as she did every week.

'I'll do no such thing,' Mary Jane's tone was indignant. An ever-growing crowd gathered on the pavement outside Molly's house, their excitement, a barney between two women, was obvious in the rapid plumes, which they were breathing in the cold night air. Mary Jane worried that they, too, would turn on her, but she wasn't going to pay up without a fight.

'Now, now, ladies,' said a soothing voice at the back of the crowd, 'this is no way to behave in front of the children.'

'You mind your own flaming business,' Cissie shouted, and it was only when the crowd hushed and parted to show the parish priest, Father Flanagan, that she closed her big mouth.

'You've a mouth like a foghorn, Mrs Stone.' Father Flanagan's black cassock was rippling in the cold breeze, his face starkly white under the gas lamp.

'I was just saying, Father,' Cissie stammered. Everybody was scared of Father Flanagan. 'She owes me a week's rent.'

'Does she, by God?' Father Flanagan peered at Cissie from under bushy white eyebrows. 'And who might *she* be? The cat's mother?' It was plainly obvious to all who gathered that he did not particularly like this woman.

'Hello, Father,' Mary Jane said with quiet reverence, 'I am sorry that you have been dragged into this commotion. However, Mrs Stone has thrown all my things onto the street.'

'And do you owe Mrs Stone this money?'

'I do not owe her a penny, Father,' Mary Jane said.

He shook his head of thick white hair and said nothing for the moment. This young woman looked him in the eye, and she spoke with an assurance he admired. She was not the usual poor Irish immigrant fleeing the Home Country and knocking at his door for assistance. This one had something about her. She sounded educated, assured, giving him cause to wonder why she had come to live in one of the poorest areas of Liverpool. He knew she had built up a good few customers with her pies and bread – in fact, he had tasted them and would not have been ashamed to serve them to the King himself. But that husband of hers. Well, he was a different subject altogether.

'She did a flit while me back was turned,' Cissie said, and Father Flanagan silenced her with a look. Her eyes were everywhere except on him, she could not look him in the eye like Mary Jane could.

As he suspected, Cissie began to unravel under scrutiny and a moment later she was babbling like a proverbial brook. 'It was like this, you see, Father... I was good enough to put her up, and not many would do so in her condition... And anybody can see that ring is not a proper wedding band... Her man has bolted and has left her in the lurch! And in turn she has left me out of pocket too!'

'Have you quite finished blackening this poor woman's character, Cissie?' The crowd had swelled a little more and Mary Jane noticed Cal Everdine locking his side gates. He looked neither left nor right but straight ahead until he closed his front door. Mary Jane's shame caused her colour to rise, he must have seen and heard the uproar.

'Did you pay any money in advance of getting your key?' Father Flanagan asked in deceivingly gentle tones.

'A fortnight's rent in advance, and then another week's rent every Sunday after. I assumed the first two weeks' rent must have been a deposit against breakages, but nothing was broken while I was there.'

'Indeed,' said the priest, turning to Cissie, who looked a little shame-faced, 'if she paid you two weeks rent in the first instance, then another week's rent every week thereafter, Mrs Stone, this young lady owes you nothing.' Father Flanagan leaned forward, his face the colour of a stormy day, his words like thunder. 'If I am not mistaken – and I'm rarely mistaken – you owe her!'

'But... But...' Cissie could not get the words out.

'There are no "buts", Mrs Stone, that is an end to the matter,' said the priest. 'Pay the lady the rent you owe her.' Cissie said no more as she drew a small purse from the pocket of her skirt and grudgingly shoved the money into Mary Jane's hand, then flounced into her house, slamming the front door.

'Thank you, Father,' Mary Jane said as Father Flanagan nodded and replaced his black biretta.

'You're welcome,' he smiled, 'and don't forget, be early for mass tomorrow.'

'Come in here, love,' said Molly in her kindly motherly voice as Mary Jane, thankful she got her money back, decided she would light a candle for Father Flanagan at mass the following morning. 'You can stay here with us.'

Before entering Molly's home, she looked across the street and could clearly see Cal Everdine standing at his window. He was looking at her, not moving. His presence quiet but commanding, and Mary Jane was immediately consumed with a gnawing guilt she experienced whenever she saw him. Because she knew the emotions he evoked, were not the same as the ones she had for Paddy. And look where that got her, she thought, knowing her life was changed forever.

* * *

The following morning's eight o'clock mass at Saint Patrick's Church saw Mary Jane genuflect and slip into the back pew, feeling the growing weight of her stomach as she lowered herself onto the highly polished kneeler, her head bent resting on entwined fingers, her eyes closed. She begged the Good Lord above for mercy on her soul, forgiveness for her sins and for Paddy to rest in peace, knowing she could not take communion until she had been to confession. Ahead of her, in the rows of benches leading up to the alter she could see Ina King and various other women from Beamer Street, pious in their supplications, paying lip service to the Almighty, until they got outside and pushed past her as if she wasn't even there. Certainly, they'd know that to deliberately ignore or humiliate another was sinful, too?

18

'Better?' Molly said as she scooped up the newspaper that held the thin slivers of potato peelings, and Mary Jane smiled.

'I've a feeling, Molly,' she said. 'Something tells me nothing can be as bad as the last few months.'

'Good on you, lass. Hard work overrules self-pity any day.' Molly took the freshly peeled potatoes and put them under the cold running water from the copper tap. 'You'll feel as if your world has gone a bit lopsided after Red buggering off like that, and that's to be expected.' She sighed as she shook the colander vigorously, dripping cold water into the stone sink. 'Happen, you'll get over it, though. You're not the type to stand still and let life happen. You'd rather grab it by the throat and shake the escapades from it.'

'You seem to have an awful lot of faith in me, Moll,' Mary Jane said, watching her friend fussing around the kitchen, offering pearls of wisdom, and she felt better than she had done for a long time. Molly was right. A gauzy notion hovered inside her head, just out of reach, and after a long time it began to form into a solid idea.

'You can have a quiet moment to think of what is gone, by all means, but don't let Red's desertion get the better of you,' Molly said. 'There's many, like yourself, has been through the loss of her loving husband.'

Mary Jane suspected there were more widows in England after the great war than there had ever been. 'I really admire how you manage to stay so positive,' she said, her heart full of respect.

'Don't get me wrong, lass,' Molly said, 'when my Albert were taken, I couldn't even see trees – never mind the woods. I was poleaxed with grief. But when you've got hungry mouths to feed, as well as your own,' she shook her head, 'you can't indulge in the luxury of a good old wallow for long.' She gave a sad kind of smile and continued, 'The little ones get scared when they see their mama cry. We're the ones who're supposed to make things better, not worse.'

'If I'm honest, Molly,' Mary Jane said, 'I count myself lucky Red left me, before he put me in the poorhouse; the man was a right bloody sponge.' Mary Jane slapped her hand over her mouth to stop another curse breaking free. Her eyes were wide when she looked at Molly, who showed no hint of shock.

'What are you going to do next,' Molly asked, 'with no man, no money?'

'Oh Molly,' Mary Jane gasped, 'I'm not going to let a little thing like Red's desertion spoil my life. I'll think about what I'm to do next, over the coming days, and I'll cross the bridge when I come to it.'

'I were like a thing possessed after the shock of losing Albert,' Molly said, glad that Mary Jane was her usual cheery self and thinking of her future, 'I turned out all his clothes – not that he had many, and I nearly ripped up me one and only wedding photograph, but our Daisy stopped me, thank goodness. I was so angry with him for putting himself in front of a toffee-apple like that and getting hisself blown to smithereens '

Mary Jane knew that a *toffee apple* was the name given to trench mortar bombs and her heart lurched. 'You were beside yourself, Molly.'

'It was only when I tried to rip up his Sunday shirt, the one he wore for chapel, that I saw sense,' Molly spoke as if talking to herself. 'I could smell the carbolic soap and pipe tobacco... It was him.' She gave a little sniff and was quiet for a moment. 'I hugged that shirt to me bosom and I cried, great heaving sobs. So much so, I nearly made meself sick.'

Mary Jane listened with rising fascination.

'I gradually stopped sobbing. And it was like he were standing there, looking at me, his voice filling our bedroom. *Molly, lass,* he said, *don't be such a soft ha'porth, you've got a babby downstairs scared to look at you. Now, what way is that to rear a child?'* Tears rolled down Molly's softly lined cheeks, her lips pressed together in a pensive half-smile, while Mary Jane sat listening. Moments later, as if waking from a nap, Molly suddenly sniffed, smiled brightly and pulled a handkerchief from the sleeve of her cardigan. She wiped her bright button eyes and trumpeted into her handkerchief. In seconds, she was her usual chatty self. Right as ninepence.

'Was he a good husband?' Mary Jane asked, and Molly told her he was one of the best.

'Even though he was always getting himself into scrapes.' She gave a little chuckle. 'He fell out o' driver's cab and broke his toe the first day on the railway. He still drove that train though; the man was a likeability.'

'Liability?' Mary Jane asked, quietly correcting, and Molly smiled.

'I know what I mean,' she said. 'After he got himself blown

up, I got a job in the munitions factory, I was earning good money too. As yellow as a duck's arse, I was.' Again, she gave vent to easy laughter, which, Mary Jane now realised, hid a multitude of sorrows. 'Then, after the fighting ended, the men came home from the trenches, wanting the work.' She shrugged her shoulders, 'Well, they had a right. They'd been putting themselves in mortal danger for our country.'

'What did you do?' Mary Jane was captivated, listening attentively to this big-hearted widow reminisce about her difficult life; trying to keep her and her family fed and warm, without a scrap of self-pity. Having lost a mother with whom she could go and share problems or joys, Mary Jane was enraptured; this friendship was a rare treat indeed.

'I scrubbed steps and took in washing,' Molly said practically, 'the usual stuff. A baby on me hip and a scrubbing brush in me hand.' She lifted her chin, 'Then there was Mr Platt of course...' Her eyes took on a strange far-away look.

'Mr Platt?' Mary Jane didn't want to pry but had to admit she was curious.

'He was me lodger.' Molly made the sign of the cross over her motherly bosom and Mary Jane did likewise. 'He had the use of the back bedroom and the parlour, I'll show you, shall I?' She took Mary Jane into the well-furnished parlour. 'He died; God rest he's soul.' There was a hint of finality to Molly's voice. 'All this furniture was he's.' She did not say 'his', and with a single sweep of her hand, she included: the robust three-piece suite complete with white lace antimacassars covering the back of the two brown leather chairs and matching sofa; the glass cabinet containing a porcelain, gold-rimmed tea set and two framed photographs; a highly polished upright piano snuggled in the recess at the side of a Victorian tiled cast-iron fireplace, and on the floor was a large multicoloured rug bordered by dark brown linoleum. The cosy room was one of the best Mary Jane had ever seen, reminding her that the small cottage back in Ireland would have fitted in this one room alone. 'He brought all of this furniture with him,' said Molly, breaking into Mary Jane's thoughts, 'but not the bedroom stuff. That was my Albert's mother's.'

'Did Mr Platt...?' Mary Jane hesitated, not sure she wanted to know where Mr Platt had died.

'No, he didn't die in bed; it was the drink that took him.' Again, Molly made the sign of the cross on her well-upholstered bosom.

'He was a drunk?' Mary Jane asked, sympathetically, and Molly shook her head,

'No, he was knocked down by a dray horse!' Molly looked slightly alarmed when Mary Jane failed to combat the herculean restraint and burst out laughing. Moments later, Molly did the same and before long they were wiping tears of uncontrolled mirth from their eyes, and when Daisy came into the parlour to see what all the commotion was about, she started laughing too. Although she had no idea why she was laughing, all she did know was that the whole room seemed to be infectious with laughter.

'I was thinking,' Molly said when sobriety returned and they went back to the kitchen, 'and just say if you don't like the idea, it's no skin off my nose.' She busied herself at the sink, throwing the words over her shoulder, 'You could move in here if you like. The parlour's yours if you want it.'

'You would rent me the parlour?' Mary Jane's breathless words came out in a rush when she could trust herself to speak.

Molly gave a little nod of her head. 'Aye, and the back room upstairs.'

'Oh, Molly, I'd love to say yes, but the money I got from Cissie Stone will have to go to pay the butcher's bill.'

'Don't let that be a worry to you,' Molly said, and Mary Jane laughed again, thrilled at the power of good this woman was doing for her. Suddenly she felt as if she could handle anything that life threw at her.

'When will the rooms be available?'

'Straight away is fine by me,' Molly said, looking down at Mary Jane's meagre belongings. 'You can put your things in the room now if you like.'

She had only the few bits of clothing and the clock, nothing much, thought Mary Jane, knowing the most difficult part of leaving Cissie Stone's house was getting back the basket of fruit, which Cissie had tried, and failed, to claim along with the clock which Cissie gave up when Mary Jane threatened to tell the priest she had stolen it. Not sure whether to laugh out loud or to hug Molly, in the end Mary Jane did both. She was going to enjoy living here.

'About the rent?' Mary Jane asked, and when Molly told her the price, her jaw dropped. Not only were the two rooms a shilling cheaper than Cissie Stone's miserable attic, but they were also fully furnished, had plenty of light and heat, and the whole house echoed to the sound of happy chatter and easy laughter. 'I'm too excited to think straight.'

'Aye, well that might be because the curious and giddy children know there's a new face in the house, but they'll soon settle.' Molly cast a knowing glance to her younger children, who were impatiently waiting for the apple and blackberry pie that Mary Jane had baked to follow their roast dinner of beef brisket that filled the house with a mouth-watering aroma.

'I'll tell you what, Molly, I manged to get plenty of fruit yesterday, so I'll make some fruit scones and tarts. How's that?'

'That will be wonderful!' Molly let out her easy chuckle, and Mary Jane heaved a sigh of relief.

'We can always find a way if we look hard enough,' Molly said, and Mary Jane nodded in agreement. And I will continue to bake some pies to sell,' Mary Jane said, knowing how people wanted her pies, pastries, and cakes.

Molly pounced on the idea. 'I've got the kitchen if you've got the ingredients.'

'It's as though it was meant to be, Ma wouldn't mind me selling her clock to secure my future,' Mary Jane said, knowing the legacy was worth a lot of money.

'That's a grand clock, Mrs Redfern,' said Daisy, and the name caused Mary Jane's insides to implode.

'Call me Mary Jane,' she said, 'I don't stand on ceremony.'

* * *

'My Albert was a none commissioned officer, before making me a widow,' Molly said later. Molly spoke as if Albert had got himself killed deliberately. She patted her salt-and-pepper-coloured hair, set in deep waves, which her eldest son, Davey, had treated her to since he started work in the cardboard box factory, next to Beamer's Electricals.

'The time has gone so quick,' Molly told her, 'it seems like only last week, I was giving birth to our Bridie.' She pursed her lips and made a short indignant noise, as if blowing out a candle.

'It must have been difficult for you?' Mary Jane, usually so good at giving support, could not begin to imagine how poor Molly had single-handedly raised her children. All of them a credit to her. But she knew she would find out soon enough and hoped she could be as good a mother.

'I knew the very moment my Albert died.' Molly's tone gave Mary Jane no reason to doubt her, not even when she said; 'I'm sensitive to changes in the atmosphere.' Molly lowered her voice, 'I can tell when something is going to happen...' Molly lifted her starched nets over the kitchen sink and looked down the back yard, and Mary Jane could have sworn Molly was shedding a tear when she said quietly, 'His passing felt like the light had gone from my heart.'

Even after all these years Molly still wept for the loss of her husband. Yet, it had only been months since Paddy was killed and Mary Jane couldn't remember the last time she shed a tear for him and felt the ever-present shame grow inside her. She was such a terrible person.

Suddenly, Molly brightened, her smile lighting up her round, maternal face when she turned from the window and said: 'It's them what keeps me going now, my children. They bring me comfort beyond measure. Without them, I am nothing.'

'It's a big responsibility being the centre of someone's world, I imagine.'

'Aye, I suppose you're right, love,' Molly sighed, 'I never thought of it like that before. I just want to do the right thing, bring them up properly, and let them know they have as much love today as they did when their father was alive.'

'I'm sure they do,' Mary Jane said. 'You're a good mother, Molly, and the children adore you.' You already have your work cut out, looking after your family without me being a burden too.'

'You're not a burden, lass,' Molly said as she went to the pantry and took out a bowl of eggs. 'In fact, you being here will help me out.'

'In what way?' Mary Jane asked, not sure she had anything to offer this big-hearted woman.

'Our Daisy has always wanted to bake instead of serving in a teashop and when she saw the way you managed to go about it, she was impressed,' said Molly. 'The only thing is, I've never been much of a baker. Could you give her a few instructions?'

'It's not easy,' Mary Jane pointed out. 'The work is laborious, and you must be an early riser, but there is nothing like the satisfaction of knowing someone appreciates the hours and the work you have put in, who comes back time and again.'

'That's what she wants,' said Molly. 'She doesn't want to take orders for the rest of her life. She wants to make her own decisions. Be her own mistress.'

'I've got competition,' Mary Jane laughed, 'but I admire her spirit, and I understand completely.'

Molly nodded her head in agreement, then she said brightly, 'I'd be made up if you could help her,' as if Mary Jane was the one who was doing the favour. 'We don't have much in the way of riches, but we've all got each other.'

'I would love to help her, Molly.' Mary Jane's spirits soared; she hardly remembered her own mother, just a few snatches of well-known phrases, or a passing aroma that brought back a fleeting sense of contentment, so she could barely believe that she was not only gaining a place to live, but a happy contented family into the bargain. 'Are you sure you don't have enough on your hands, considering you've five mouths to feed and very little prospects.' There was a silence in the room and Mary Jane wondered if she had said something wrong.

'Who says I've no prospects?' Molly's careworn face creased into a web of fine lines, and for the first time, Mary Jane realised she wasn't the only one who might have been carrying the weight of the world on her shoulders. She put her hand to her mouth, horrified when she realised what she had just said!

'Oh, Molly, I didn't explain myself properly! What I really meant was that I don't want to add to your burden!' Mary Jane jumped up and, in the process, accidentally knocked over her cup, spilling hot tea all over the beautiful white tablecloth. 'Molly, I am so sorry! I didn't mean to cause offence!' She was mortified and would not hurt Molly for anything.

'You didn't upset me, you daft ha'porth,' Molly answered, bustling to the sink and fetching a clean dishcloth, 'but let me tell you something. which I learned early on after my Albert died.' She dabbed at the spilled tea. 'I don't take kindly to pity – nor to feeling sorry for myself, what's the good in that?'

'None,' Mary Jane said, taking the dishcloth and mopping her mess.

'All I meant,' said Molly with a sigh, 'was that I had no intentions of lying down and letting my worries get on top of me... I suspect you're that way inclined, too?'

'I suppose I am,' Mary Jane stopped dabbing when Molly picked up the teapot and tilted it over her cup.

'So let's grab life by the shirt tails and hang on for the bumpy ride!'

'We have to, it's the only way!' Mary Jane laughed. 'Otherwise, what's the point?'

'Aye,' Molly said, offering the cup to her friend. 'Well, get this down you and watch what you're doing next time.'

'I promise to be a bit happier, and let's face it, I couldn't get much worse.' Mary Jane's amused smile lifted her face. 'I've had so much building up inside me these last months and haven't been able to talk to a soul.' She stirred her tea. 'If it hadn't been for you and Daisy, I might have exploded words all over the place.'

'Aye, and that's another mess you'd make,' Molly offered, sitting at the other side of the table. 'There'd be big pools of unexplained words.' They both looked at each other, and in no time, they were both laughing at the absurd notion. 'Mind you,' Molly said in that straight-talking way of hers, 'nobody would have a clue what you were going through. You always looked so sure of yourself. I think a lot of folk were jealous of you, especially having a good-looking husband – even if he was a wastrel.'

'I like to keep myself to myself,' Mary Jane said.

'And who could blame you,' Molly answered, 'but that's what goads that lot out there,' she nodded towards the street.

'I had no intentions of filling their mouths with gossip,' Mary Jane said, putting her cup on the saucer.

'They thought you'd something missing in the upper story.' Molly tapped her steel-coloured hair. 'But you'd no choice – I told them. I said, not every girl knows she's marrying a prodigal. Beg pardon for saying.'

Mary Jane shrugged her slim shoulders. She could not stop the neighbours reaching their own conclusions.

'I soon put them wise, though. I told Ina King "*the girl's got no choice, just like the rest of us, but I don't see her knocking on any of your doors begging a bit o' sugar or marge.*" That soon hushed their jangling.'

Mary Jane, relaxed now, wondered if she dared tell Molly that Red was not her real husband, but something stopped her. Molly had every faith that she was a wife scorned and left to fend for herself. Would she be so hospitable or so friendly if she knew the truth? Mary Jane doubted it.

'Hello, Mam, what's for tea, my belly thinks me throat's been cut!' Davey took off his cap and muffler and hung them on the cellar door hook, and the brief interruption brought

Mary Jane quickly to her senses. Whatever was she thinking of? What possible good could come of divulging such shameful information? Telling Molly everything might be a load off her conscience, but more than likely, the news would lose her a very valuable friendship! And right now, that's the last thing she needed. The guilty lie ate away at her from the inside. But she had to save her reputation at all costs. Wasn't it bad enough Red had been fodder for gossip since he arrived in Beamer Street? Well, now that he had upped and left her to it, she was going to change the way people round here thought of her. She wasn't like Red with his indolent ways and his grasping nature. While she had a good pair of hands on her she intended to work for what she needed.

'The only ones you have to care about are yourself and that little one you're carrying,' Molly was saying, 'you'll have it all to do and more when it gets here. Everybody else can go to hell in a handcart.' Molly stood up and said, 'right, that's enough gossip for half an hour, I've got tonight's tea to cook.'

'Let me help you,' Mary Jane said and hugged her friend. One day she would tell Molly the truth. But for now, she had revealed enough.

'Pass me those spuds.' If she was going to take up space in Molly's kitchen, Mary Jane would make herself useful. As they worked, they were both quiet, lost in their thoughts. In harmonious silence, she was peeling a small mountain of potatoes, while Molly was plucking the chicken, each of them mulling things over and for the first time in months Mary Jane felt strong enough to consider what had actually happened that day when she left Cashalree for good.

Mary Jane knew if she had been stronger, she would have refused to leave Ireland. She should have gone back home. Faced her fear. Stood up for Paddy in the way he was going to stand up for her. Nevertheless, she certainly did not feel the same way about Paddy as Molly felt about her Albert. When Molly spoke of her Albert, her eyes and her voice softened. Lost in the love they once shared.

Safe in the knowledge she would marry him, cook for him, clean his house, warm his bed, Paddy never took her dancing, except for that one night when he seduced her in the hayloft. He never bought her chocolate, like she'd seen other men do for their girls, never walked out with her, in the same way other girls were courted.

'Is everything all right, Mary Jane?' Molly's forehead pleated in concern and Mary Jane nodded, not realising her breathing was becoming more rapid with each new thought.

'I was just thinking,' she said. 'Sometimes my thoughts run away with themselves.'

'Of course, they do,' Molly said kindly. And something in her heart told Mary Jane she was adding to her wickedness by cultivating the lie. She knew deep down that one day she would be punished for her brazen ways. God was slow, but he was sure, of that she had no doubt!

* * *

Cal Everdine saw Mary Jane putting empty milk bottles on Molly Hayward's step when she looked up suddenly. Even in the light of the gas lamp, he saw her green eyes flashing defiance, as if they could pierce his buried secrets and see the worthless man he truly was.

He refused to retreat behind the net curtain.. Some magnetic draw held him fast. In a moment, she turned and went back inside Molly's house, closing the door tightly behind her.

Lowering the blind, Cal turned from the window, resting his back on the paperless wall. He had heard the fracas between Mrs Redfern and Cissie Stone. Even the local clergy had become entangled in the altercation, and he had longed to go down to the street and end the matter. But that might start tongues wagging. What business was it of his, they would say. He had nothing to do with Mary Jane.

So, he thought, Mary Jane's husband had done her a great service and left her. He had heard the bastard had left her penniless. Cal could feel the tightening in his guts. If she was his, he thought, Mary Jane would want for nothing. Looking around the sparsely furnished room, it was as if he was seeing it for the first time. As she would see it when she came to use his oven each day. Nothing of comfort or pleasurable. Just a barely furnished room and a gas mantle hanging from a ceiling chain in the middle of the room. Cal had more money than he could spend in a lifetime: his inheritance, the incomes derived from his many properties, and the rich proceeds from the silver mines in Canada. Yet he lived like a pauper. Penance for past wrongs. He clenched his huge fists so tightly his tanned knuckles turned white. Why should he live in comfort when he had nobody to share it with? If he had married someone as feisty and as beautiful as Mary Jane... But he hadn't. And he realised there was no point in dwelling on the tumbling, russet-coloured hair, or eyes that could change from gentle green to flashing emerald in mere moments. Cal knew he had no right to feel this way.

'She is a married woman, you fool.'

19

'Well, I'll leave you to get settled, it's been a long day and I'm sure you're tired,' Molly said, ushering Daisy from the room. 'And if my lot disturb you, just let me know. I won't allow them to make a nuisance of themselves,' she said cheerfully before closing the door behind her.

Mary Jane sat by the fire and felt the comforting heat envelope her. She loved to be surrounded by people, lots of them. But sometimes she just liked to sit quietly and ponder. Even though she should be sick and tired of her own company by now; Red's company was the famine, while the Haywoods' was most certainly the feast.

Resting her head on the back of the chair, she closed her eyes. This was the finest room she had ever inhabited. The clean smell of mansion polish and freshly laundered curtains – everything was perfect. She could hardly believe her luck. She could never repay the kindness Molly had showed her today.

* * *

Mary Jane woke early to the sound of children's whispers outside the bedroom door, and for a moment she wondered where she was. There it was again!

'*Ssswww, ssswww, ssswww.*'

When she opened her eyes, she knew for certain she was in another world. This was a million miles from the house next door. She didn't need to wipe the sleep from her eyes to see that it was clean. The fresh scent of wax polish that had lovingly brought the furniture to a burnished sheen pervaded the cosy bedroom and reminded her of home.

Turning her head on the feather pillow, she reached for the glass of water on the bow-fronted bedside table which Molly had thoughtfully placed there the night before. She had told Molly she often woke in the night with a throat as dry as the bottom of a budgerigar's cage. After quenching her thirst, Mary Jane flopped back into the most comfortable bed she had ever slept in, revelling in the luxurious mattress that was free of bugs or fleas, and no springs poking through to pierce little holes in her legs. Pushing back the covers, she swung her legs out of bed, and her toes danced on the cold linoleum searching for her shoes.

'Come away from that door this minute! You little hooligans!' she heard Molly say and Mary Jane smiled when she heard them all scuffle down the stairs.

'Go and play with your wooden train while I get the breakfast on the table – and don't wake Mary Jane!'

Mary Jane suspected there was little chance of children being quiet first thing in the morning; they were far too excited about their new lodger. She loved Molly's boisterous family and imagined that they were her own. They were not well off, but they were kind and considerate and treated her the same way they treated Molly, who ruled this house with a firm hand and lashings of love.

The children were Molly's most precious commodity and she made sure they knew they were loved and well cared for. It was a fine balance at a time when there was no man about the place. Although, Mary Jane noticed, the younger children paid the same heed to their older siblings, Daisy, and Davey, as they did to their mother.

'Don't worry about me, Molly,' she called, opening the bedroom door, 'I've been awake for ages.' Mary Jane popped her head outside to see the two beaming faces of seven-year-old Freddy and five-year-old Bridie. Edging them along the landing with her buxom hip, Molly told everybody their breakfast was nearly ready as Freddy and Bridie ran downstairs, laughing and whispering among themselves. 'Take no notice of those two giddy kippers,' Molly said. 'They'll soon get used to you being here. If they get in your way, just give them a little job to do, they'll soon scatter.'

Mary Jane laughed, she loved Molly's down-to-earth approach to life, knowing she was going to be happy here. How could she not? Even though this house was the mirror image of the one next door, it was as different as it was possible to be. This happy house, although as big, was bright and full of love, not filled with shadowy people who only came out at night.

'These houses overlooked the beach in days gone by,' Molly said conversationally as she dished up hot porridge for the little ones, and bacon, egg, sausage and tomatoes for the older siblings. 'They were in amongst the sand dunes, weren't they, Davey?' she asked her son, who nodded. 'I sometimes try to imagine what it must have been like to be lady of the manor.' Molly laughed and her rosy complexion turned a deep pink when Freddy jumped down from his chair, gave an exaggerated bow and said in lofty tones:

'Very good, milady.'

Molly's youngest daughter, caught up in the frivolous moment, said brightly, 'You are the lady of the manor, Mum!'

'That's as maybe,' Molly said, sitting down to her own breakfast, 'and seeing as you're so chirpy this morning, I'll let you lot do the washing-up.' Squeals of outraged protest chorused around the table, and Molly laughed, assuring them that they had been excused the chores, whispering to Mary Jane that the last time she allowed them to 'help out', they nearly broke every piece of crockery, soaked the kitchen floor and half drowned each other. Although, the two youngest were quick to leave the table, when they'd had their fill, just in case Ma changed her mind.

'Imagine owning all of this,' Mary Jane said, gazing around the spacious kitchen that had once been the servants' quarters.

'I know,' Molly answered, 'but when the docks were built the merchants wanted somewhere a bit more attractive than cranes and warehouses along the docks.' Her eyes widened with good humour 'So wasn't that our good fortune?'

'I love these high-ceilinged rooms,' Mary Jane said. 'Having come from a little rural village, we didn't have anything so grand.' Every time she mentioned Ireland, she was filled with longing to go back home.

'They come in handy when you've a big family,' Molly said, 'and there's plenty of those around here.'

'You'd need this space to fit them all in, for sure,' Mary Jane added, imagining how her own family would have fared. 'My brothers are huge, but, like goldfish, they'd have grown even bigger if they had this much room to grow in.' Mary Jane paused and then said in a lower tone: 'I never thought I'd ever say so, because they were always in my way, but I do miss them.' Realising the conversation, which had started so innocently, had suddenly taken a maudlin turn, she cheered up and laughed. 'Listen to me prattling on like a fixated eejit. You don't want to hear me meandering down memory lane on my first day.'

'No, I like to hear about other people's family, you never speak of yours,' Molly said, buttering a piece of toast.

'Red didn't like me talking about my brothers – I've three of them, Aiden is the eldest, then Bly and then Colm.' She was pleased when she saw the surprised look on Daisy's face.

'A.B.C.' Daisy smiled, then her eyes widened.

'The big fellas – that's what everybody called them – had their own way of doing things and nobody dared to discommode them, they are very respected.' Mary Jane's eyes softened; she could not believe that her own flesh and blood would do something as terrible as kill a man. It wasn't in their nature. After a moment, she realised they were waiting for her to continue talking. 'The youngest, Colm, had a pet pig, which the other two threatened to eat if he failed his exams.' Mary Jane laughed. 'And he was so attached and fearful for it he let it sleep in his bedroom.'

'That's wonderful.' Bridie clapped her hands in delight 'I would be in heaven!'

'She's animal-mad, this one,' Molly interrupted. 'If it's small and furry or has four legs you can bet our Bridie will try to sneak it into the house.'

'Ma won't let us have animals,' the young one said, looking under her dark lashes. 'She says they cost too much.'

'What I said, if you heard me right, Missy, was that I couldn't bear to lose one – they don't last long, like we do, you know!'

'Mary Jane and her brothers had the right idea,' Davey said practically. 'If you are going to have a pet you might as well have one that will show a nice return on your investment of time and money.' Bridie shrieked with horror at the idea. And Molly ordered Davey to drop the subject and she patted her youngest daughter's back, making maternal sounds of reassurance.

'How do you fancy a bacon sarnie, to cheer you up?' She looked quite perplexed when they all started laughing, having no idea what she had just alluded to. 'Oh, my word!' The penny dropped; Molly spluttered her apologies. 'I didn't mean... I just meant... I haven't a clue what I meant!' She wiped her pink-tinged cheeks with her apron and, throwing back her head, let out a rib-aching laugh.

Mary Jane wiped away tears of joy with the pad of her hand and putting her anxiety to the back of her mind, sure she was going to love living here.

20

LIVERPOOL – OCTOBER 1921

'Molly, can I ask you a great favour?' Mary Jane had been enjoying Molly and her family's hospitality and had been so busy making her bakes in Cal's kitchen, she felt she was neglecting her promise to Molly to teach Daisy the finer points of baking. She wasn't comfortable with the feeling, knowing Molly had been a good friend to her as well as charging much less rent than Cissie Stone, while providing a lot more comfort. But that wasn't the reason she hadn't been giving Daisy instructions, Mary Jane needed to be busy. Doing things. Keeping her mind on the here and now, instead of dwelling on her yesterdays. Dear God, she needed to stop thinking about her yesterdays, they brought back such bad memories.

'What kind of favour?' Molly's eyebrows furrowed in a mock sombre expression. 'In my experience, favours can cost, one way or another.' Then, showing Mary Jane she was not serious, Molly laughed, 'But I'm willing to risk it.'

'It's a huge favour,' Mary Jane said. 'I will pay for the extra gas, of course, but I need the use of your stove - and a couple of days, if Daisy can spare the time.'

'There's no need to cook your own food, lovely,!' Molly said in her usual pragmatic way. 'I do the cooking, you know that and it's no bother, the more, the merrier; it won't make any difference to me. I have the tea on already, love. We're having liver and onions, lots of iron for the little one,' she added, nodding to Mary Jane's thickening waistline.

'I don't mean for the tea.' Mary Jane shook her head almost apologetically, 'I need more oven space, I can't bake enough pies and bread in CaI's kitchen, and I was wondering if Daisy could spare me some time, as she is working part-time now.' Mary Jane knew Daisy had her hours cut at the teashop, 'I thought she might be looking for a couple of days helping me.' Mary Jane stopped talking when she noticed Molly's quizzical look.

'So, it's Cal now?' Molly queried. 'Whatever happened to Mr Everdine.'

'He's Cal's father,' Mary Jane answered, straight-faced, before the two women filled the room with laughter.

'I am grateful to you and Cal for the kindness you have shown me over the last few difficult weeks – I don't know what I would have done without either of you.'

'I'm sure he appreciates a home-cooked pie when he gets home.' Molly was so glad Mary Jane was happier, less haunted looking.

'Do you think Daisy will help me out, I will pay of course.' Mary Jane was trying to evade the subject Molly could tell.

'Nobody's ever asked her to bake before, she usually bakes a few fancies for the teashop, but that didn't do her any favours.'

Mary Jane felt the keen stab of disappointment, knowing that although Molly would help her any way she could, she did not sound keen to lose Daisy's help around the house, and Mary Jane hoped the offer of payment would change her mind. 'I promise I will make it worth Daisy's while, and I did promise to train her.'

'Oh I'm not putting a spanner in the works,' Molly put a motherly hand on Mary Jane's, arm. 'It's just that, our Daisy was so disappointed when her hours were cut, she did mention that she didn't want to bake ever again.'

'I'll soon change her mind,' said Mary Jane. 'I can't let her natural talent go to waste.' Back home in Cashalree, she had sold her pies from the kitchen window, much to her brothers' chagrin, thinking she was lowering the tone of the village. But they soon capitulated when the tantalising aroma drew people to the window from afar. She put the money aside, saving for a rainy day, determined she was not going to become a nurse or even a doctor as her parents had once wished when they were alive. But all she wanted to do was bake, and if she could make a living from it, all the better.

Although she had not anticipated the same level of custom here in Liverpool as she did back home, Mary Jane did not expect her reputation to travel so fast she was unable to keep up with the work single-handed.

'Do you think it would be a good idea to ask her?' Mary Jane's voice sounded hesitant, even to her own ears.

'How many pies?' Molly asked, interrupting her thoughts.

'About two dozen.' Mary Jane saw Molly's eyes widen and then some more when she said... 'A day.' Mary Jane felt the need to explain, 'Baking is all I want to do, it's where I am at my most happy, and it is how I can best earn my keep.'

'You're not wanting to go out selling pies every day, in this weather?' Molly's abundant chins wobbled as she spoke, knowing the days were growing colder and Mary Jane was growing bigger.

'I shouldn't have asked.' Mary Jane was sure she had overstepped the mark.

'It's not that I don't want to help you,' Molly said hesitantly, lowering her voice, 'but this house is rented, I can get away with having a lodger, because the land agent will think you're family when he comes to collect the rent. But the rent book clearly states I cannot run a business from the property.'

'Oh, of course… I understand.' Mary Jane could taste the disappointment. She had been so busy making her own plans and gave no thought to the consequences for poor Molly. 'Don't give it another thought.'

'Although,' Molly said, tapping the side of her nose, 'I'm sure it would take a while before somebody cottoned on.'

'I couldn't put you in that predicament, Molly, what if somebody told the landlord? You'd be put out on the street.'

'Don't talk so daft, who would do such a thing?' Molly had such a trusting nature and a huge heart, but that did not give Mary Jane the right to take advantage. 'Anyway, you might be doing me a favour as far as our Daisy's concerned,' Molly said. 'I think she'll jump at the chance when you ask her.'

'Are you sure?' Mary Jane asked, her spirits soaring. 'I don't want you getting into trouble with the landlord,' she whispered so the children would not hear.

'I wouldn't know the landlord if I fell over him,' said Molly. 'Mr Jarvis, the rent collector comes every Friday, takes the money, signs my rent book and goes again.'

'I'll make sure I'm not selling from the parlour window on a Friday then,' Mary Jane said and laughed out loud.

'I like the idea, though.' Molly answered, and Mary Jane could have whooped with joy as hope fluttered in her heart, an excited energy lifting her spirits. If she sold enough pastries, she could afford to pay Molly the going rate and stay in this warm, decent house until her baby was born. What happened to her after that, she did not know. However, that would be another bridge to cross when she came to it.

'I've seen women selling all manner of things out of baskets, along the dock road,' Molly chuckled to herself, 'but I can't recall seeing any selling pies out of a parlour window.'

'Oh Molly, thank you,' Mary Jane said, 'you won't regret it, I promise.'

'Well, I'm sure that baking a few pies to sell won't do any harm,' Molly said, spooning carrot and turnip onto every plate, before bustling around her ever-busy kitchen. 'And if you like, you can bake one for our tea tomorrow.'

'You're on.' Mary Jane could not wait to expand her production of bakes. 'I'll go around to the butchers for some more supplies.'

'Watch that fella on the top road,' Molly told her, 'he'll diddle you as soon as look at you.'

'He can try,' Mary Jane's heartfelt laugh filled the kitchen. 'But I've met a fair few in my time. I know their tricks.'

* * *

'Let's sit down and eat,' said Molly as she put her plate of food on the table, later that day.

It was Mary Jane's opportunity to talk to Daisy about her proposals to expand her business.

'I'll start with something simple, Daisy,' Mary Jane said, tucking in while the children, quiet as mice, listened to the grown-ups talk. 'Would that be all right?'

Daisy nodded, eager to get started and the whole family

nodded too. All keen to see Mary Jane succeed, and even offering their services, giving her a boost of enthusiasm.

'I could make a few cakes, too, if you like,' Daisy offered, and Mary Jane nodded enthusiastically. 'There's also the banks near the town hall, and the insurance offices in Dale Street where we can make sales.'

'Then there's the offices in the Liver Buildings!' said Davey, who rarely got involved with adult conversation, preferring to read. 'Loads of people work there.'

'And the cafés and canteens along the dock road,' Molly was caught up in the vivacious excitement. 'I'll put the word out. We can take orders!'

'And deliver,' Mary Jane laughed. 'Although, we will have to find out how we can be in two or three places at one time.' Five sets of hands waved in the air and declared that they would deliver the pies. Even the youngest, five-year-old Bridie, in her gravy-stained pinafore, waved her chubby little hands and cried, 'Me too, me too!'

'I'll parade along the dock road with Mr Everdine's hand-cart, while Bridie has a ride on the back of it,' Mary Jane announced. She went on to explain that at the market, her pies usually sold by word of mouth. 'The first lot will go for next to nothing.'

'Is that wise?' Molly asked, her lips set in a straight worried line. 'Will you cover your costs?'

'I've got an idea which will cover the first lot if I start small, on this very doorstep,' Mary Jane assured her. 'I'll send a free pie to Ina King, to feed her brood.'

Molly nodded in agreement, knowing Mrs King had nine children. 'A large plate pie would be a welcome addition to her table, I shouldn't wonder. Her husband works for the Corporation...' Molly said, and gave Mary Jane a knowing smile. 'She's a terrible cook, have you seen the state of her little'uns – they're like laths.'

'Ina's got the biggest gob this side of the Mersey, she won't let a gift like that go unmentioned,' Mary Jane said, tucking into creamy mashed potato, which Molly had heaped onto her plate.

Molly's eyebrows met, and she was still for a moment, holding her knife and fork either side of her plate. Suddenly the penny dropped. 'Ahh, so that's the reason you're giving her free food?'

'Two reasons.' Mary Jane nodded. 'She'll accept the pie without question, telling everybody she meets. Then she will give it to her husband, and if I am right, she will pass it off as her own,'

'Of course, she will,' said Molly 'She's a sly one that Ina King. But how will that help you?'

'Well,' she answered, 'before long, her husband will want another of her pies, telling his workmates how good a cook his wife has become, and he will want to take one to work to show it off.' Mary Jane's smile was wide, safe in the knowledge that she would sell one pie at least!

'Mr King will compliment her on her improved baking skills, stop throwing his plate against the wall, and Ina will be rushing over to buy another pie.' Molly smiled at this vibrant young woman who certainly had her head stuck on the right way, and who had no pretensions, just a solid assurance of her own ability.

'And when she comes back for more,' said Mary Jane, 'she'll be prepared to pay full price, like everybody else.' She tapped her head and nodded, 'Up there for thinking, Molly.' Then she pointed to her feet 'Down there for dancing, that's what my brothers say.'

Molly was glad this forthright woman had chosen to come and live here. Her ideas were bigger than the sky. 'I wish you every success.'

21

LIVERPOOL - NOVEMBER 1921

Nervously tapping her foot, Mary Jane waited for a response to her loud banging on the dull brass knocker, knowing a bit of elbow grease and a tin of Brasso would bring it up a treat, to look bright. The weather had taken a turn and considering it was two weeks into November, the evening had a bite that didn't go around, it cut straight through her and brought smoke from every household chimney, as the wind dropped allowing a spot of sleet to land on the tip of her nose. Mary Jane leapt onto the step that led to the paint-chipped door and managed to dodge being carried along by a herd of working men who were hoping to secure a twilight shift on the docks. They were heading down to the pens in a cloud of tobacco smoke wafting over their flat caps, in the hope of being taken on, the same as they probably did this morning and then again this afternoon,, and the thundering rumble of hobnailed boots on cobbles drowned out any anxious thoughts she might like to dwell upon.

Mary Jane knew she could have used the key, which Cal

had given her to let herself into his kitchen, but it didn't seem right to do so at the end of a working day.

As the din began to wane, Mary Jane could hear the sound of hurrying footsteps descending the stairs on the other side of the bottle-green door. Seconds later, she heard the key in the lock and the scrape of the bolt before the door swung open.

'Are you early or am I late?' Cal Everdine's deep voice had a masculine rasp, although it did not sound harsh, in fact it sounded very light-hearted and Mary Jane bristled at his rumpled appearance: his hastily buttoned shirt was done up all wrong and his abundance of raven black hair, dripping water on the floor and down his shirt.

'I beg your pardon?' Mary Jane countered, oddly fascinated by the sight of his bare feet on the rough floorboards, fixated on the little spirals of dark hair on his toes. She had never seen her brothers walking around half-clothed and wasn't sure it was decent to see Cal Everdine do so either. 'You will get splinters if you don't put something on your feet.' She felt it was most peculiar for a man to answer the main door of his abode in his bare smacks.

'I was in the bath, it's at the back...' He stopped talking for a moment as if to recollect his thoughts, and when he spoke again his tone was less hurried. 'To what do I owe the pleasure at this time of night?' he asked, and Mary Jane's eyebrows gathered in a confused pleat. Although the darkness of the night had drawn in hours ago, it was still only seven o clock. He opened the door wider and stepped aside to allow her access to his living quarters and Mary Jane wondered if she was doing the right thing after all?

However, she was here now so there was no point in waiting until morning.

'I have come to ask you something,' she said, stepping into

the passageway. Her tone matching his as her eyes trailed the distempered walls and gloomy staircase, which she was now familiar with, the wooden stairs bare of any covering, not even a bit of linoleum, and the place looked neglected and forlorn, desperately in need of a woman's touch. She could feel his eyes boring into the back of her head as, with an outstretched hand, he motioned for her to climb the barren wooden stairs. Her glimpse of the sparsely furnished living room did not inspire Mary Jane with confidence. If she were asked to describe Cal's living arrangements, she would certainly not call them cosy or even comfortable. Quite the opposite. She would say it was a lonely place, a desolate, unforgiving place.

'Thank you so much for the delicious pie, you left on the kitchen table.' He smiled, seemingly oblivious to his austere surroundings, and she noticed how his eyes sparkled when he smiled.

'That's not why I have come here,' she said her eyes sweeping the barren room she rarely entered, its only saving grace were the plentiful, although curtainless sash windows, three at the front overlooking Beamer Street and three at the side overlooking Beamer Terrace. With a bit of furniture and a lick of paint, these rooms could be magnificent. Turning quickly to face him, she said: 'I have come to ask if you could give me the name of your landlord.' The click of her elegant heels echoed on the stark floorboards as she went from one window overlooking the houses opposite, to the other window overlooking 'the terrace' as it was known locally. The blinds, pulled halfway down were so threadbare she could see moonlight and the glare of the gas lamps through them. The blinds were just flimsy bits of material, serviceable, not in the least extravagant nothing to make the place more homely.

Cal watched in silent amusement as she surveyed his

home, and for the first time since he moved in, he saw his living conditions through her eyes, realising how stark the place was and his amusement dissipated when he tried to ignore the shameful surge of emotion he fought to push down again and again. A feeling he was worthless and utterly alone. Unworthy of the comfort he craved. 'Would you like a cup of tea?' he asked politely, and Mary Jane suppressed a gasp when she shook her head, not comfortable being waited on by a man.

'The landlord's address? You see I am very grateful for the use of your oven,' she said trying to push down the nervous energy building inside her, 'and I am grateful for all the help you have given me, but you see...' She moved to the window, her back to him. 'The thing is, I need more space if I am to grow my business.' She heard his deep sigh behind her, as if he was mulling the idea over. Maybe she should have waited until the morning, but being impulsive, she took action before thinking the whole thing though.

'I am not throwing your generosity back in your face,' she blurted, turning quickly to face him, 'I need more space – speculate to accumulate, so to speak...' She was waffling, and it was about time she stopped talking.

'I can show you the premises,' Cal said eventually and saw her eyes light up. A sight that brought him the most unexpected and extraordinary pleasure.

'That would be marvellous,' she enthused, not even knowing where she would get the money from to pay a week's rent on the place.

Cal went off to fetch the keys. It had been many a long year since he had felt such a surge of joy, it took him by surprise.

Taking the keys from the glass-fronted cabinet that held

only the merest of necessities, he made his way back to the front room.

'Have you always lived here?' Mary Jane asked conversationally when he entered the room. He said nothing for a moment, as if the question had taken him by surprise. 'I'm sorry, my natural interest in people comes across as being a bit intrusive, I'll shut up now.'

A voice inside his head gave a terse reprimand and he tried to expel the nagging memory of those far-off days when he was just a boy of sixteen and his father, who owned silver mines in Canada, sent him there to train in engineering. 'I was born here, but went to Canada for seven years…' Cal said, knowing in all that time he had not received one letter. Not even a note to tell him his beloved mother had died after he left England. When he got back home with an engineering certificate under his belt, he discovered he had a new mother. A complete stranger. But he was not going to burden Mary Jane with such information, giving no inkling about living in the house directly opposite, which now belonged to Cissie Stone. 'I was away for many years and came back to join the war.' Unable to stay under the same roof as a woman who took his mother's place, he had no intention of working for his father and carrying on the great Everdine businesses. He would find his own way. Do his own thing he had thought before moving out of his father's house and going back to Cobalt, Ontario. He would have liked to tell Mary Jane about his life in Canada, but even though it had been so long ago, he still felt unable to talk about it, even now. He doubted she would want to hear his tales of woe. If what he had been told about her husband leaving for America was true, she had enough troubles of her own.

'This way,' he said, leading her to a door in the passageway, which he unlocked and descended the wooden stairs, sweeping away the cobwebs with the back of his hand. 'This place hasn't been opened for years,' he informed her before unlocking the door to the shop, his thoughts having been poked, burst into life, and he remembered the days, working on the railway, before prospecting for silver in the hills of Canada. He won shares in a silver mine playing poker. There was not much else to do when he was just twenty-one years old. Then he had met Ellie and a month later they married.

As Cal unlocked the door at the bottom of the stairs, Mary Jane's heart sank. What if it was in a bad state? She didn't have enough money to do it up – in fact she might struggle to find the rent.

'I take it you will be using it as a bakery?' he said lighting the gas mantle with ease, his tone assured, as if she had already agreed to take on the rental of the shop. Leading the way further into the huge bay-windowed shop, that didn't look this big from the outside Mary Jane's eyes widened.

'This is marvellous,' she gasped. 'Excellent, in fact. I could bake so much more in here.' Mary Jane's positivity held no trace of conceit. Her eyes took in every inch of the room. 'I could whitewash the walls and put in shelves, and a long counter to show off the day's bakes.' Her hands drew an invisible outline of where everything would go, her head bursting with ideas. 'A straight-backed chair here, by the counter, for the customer to ponder on what is needed. I would employ a delivery boy, obviously and up here...'

Now it was Mary Jane's turn to lead the way. Continuing up three wooden steps, 'I would have the ovens in here, all my bakes will be fresh every day.'

'So, you'll have more than one oven, that's good,' Cal

smiled, her enthusiasm was infectious. These premises had been closed for too long. He could see how a bakery would be a godsend to an area like this.

'I'll need more than one oven if I'm to supply this lot,' she said, with the sweep of her hand. 'The place is desperate for a woman's touch and at the end of the day, I will sell off any left-over baked goods cheaply, so I don't clutter the place up with bread and pies that would go stale overnight.'

'How soon would you be looking to move in?' Cal asked and suddenly Mary Jane's expression changed. His words had brought her down to earth with a bump. The bubble had burst. She could afford the rent if it was cheap, but then she needed to put in fixtures and fittings, pay a carpenter. Would she have enough money? *Damn you to hell for taking everything I worked so hard for, Christie Redfern!* Mary Jane's fingers curled tightly into the palms of her hands. Looking around again, she could almost see the tables, with bright tablecloths, and little vases of flowers on each displaying her bakes. But it was a dream, and it would remain unfulfilled until she could get enough money together. She felt worse now than she had done before she ever set foot in the place. Because before she could only imagine what this place could be like. Now she knew.

'I think I may have wasted your time, Mr Everdine,' she said. 'I got carried away...' Mary Jane knew she had to be honest. 'I don't have the money to open this place as a going concern, not yet.'

Seeing the expression of disappointment in her eyes, some kind of madness overtook Cal, and he was powerless to resist helping her. 'I know the landlord very well,' he said, 'and I'm sure he would rather see this shop open and thriving, instead of growing damp and musty.'

'I did have the money, before...' There was that flash in her eyes, but it died quickly. And Cal was not at all surprised, he wanted to help her even more. He surmised her indolent husband would have done his best to leave her with nothing. The look of regret in her eyes tugged at something lain dormant for many years.

'It's strange you should enquire about the shop,' he said, 'because the landlord is so eager to open this place up before Christmas, he is prepared to offer a month rent-free.'

'Why? What's wrong with the place?' Mary Jane gave him a sideways look, unsure whether to believe him or not.

'Although, if you don't think you are up to the job...' He understood her reticence. She was a proud woman, and he suspected she did not take kindly to charity.

'I am up to the job, have no fear about that,' Mary Jane's clipped tone betrayed a rare bout of apprehension, but she recovered quickly. 'I sell my produce to satisfied customers, who come back day after day – even you said how delicious my bakes are.'

'I have never tasted better,' Cal answered.

'I will have the money at the end of the first month, of that I have no doubt whatsoever. If the landlord is willing to wait a month for the rent, I will be able to buy what I need to start off, at least.'

Cal Everdine accepted the fact that living alone did not mean he was lonely, and the truth of it was, he had never considered another person for many years. All he knew was he wanted to make this beautiful woman's life a little easier, in a way he never thought he ever would again. Although that had not been his initial intention. The sole purpose of offering this feisty redhead a start was to save her from destitution.

'Also, I have a favour to ask,' he said, and his direct gaze put

Mary Jane on her guard. She had heard about men who asked for favours. And not all of them were proper or respectable.

'What kind of favour?' Suspicion laced her words.

'I wonder if you will do me a good turn, and cook a meal for when I get home each night?' After a moment's thought, he said quickly, 'I am prepared to pay a pound a week – is that enough for six evening meals?'

Mary Jane could not believe what she had just heard and asked him to repeat himself, which he did.

'I understand you have much to do, but I do not want you to labour for nothing.'

She looked at him for a moment, her facial expression inscrutable, every nerve in her body fizzing. A cooked meal a night, for the princely sum of twenty shillings. By the time she had taken her rent out of the weekly sum, she would still have plenty left. 'That is way over the odds for a cooked meal,' she said, having never earned that much selling her pies and pastries, but she could not live with herself if she took his money and not said anything.

'You are not a domestic servant.' His voice was low, determined. 'You are an artisan, a woman of talent, and I am prepared to pay for such aptitude, and I would thank you to raise your self-esteem to a higher plane.'

Wary now, Mary Jane stretched her back as far as her spine would allow, knowing she would never be tall enough to look him straight in the eye, and an awful thought went through her head. 'And what is it you expect me to do for that kind of money? You don't expect me to live in, do you?' Mary Jane was still not certain of his true intentions.

'No, I do not expect you to live in. The thought never crossed my mind.' He sounded a little hurt.

'In that case, I have something I need to tell you,' Mary Jane offered, 'it might change your mind about putting in a good word for me with the landlord.' It was only right she should tell him the truth. Mary Jane took a deep breath, feeling she was about to talk herself out of a lifeline, but unable to lie to get what she wanted. 'I am due to have a baby at the end of January, but I can assure you I am fit, robust and have never shied away from any task I set my mind to.' Her words were coming faster when she saw the steel glint in his eyes. 'I must earn enough money to give my child the best start I can, and with Christmas only six weeks away this will be one of the busiest times when I can build my trade.' She ignored the set of his jaw, no doubt he felt he had wasted his time on a woman who only wanted to make some money for Christmas, but she must assure him that was not the case. 'I give you my promise I will cook you nourishing meals right up to the time of my confinement.'

For a long time, Mary Jane could hear only the heavy sound of silence, and her resolve began to dissipate.

'A baby?' he said eventually, momentarily forgetting her pregnancy and stretching his neck as he walked over to the window, he looked down into the street. *A baby!* He leaned against the frame of the sash window and his eyes slowly closed, hiding the pain he still felt to this day.

'Yes,' Mary Jane's voice was low, knowing she would have to explain herself. He had been so kind, offering to put in a good word with the landlord. 'You see when Red... Mr Redfern left,' her insides turned, and Cal turned to face her so quickly, she blanched.

'That drunken scoundrel is the lowest of the low, leaving you to fend for yourself knowing you were carrying a child.' The words sounded hypocritical to him. He should not judge any fellow. Not after what he had done. But her husband, the lowest of the low, did not deserve a woman like Mary Jane. 'Horsewhipping would be too good for him!' He had not realised his words were spoken out loud until she answered.

'I can assure you the feeling is mutual, Mr Everdine,' Mary Jane was glad Red was no longer part of her life, and she appreciated that Cal Everdine had not called Red her husband, nor that the child was his – that way, she did not have to lie again. 'I can guarantee my work will not suffer. I am strong and I am determined...'

'I have no doubt about that.' Cal's words were strained as he turned away, looking down to the street, his fists clenched. Cal wondered if he could bear to watch her, day after day, all the while preparing to bring a new life into this Godforsaken world... But he had no choice. He had offered her a chance, and she accepted. As a man of honour, albeit dubious to his way of thinking, he must stand by his word. He suspected – no, he knew how proud she was. Mary Jane would give of herself time and time again to make life better for her and her child.

'I will do a good job,' she said, hopefully, mistaking his silence for a change of heart, watching as he shrugged powerful shoulders that seemed to carry the weight of the world. He was a mystery. Living alone in a sparsely furnished flat above an unused shop, with barely any belongings or comforts to speak of.

'As long as I have a hot meal at the end of the day, you can do as you please.' His words were abrupt. 'I hope it works well for you.' His long strides ate the floor and the sound of his boots reverberated on the dusty wooden floorboards.

Mary Jane's throat constricted, and she did not know why she felt like a child who had been scolded for an offence they had not committed, watching as he opened the door and, standing back, made way for her to exit. She was determined not to show him how much his words had stung her. Mary Jane stood her ground and swallowed hard.

'If it's all the same to you, I would like to give this place a thorough clean before I start cooking in it.'

'There is a room at the back you can prepare your bakes.' His words gave her the impression he was not very pleased with her impending arrangements. 'Another stove can be installed when you are ready for it.'

'Everything will be done properly,' she said, knowing she was not going to cut corners. Until the place was as good as she could get it, she would use Molly's kitchen as well as Cal's oven.

'There is another back kitchen,' he said, leading the way. The kitchen was along the landing at the back, and when Mary Jane looked into the room, all she could see was a deep sink with a wooden drainboard, a bare wooden table on one side and a small cupboard on the other.

'This could be kitted out with shelves and cupboards,' he said simply.

Although, any awkward feelings were quickly dispelled, and soon she was firing instructions like a seasoned sniper. He could still hear her from halfway along the landing.

'I will need cutlery, and crockery. A teapot – who has ever heard of a business without a teapot? I need some cups that are fit to drink from – these have got more chips than Mr Tim's fried fish shop, and I could do with a few pots and pans here too...'Mary Jane was surprised when she heard the door downstairs close with a bang. And looking out of the window over the sink, she watched him open the huge double gates and lead his horse from the stable.

'Well, would you look at that!' she said to the empty shop,

knowing that first thing the following morning she was going to do something she swore she would never do.

* * *

'Would you look at the cut of that one,' Ina King said to her companion when she saw Mary Jane entering the pawnshop on the corner of Vauxhall Road. 'It looks like Missus High and Mighty is just like the rest of us after all!'

'I 'eard she's traipsing up and down Mr Everdine's flat every day... And her a pregnant woman who can't keep hold of an 'usband.'

'I can imagine why that would be the case, you know what I mean?' Ina King didn't elaborate as she shrugged her skinny shoulders, talking to the back of her neighbour's head.

Every muscle in Mary Jane's body tensed, trying to ignore Ina's vicious tongue. She was the last person Mary Jane wanted to see and it wouldn't take long for her neighbour to spread malicious gossip. However, she would not let these women see their comments bothered her as she stood in the pawnshop line behind them.

Mary Jane had intended to be first in the queue, when there would be nobody here who would recognise her. Never having had to visit one before, she felt ashamed knowing the teeming streets near the dockside were rife with women looking for a way to find enough money to put a meal on the table, so when she rounded the corner and saw the long queue before the shop had even opened, her heart sank.

Cal's news, that the landlord was willing to wait a month for the rent, came as a great but welcome shock. Mary Jane needed enough money to start her off in business, knowing it was a fine thing to have the premises, but she needed to fill them too.

Uncle Bill, as the pawn broker was known locally, gave an encouraging nod of his bald head when she showed him her mother's clock, but Mary Jane could not hide her sinking disappointment when he offered nowhere near the price she had expected. However, she did have a choice, whether to accept what *Uncle* was prepared to offer, or try elsewhere. The pawnbroker shrugged his shoulders when she refused his offer.

'It don't matter one way or another that the clock has an onyx casing or that its circular face is rimmed with gold,' he said sympathetically. 'If you don't redeem it and your pledge runs out, it could sit in the window for months, because nobody round here will have the money to afford it.' Leaning forward he continued in a low voice so none of the other women in the queue could hear him, 'it's a fine piece, I grant you. Why not try Ruby's Emporium? The new owner gives a good price.'

'Thank you,' Mary Jane said and, picking the heavy clock off the counter, she headed for the door, refusing to give in to the humiliation she felt.

On her way back to Molly's house, she reached the empty shop. Mary Jane had never considered herself superstitious. She was far too practical for all that nonsense. However, she felt something was urging her to keep hold of the clock and she imagined it sitting in the window. *Time for tea?*

A shop like this could be her future. A lucky omen? Perhaps. The shop had been sitting empty, since she moved into Beamer Street. as if waiting for her. Surely this was a sign. But how was she going to get the money for the fixtures and fittings? That was the big question and, as yet, she did not have the answer.

* * *

Cal regretted not dragging that no-good husband of hers into the street when he had a chance and thrashing him until he begged for mercy. But what good would that have done? He knew the women of the dockside streets were spirited and preferred to look out for themselves – they did not take kindly to interference from outsiders.

He had no choice but to let her be. Mary Jane did not need platitudes. She needed a good man behind her. Not one prepared to see his expectant wife walking the streets of Liverpool, toiling from dawn 'til dusk, just to keep body and soul together. And, he told himself, that was the main reason – the only reason – he had offered her the shop rent-free for a month and intended to do all he could to help her.

He clicked his tongue and flipped the reins for the horse to move slowly on, forcing his thoughts from the direction they had been heading. His chest tightened and that familiar ache at the back of his throat threatened to overwhelm him until he swallowed it down and took in a deep, calming stream of damp morning air. He did not want to revisit that past guilt any longer. There was nothing he could do. He knew that now.

* * *

In spite of her worries, Mary Jane did not feel afraid any more. And she realised that a new feeling had settled in her heart. It was called hope, and it fluttered through her like a butterfly. She must be optimistic for the child's sake and cultivate the positive attitude that once was as natural as breathing. Long before she had to worry about Red. He was gone now, and she must aim to regain the confidence that had once sustained her.

I know I've done wrong, Lord,' Mary Jane offered up a silent prayer, '*but if you can see your way clear to letting me make a fresh start, I won't let you down.*

22

Mary Jane was surprised when she saw the shop walls had been whitewashed and realised Cal must have spent all night painting. The place looked light and bright – a far cry from the dismal place it had been yesterday.

She took off her coat and spent the rest of the day scrubbing floorboards, polishing windows, black leading the huge oven until it gleamed, and when she finished, her mouth was so dry, she felt she would choke .In the back room that served as a small kitchen with a sink, a cupboard and not much else, she found a cup that had no cracks, but neither did it have a handle, although that was of no concern She was downing a refreshing cup of ice-cold water, when she heard the inside door to the shop open.

'Come and have a look at this,' Cal said, not waiting for her to reply. 'Tell me if this is to your liking.' Mary Jane's eyes nearly fell out of their sockets when she saw the contents of the flat-backed cart standing just outside the door. 'I've got a few of the neighbourhood kids to help me bring this lot in,' Cal said, nodding to the cart. 'Just a few bits and pieces I picked up along the way.'

'A few bits and pieces!' Mary Jane's eyes were as wide as side plates as a long line of neighbourhood boys doffed their caps as they passed her, bringing long planks of wood on their shoulders through the empty shop.

'Mahogany for the counter, shelves and cupboards,' Cal said, marshalling other boys carrying bright new linoleum for the floor.

'Well, you didn't get this lot off the market,' Mary Jane sounded a little breathless, her eyes devouring everything. Cal seemed to be enjoying himself, firing questions on where she wanted everything to go. And in anticipation of a good tip the boys were very obliging.

'A gas cooker is being plumbed into the supply first thing tomorrow morning,' said Cal, 'and I have bought some kitchen utensils as a shop-warming gift – here is the teapot you find so hard to live without.' When he smiled, his warm eyes seemed to dance with mischief and delight, and for the first time in years, he felt his day had a purpose. 'And just to show I am a civilised man; I also acquired a milk jug and sugar basin.'

'Oh, Cal, you shouldn't!' Mary Jane could hardly breathe for the excitement bubbling up inside her. 'But I am so very glad you did.'

* * *

'You should see the wood for the shop furnishings,' Mary Jane gasped from the other side of the dining table, when she finished her work and returned to Molly's house later, 'I have never seen the likes – it wouldn't look out of place in Fortnum and Mason.' She had no idea what Fortnum and Mason looked like, but she had heard it said that it was one of the most prestigious shops in London.

'I heard a rumour he had a few bob,' said Molly and then stopped abruptly. 'Not that I believed a word of it, it's what everyone was saying when he first moved in.'

'And how would they know?' Mary Jane asked, never surprised at the gossip, which was bread and butter to most people around here, proving that no matter where folk lived, either in a huge port town like Liverpool or a small village like Cashalree, there would always be a healthy dose of information sharing or – as everybody around here called it – jangling.

'Have you not heard from your brothers?' asked Molly, who was bustling in and out of the kitchen, never beating about the bush if she wanted to know something. Mary Jane shook her head and felt the rush of adrenaline that made her heart pump at the mere mention of her brothers. Molly knew about them because Mary Jane had felt the need to discuss her family, but she did not tell her friend the whole truth about why she had to get out of Ireland so quickly – or, rather, why Red had insisted so. Her thoughts were interrupted when Molly disappeared, coming back to the front parlour a few minutes later with a jam sandwich cake, which Daisy had baked yesterday specially for Mary Jane's birthday.

'I didn't tell you it was my birthday!' she exclaimed, her face beaming with delight and embarrassment.

'You mentioned it being a week after bonfire night, so our Daisy took a guess.'

'That is so kind of you, Daisy. This cake is delicious,' said Mary Jane, as small, eager hands accepted their plates.

'It is not as good as the cakes you bake,' said Daisy, her flame-coloured cheeks glowing at the compliment.

'You're a natural.' Mary Jane wasn't just paying lip service to

Daisy because she had baked her a cake that melted in her mouth, she knew Daisy had the gift. 'I truly believe you have a talent and you're wasted serving in a dockside teashop.' Mary Jane meant every word. 'And what's this?' she asked, when Molly handed her a schooner of dark red liquid.

'One little drop of port wine won't hurt you,' she said, offering Mary Jane the birthday drink. 'I never touch the stuff any other time, but my Albert always brought me one on my birthday to wash down the cake. Then, when the children had scoffed all before them and had gone to bed satisfied, we would sit here by the fire and count our blessings.'

'You have many blessings to count from what I can see,' said Mary Jane. 'The children are a credit to you.'

'We were the lucky ones,' Molly said proudly, stroking the old but well cared for furniture. 'Albert worked on the railway, so his employment was guaranteed, unlike the men who worked on the docks and had to hire themselves out each day.'

Mary Jane rolled her eyes, knowing it was the hiring bit that suited Red, he did his best to avoid it at all costs. Sitting around the table with the Haywoods, who surrounded her like a warm blanket, Mary Jane took Molly into her confidence. 'Red only went down to the docks when he ran out of money, or if I wouldn't give him any.' She picked crumbs off her skirt. 'Even when he was taken on in the morning, he rarely did an afternoon shift, because he'd be in the pub drinking with his cronies.

Molly tutted and shook her head. 'It's a shame, it really is. You deserved better.'

'Oh, I'm not so sure about that.' Mary Jane could feel her cheeks grow hotter. Putting the warm flush down to the port.

'Do you miss him?' Molly asked in that motherly way, and Mary Jane sighed.

'I miss him like someone misses mumps.' They both threw their heads back and laughed, and Mary Jane relaxed in the company of this lovely woman and her family. 'He was a pain in the neck that I could not wait to be rid of.' She cradled her empty schooner before putting it on the table, and shook her head when Molly rose to fill it. 'I could not eat or drink another thing,' Mary Jane laughed. 'My skirt is cutting in; I've been so greedy.'

'Away with you,' Molly said, 'you eat less than our Bridie and she's only five.'

'To be fair, Ma,' said Davey sitting opposite, 'Bridie is a gannet.' He laughed, ducking when Molly swiped him with the tea towel.

'You'll have to excuse my eldest boy, Mary Jane,' Molly sounded mortified. 'I don't know where he gets it from, I really don't.'

But Mary Jane held up her hand, hardly able to get the words out for laughing. 'Don't apologise, Molly, I'm having a wonderful time – this is one of my best birthdays ever, and I didn't expect that last week.'

'I can smell bun loaf,' Daisy sighed, and Mary Jane jumped up to check them, while the young ones knelt on the mat by the range, engrossed in their peg soldiers, marching them across the floor, like their brave dad whom Molly talked about, every single day. Distractedly, Mary Jane took the bun loaves from the oven, and looking up, she read the labels on the bells that lined the wall of the kitchen, one for every room.

'The kids loved those when we first moved in,' Molly informed her. 'They had me running all over the house, they did.' She laughed again, and Mary Jane noticed she did that a lot. It made her heart glad, knowing it was a far cry from the misery on the other side of the wall.

Placing the baking trays on the table, around which the family sat each night to share the day's exploits, Mary Jane turned out tomorrow's bread and bun loaves onto wire racks to cool. She would take some over to Mr Everdine to put in his carry-out. The name the locals gave to the sandwiches wrapped in brown paper, for their morning break.

'Don't nobody dare touch those, do you hear me?' Molly told her children, but none of them answered, they were too engrossed in their peg soldiers. While Daisy put away the washed, blue patterned plates into the Welsh dresser standing along the far wall, Mary Jane knew that if ever she was lucky to have a place of her own, she would want it to look exactly like this.

'Wouldn't it be wonderful to work in a kitchen like this all the time?' she said.

'I wouldn't go that far,' Molly laughed' When you've my lot to fend for.' Ignoring her daughter's look of indignation, she turned to Mary Jane. 'How did your first day go in the shop? ... and Daisy Haywood, will you stop giving me looks, you know as well as I do, you're dying to hear all.'

'Oh, Mam, you are so... so...' Daisy laughed.

'To be honest,' Mary Jane replied, not a bit put out at the questions, 'once I had swept and washed the floor, cleaned the windows and gave the whole place a thorough clean, there was nothing else to do. I put a hotpot in the stove for when Cal comes home from work and that was that.' Mary Jane's eyes widened. 'I was tempted to strip off and have a good soak in that huge bath in the back room and was wondering if I dared to have a dip, when himself turned up with the huge pile of shop fittings.'

'He's got a bath?' exclaimed Molly. 'What's it like? Does it have taps and hot water? Surely not!'

'It does, Molly,' Mary Jane conceded. 'The water is heated by a back boiler, which sits quite comfortably behind the range.' She watched Molly slowly shake her head in wonder. 'I'll let you in tomorrow to have a look at it.'

'And you were tempted to have a good soak?'

'Isn't it a good thing I didn't, when himself came home early.' Mary Jane gasped. 'Imagine the uproar if he caught me wallowing in his hot water.'

Molly squealed and they both laughed until tears ran down their cheeks. When the hilarity subsided, Molly said, 'Our Davey told me about the fixtures and fittings, how he helped him move it all in.'

'He did,' said Mary Jane, still smiling at the outrageous thought of Cal Everdine walking in and catching her in the bath. 'Who'd have thought he could afford the likes of the stuff he brought back, when he didn't have so much as a teapot before!' Mary Jane's eyes had a *can-you-believe-it* expression. 'I have never known a home without a teapot.'

'You'll soon whip that shop into shape,' said Molly. 'Sometimes a place needs a woman's touch.' Molly picked up little Bridie's dress, and sewed the hem, which had come down when she was out playing in the street. Always on the go, Mary Jane admired the woman who was busy from the moment she got up to the time she went to bed, and Mary Jane was of the same type.

'His home... no, his dwelling, is so sparse,' Mary Jane mused, 'yet he brought some lovely stuff back for the shop. He has a good eye for colour too.'

'I suppose living on his own, with nobody to please but himself, out with the lark and home with the night-owl, there isn't much call for nice things,' Molly answered.

'You don't think he'll expect me to pay for it all in one go, do you, Moll?' Mary Jane would not like to think she had put him in debt.

Molly shook her head.

'All the same,' said Mary Jane, 'there was very little in the way of comfort, except that big bath, the biggest I have ever seen!' Back home, as well as here in Liverpool, most people only had the use of a tin bath, usually hung on a six-inch nail out in the back yard.

'What I would give to have a nice long soak at the end of the day,' said Daisy and Mary Jane nodded, while Molly shook her head.

'Hot water from a tap, I have never seen the like in all my born days.'

'I would love to have a look at that,' said Daisy. 'Imagine the luxury...'

'And not even a rag rug on the floor,' said Mary Jane. 'What do you think about that?'

'I think a bath trumps a rag rug any day.' Davey's far-away look did nothing to hide the thought of all that hot water when all they had was a cold tap out in the scullery. If you wanted a warm wash, you had to heat the water in a pan on the range beforehand, and as he was always in a hurry, he woke himself up with a splash of ice-cold water from the tap.

Mary Jane, watching Molly sewing neat stitches in her youngest daughter's dress, decided she would buy some material and make new curtains for Mr Everdine's windows, as a thank you for his help and she would buy a bit extra to make a rug for in front of the fire. She would like to make the place nice for him, after all the generous wages he paid her to cook a daily meal. Having so much money, she was eager to make sure Molly was not out of pocket, too. 'I insist on giving you the same amount of rent I paid to her next door,' she told Molly.

'Does money burn a hole in your pocket, Mary Jane? You cannot wait to part with it.' Molly laughed, until Mary Jane told her what Cissie had been charging her.

'The thieving hag.' Visibly outraged, Molly tutted and glared at the wall that separated both houses, 'She ought to be ashamed of herself.'

'Not all the money went to Cissie, I suspect,' Mary Jane replied. 'Red insisted on going down to pay her, saying it was the man's duty.'

'It's a pity he didn't think it was his duty to earn it,' Molly said, then clapping her hand over her mouth, she apologised: 'Mary Jane, I am so sorry, please take no notice of me, my mouth runs away with itself sometimes.'

'Don't give it another thought, Molly. You didn't say anything I hadn't already known.' She recalled how Red went out early, washed, freshly shaved, and wearing clean combinations on the night the rent was paid. 'I knew when he went out, he would not manage the extra flights of stairs, that would take him to the attic room, on his return. He often ended up in Cissie's bed and had no hesitation in telling me.' Mary Jane would say no more about him, nor tell Molly her standard reply was to tell him he could do as he pleased.

Molly blew out her cheeks. 'Cissie Stone is no better behaved than an alley-cat.'

'Let's not talk about them,' Mary Jane said. 'We've had a grand day and I don't want to spoil it.'

'On the other hand, I don't mind at all,' Molly laughed her easy chuckle. 'I like nothing better than a good old gossip about the neighbours!'

'Molly, you are a case,' Mary Jane said, wondering what her lovely friend would make of it if she knew the whole truth. She longed to tell her. But not yet.

* * *

The delicious aroma of succulent steak and kidney nestled in golden flaky pastry mingled with the delightfully appetising waft of freshly baked bread in the shop the following day, causing children from roundabout to linger in the doorway of Mary Jane's door, until five-year old Bridie Haywood robustly scattered the drooling children off the black and white tiled step. Each pie Mary Jane baked tasted better than the last, and the Haywoods who were all there too, savoured to their heart's content.

'Our own mam bakes a scrumptious pie too,' Davey added quickly when he saw Molly's fixed smile barely disguise a fleeting glimpse of disappointment. Nobody could beat his mam's cooking, he had thought – but he had to admit Mary Jane really was an expert baker.

'I have never put in a filling as good as this,' Molly exclaimed.

'Are you sure, Molly? You're not just being kind, are you?' Mary Jane had to be certain these pies would be good enough to go into her shop.

'I'd walk from one end of Liverpool to the other, for a pie like this,' Davey said, as tasty gravy dribbled down his chin, and he was admonished by his mother for speaking with his mouth full.

'I'll have no son of mine acting like a common lout who speaks with a gob full of pie,' Molly chastised her son, who nodded and apologised – as soon as he swallowed the last bite. 'With my help and our Daisy's, you will soon have a good little production line going. Everyone tells me how much they love your pies, Mary Jane.' Molly chattered away as she cleared away the empty plates and put them into the sink to wash.

'I experiment with different herbs that go into the fillings,' she said, taking out a small, lined notebook, in which she wrote her recipes. 'I used to gather them from the hedgerows, back home.'

'You'll have a hard time finding herbs growing,' Molly said, 'even weeds don't grow around here.'

'I walked to Netherford a few weeks ago,' Mary Jane said, 'and I gathered fresh herbs to store.'

Davey smiled at a long-lost memory. 'I remember Dad taking us to the countryside. I was about seven, same age as our Freddy.' Davey looked to his mother to make sure he wasn't upsetting her, but Molly was beaming at the memory. 'We were all on the back of a railway cart he borrowed and got back home really late.'

'Those were the days.' Molly's eyes were tender. 'My Albert loved taking the kids fishing in the streams and canal. A real treat.'

'We'd bring back tiddlers – little sticklebacks – in a jam jar.'

'The fish were lucky if they lasted a week,' Molly said, and Daisy laughed. 'All because our Davey liked to take them out of the water, to watch them dance.'

'I didn't know they needed water to survive.' Davey sighed, and everybody laughed.

'You've done a fine job raising four children on your own,' Mary Jane said. 'It could not have been easy without a man around to help.'

'I couldn't have managed it without our Daisy or our Davey, even if he does talk with his mouth still full.' She gave Davey a forgiving smile. 'But they have been my strength when times were hard. I don't know what I would've done without them.'

'We wouldn't see you struggle, Ma,' Davey said, giving his mother a hug.

'It's not in our nature to see anybody struggle, and your poor dad, God rest his soul.' Molly made the sign of the cross on her motherly bosom. 'He was just the same.'

'I'm sure those pies were the talk of Cashalree, as they were down the dock road,' Davey said, changing the subject knowing that when his dear old mam got onto the subject of his father it usually ended in tears.

'I'm sure they were, Davey boy,' Molly answered.

'I never had the need to go out selling before I moved here and took them to the docks,' Mary Jane answered taking a fresh batch from the stove. 'The customers always came to me.'

'And they will again, Mary Jane,' Molly said, 'I can feel it in my bones, and I am never wrong when I feel it in my bones. This pie lark is going to be a great success!'

'In that case I'm in need of some bags to put them in,' Mary Jane said, 'something a bit classy.'

'You'll not sell many if you charge the earth though, Mary Jane,' Molly warned. 'If women buy pies from a shop, the pies are wrapped in newspaper.'

'But I want people to know who made their pie, so they can come back again.' And what better way to do it, thought Mary Jane, than to have her name on the paper bag the pie came in. 'I've had a word with the butcher and told him he would be my only supplier if he could offer a fair price, and guess what? He promised me a discount if I can order enough meat.'

'You're a born businesswoman, Mary Jane,' said Molly polishing the long L-shaped counter Cal had made, which ran the length of the shop. She knew that in an area like this, where work depended on the docks, and orders were scarce if the docks were not working to full capacity, the tradesmen are eager for orders from local businesses. Rather than having to depend on hard-up housewives scraping just enough money for a bit of belly pork, or stretching half a pound of minced beef to go around a family of fourteen.

'You are right, Moll, and that's why I don't want my pies roughly wrapped in yesterday's news; they deserve better treatment than that.'

'You make them sound like the family pet,' Davey said, and then coloured red to the roots of his hair when all eyes were upon him. 'Did I say that out loud?'

'You'll get used to him, eventually,' Molly said good-humouredly as they went about their business, tidying the baking area out back. Even little Bridie helped out, standing on a chair, she washed the dishes and didn't break a single one.

'What about individual boxes, each one containing a single pie?' asked Davey, who had started work in Simpson's cardboard factory after leaving school. 'We supply boxes to all the best shops in London,' he said importantly. 'Mainly the boxes are for fancy cakes, but I'm sure they could be used for pies?'

'Perfect!' Mary Jane said. 'A plain white box with a nice blue gingham border, all fresh and wholesome.' She asked Davey to arrange an appointment with Mr Simpson, owner of the cardboard factory.

The following evening, Davey arrived home from work and, throwing his cap expertly on to the hook at the back of the kitchen door, he announced that he had secured an appointment with Mr Simpson the following morning.

'Oh, you are a good lad, Davey,' Mary Jane said as they sat down to discuss the day's activities. 'It's a fancy idea, I know, to put my pies in boxes, but if I charge a tiny bit more, a farthing or such, the boxes will pay for themselves.'

'Aye.' Davey was bright-eyed, glad he could be of help. 'And the customers always think they're getting summat extra when it's in a nice box.'

'Oh, he is clever,' Molly said proudly, 'and what about those paper bags too?'

'Go easy, Missus,' Davy laughed, 'she'll have no profits left.'

23

Mary Jane arrived at Simpsons half an hour after it opened. She would have been there first thing, but Davey advised her not to look too eager. Eagerness inflated the price of the boxes, he said.

When Mr Simpson called her into his office, Mary Jane's mouth was paper dry and her heart was playing a jaunty tune on her ribcage, but she certainly didn't allow it to show. Smiling brightly, she walked into the office, with its filing cabinets and brass telephone and stretched out her hand. A little perplexed, never having dealt with a woman buyer before, Mr Simpson waved his hand towards the chair opposite. Mary Jane remained standing, thinking Mr Simpson, appeared smaller when he sat behind the huge wooden desk, which reduced her jingling nerves, making her feel more confident.

'I believe you want some boxes? So, what can we offer you?' Mr Simpson's tone was pompous, which forced Mary Jane's hackles to rise. *Here we go*, she thought, knowing there were women who were actually dying, because men like this one, did not believe in female emancipation, believing every woman should be tied to the kitchen sink.

'A discount would be a start,' she said, in the same forthright manner, amused when she saw his grey eyebrows shoot northward. Mary Jane was determined, she would get a good deal out of the meeting, or what would be the point. 'I was thinking, something like this,' she said, 'let me show you.' She took out a paper parcel from her basket, allowing the aroma of a freshly baked pie to waft through the office. Opening the parcel, her heart soared when Mr Simpson's eyes rested on the golden crust topping. 'I wanted to show you the size I was thinking of,' Mary Jane said innocently, pleased her idea was having the desired effect, 'I want a box, big enough to hold a pie this size.' She noticed his look of longing. Not slow to seize the chance of a future sale, she asked, 'Can I tempt you, Mr Simpson? You might enjoy a nice pie for your break, or even lunch if you can resist it for that long, compliments of the cook.' Mary Jane put the pie on the desk.

'It does smell very good,' he said, his eyes devouring the pie, and Mary Jane pushed it temptingly across the desk. She knew it was too early for dinnertime, but it was probably quite a while since he ate breakfast. 'It would be rude not to sample the wares,' he said, clearly unable to resist as he took it with undue haste. A moment later, he was sinking his teeth into it, and he did something Molly would have surely chastised him for. 'Oh, my dear, this is delicious,' he said, closing his eyes, his mouth full, savouring the pie. 'Can you make some of these for us?'

'To take home to your wife?' Mary Jane was thrilled – a customer!

'No, for the factory canteen,' Mr Simpson said. 'Our usual supplier has been giving us the run-around, he needs a bit of competition. My wife would never allow me to eat something like this at the dinner table.'

'I can deliver to the canteen,' she said as calmly as her thundering heart would allow. 'How many would you like?'

'Let's call it a dozen to start with,' Mr Simpson told her.

Mary Jane decided to push her luck. Well, she thought, there's no chance of being successful if she was as timid as a country mouse. 'Let's call it two dozen and I'll knock off a farthing for every pie – on two dozen pies, that's sixpence off the price.' Her quick deduction brought a look of approval from Mr Simpson, giving him cause to stand up to shake her hand to seal the deal.

Mary Jane agreed to supply the canteen on Mondays, Wednesdays and Fridays. When she left the office, she not only had the boxes she wanted but also managed to secure a discount, and a gross of paper bags were thrown in with the order for good measure. But that wasn't all, Mary Jane, also had the option to increase supplies if the pies were greeted with enthusiasm in the canteen. Never in her wildest dreams did she think her first order would come so quickly. However, she had not budgeted for supplying the factory. How was she going to do all that work by herself? She would need to hire someone to help her. Immediately, her thoughts sprang to Daisy. She could pay her to work full time in the shop. But would Daisy want to work in a backstreet bakery when she was accustomed to working in the busy teashop?

* * *

'That was a lovely pie you passed over the other day, Mary Jane!' Ina King, friendly as you like, called across the street. Mary Jane gave a wave as she made her way down Beamer

Street. Ina, as she suspected, had spread the word quicker than the Mersey News.

'Shall I pass another one over?' Mary Jane asked, and Ina nodded, her face alight with glee.

'Could you make it steak and kidney again,' Ina asked in a lowered voice, 'in that lovely gravy? My Albert devoured it, said it is the best he ever tasted.' She looked around before saying with a hint of mischief, 'He thinks I've been taking lessons.'

'Well, we mustn't disappoint your Albert. Is one going to be enough?' Mary Jane could not stop smiling.

'We'd best make it two,' said Ina in a chummy tone, which Mary Jane had not heard before. Gone was the contempt, she had offered in the past. 'Shall I call over for it before my Albert gets in from work?'

'That will be fine,' Mary Jane said in an equally friendly voice, 'and seeing as you are a neighbour, I'll only charge you what it cost for the ingredients.' Ina King's short gasp did not go unnoticed. 'They are the very best cuts, mind, so they don't come cheap, and if you would like me to add you to the penny club, you won't go short.'

She deliberately ignored Ina King's look of disappointment. *Ina must think I'm a soft touch, but she'll find out soon enough...* Mary Jane smiled. She knew exactly what she had to do and arranged another meeting with Mr Simpson.

* * *

'Can you put a bit of writing on the boxes?' Mary Jane asked Mr Simpson at their next meeting when he saw another delicious pie – an apple and blackberry this time.

'Certainly, we can,' he answered, greedily taking the pie from the box. 'What would you like it to say?'

'Here, I've written it down.' She passed him the piece of paper, upon which was written:

Mary Jane's Succulent, Quality Pies: Devoured by Kings

'Oh, Mrs Redfern, that is perfect...' Mr Simpson laughed out loud when she told him of her meeting with Ina. 'Absolutely priceless.'

When she left the office, Mary Jane had a large order to supply fruit pies as well. She felt ten feet tall.

* * *

December 1921

A few weeks after the shop was opened, business was going from strength to strength and Mary Jane asked Daisy if she would like to work full-time. Daisy jumped at the chance to learn her chosen craft and the shop was doing very good trade. Mary Jane's pies and pastries were being bought up quickly. And at the end of a satisfying day's trading, before shutting up shop, she did what she promised she would do, and gave out any left-over stock cheaply. It was the busiest part of the day as news travelled. Good at remembering faces, she did not allow the same people to buy cheap bread and pies all the time, knowing some would take advantage. But she had an eye for a genuine, hard-up case, and never failed to help them out. 'You'll never be rich practically giving your stock away,' said Molly.

'I never wanted to be rich, Moll,' Mary Jane answered, 'I wanted to be happy, and I am.' She was standing on the front step, the same as she did every night, taking in the sights and sounds of Beamer Street, watching the children play before they went in for the night. However, tonight her back was aching, carrying heavy trays of pies was beginning to take its toll as her pregnancy was now at the end of the seventh month. Dusk had long descended when she noticed Cal coming out of the side gate. He was about to lock up when he saw her, and he paused.

'Are you all right there, Mary Jane?' he called across the street, and Mary Jane raised her hand to let him know she was.

Cal was glad business was going well. But Mary Jane was so busy baking and selling pastries, she no longer had time for their nightly chat when she brought him food. He hadn't realised how much he had come to enjoy – no, depend on – seeing her, when he finished his working day, her visits with his food were more than just the satisfaction of a home cooked meal. He devoured her daily news while he ate, and discovered more about the community than he ever thought possible. His life had taken a turn for the better. But these days Mary Jane sent Daisy or Davey upstairs with his evening meal, which, nevertheless still delicious and much appreciated, was not as enjoyable as it had been when Mary Jane sat unselfconsciously at his table and shared her thoughts and plans for the future of her and her child.

* * *

During the next weeks as her business grew, very soon, Mary Jane had enough to replenish her stock, buy extra meat, pay Molly more housekeeping and put money away for when her baby was born, knowing she would have to take a bit of time off.

'Can I look after the shop tomorrow?' Daisy asked. 'It looks like you could do with a rest. You've been on your feet since four o'clock this morning, and still haven't finished.'

Molly tut-tutted, bringing Mary Jane a well-deserved cup of tea, suspecting the girl was doing far too much for someone who only had a few weeks left until her baby was born.

'People are putting in their Christmas orders,' Mary Jane answered. 'I cannot afford to disappoint them. I need to build up my rainy-day money.' Although, she did feel more tired lately. There had been no let-up in the stream of customers. Not that she was complaining, mind. But until she had her pot of money, for when the baby came, she could not afford any respite from her relentless toil. 'I worked out that I can give you a raise in your wages,' Mary Jane said, knowing, with Daisy's help, business was certainly lively. 'You've been a godsend to me, Daisy, and I could not have done it without you.'

'I'm a rich girl since I stopped paying tram fares,' said Daisy, obviously thrilled, knowing she was learning a lot from Mary Jane. Mary Jane's reputation was growing daily and was she was getting regular orders from the offices in town as well as from Simpson's.

* * *

Everything was working out very nicely, and Mary Jane knew it was just as well, because she did not have long to go before her confinement. Her baby was due in January, so that gave her a few weeks to increase her rainbow gold; the pot of money she had been saving.

'Mary Jane,' Molly said tentatively, 'Daisy's really enjoyed helping you with the pies and so have I, but...' she hesitated, as if looking for the right words. 'She's been offered full-time at the teashop, and it might lead to being taken on full-time permanently.'

'It's only for the Christmas trade, Mam,' Daisy protested. 'I'll probably be put on short time again afterwards.'

Mary Jane knew the girl was never happier than when she was elbow deep in flour and pastry. She loved baking, and even when Mary Jane went out to meet buyers, Daisy was capable of running the shop. She was good at selling, almost as good as Mary Jane – and Molly was a natural with the customers. No shrinking violet, she could sell sand to the Arabs and snow to the Eskimos if she had a mind and Daisy was a younger version of her mother, Mary Jane would be a fool to let her go, but she had to give the girl the chance to choose her own path.

'You're young, Daisy, you might have a chance of owning the teashop one day,' Mary Jane said, rolling pastry for the following day. She did not want to let Daisy go but she must give her the opportunity if that was what she wanted to do. 'You may not want to be stuck in a hot kitchen baking pies all day long..'

'I'd rather work with you than the teashop any day,' Daisy sounded more determined than ever, and Mary Jane breathed a sigh of relief.

'I think you enjoy baking as much as I do,' Mary Jane gave an encouraging smile that said she would make things right with Molly. 'I'm sure we can come to some agreement.' There was enough work for three of them, for sure, but how long it lasted, well, that was the question. Mary Jane had promised to supply the factory until Christmas, and she had a steady demand from the offices, but if either of those dried up, she would be in trouble. 'She's good at what she does,' Mary Jane told Molly, 'she follows my recipes to the letter, nothing added or taken away.'

'I'll teach her everything I know,' Mary Jane said, 'and between us we will have a thriving business to keep us all going.'

'It'll be the best this side of the Mersey,' Molly said with pride, and it was agreed that from now on Daisy could work in the shop, which was known locally as *Mary Jane's Kitchen*.

* * *

When she got back from Simpson's Printers after placing a bigger order, Mary Jane could see Molly had been crying. Sitting at the kitchen table, the older woman held a crumpled letter in one hand, and her head in the other. When she looked up, her sparkling eyes were red and swollen and full of despair, stark against the tight, grey pallor of her normally rosy cheeks.

'They're going to evict us, Mary Jane,' she said, and the tears she had been so determined not to spill ran down her face afresh.

Mary Jane felt her heart flip. 'No,' she whispered softly, 'you must have got it wrong, Moll.'

'We've lived here since my Albert secured rooms on the top floor, just after we were wed.' Molly stared into nothing, remembering. 'We've had the run of the whole house since the old man who lived down here died, our Davey was a babe in arms.'

'Who is evicting you? The railway company?' Mary Jane knew the railway company secured the rent when Albert started driving the trains and the rest of the house became available. Nevertheless, Albert wasn't here any more. 'Have they stopped paying the rent?' Mary Jane asked, afraid that Molly and her family would be forced from their home before Christmas.

Molly shook her head not looking at her, and Mary Jane's heartbeat escalated, afraid now, but the question needed to be asked.

'Is it because of me?' she asked.

'I have a small pension from the railway; they don't pay the rent since Albert was killed in the trenches.' Molly shrugged, hopelessly accepting what life threw at her, because she had never been in a position to do otherwise. 'Even if I put all of the bits of money together, it doesn't add up to the cost of feeding, clothing, and keeping a roof as good as this over our heads... I was so glad when you said you would come and live here, and I wouldn't bleed you dry like some.'

'Oh, Molly, you should have let me know you were struggling – and here's me talking about Christmas orders and how well we were doing.'

'It's not up to you to keep us all, and anyway, I manage to pay the rent. That's not what the notice is about.' Molly took in a huge shuddering sigh. 'And before you go thinking it's your fault, we love you being here, we really do. The house has never been so alive, and the children love helping out.' She paused for a moment then said, 'But that's the whole problem.'

Mary Jane held her breath when she read the letter. *She* was the cause of Molly being evicted. Her eyes skimmed the words again hardly able to believe somebody had told the landlord that Molly was running a business from her rented home.

'We're going to be turned out, it says so there, in black and white.' Molly got up and paced the room, hardly able to breathe. She gasped, 'We'll be on the streets.'

Mary Jane caught her friend's shoulders and pulled Molly to her, shushing her like a child. 'You will not be put out onto the streets Molly.' Mary Jane's words were tipped with steely determination. 'I'll put a stop to this nonsense, so don't you worry about a thing.' How she was going to stop the eviction taking place was another matter. However, she would do everything she could to restore Molly Haywood's good name. 'Who is your landlord?' she asked.

Molly shook her head, her voice a querulous tremor. 'We have never seen the person who actually owns the house. Landlords don't set foot in a place like this unless they have to. They're too busy protecting their ivory towers!'

'Don't cry, Molly, this is my mess, and I will clean it up, you wait and see.' Mary Jane soothed her friend. 'I may have a way out of this...'

'But, Mary Jane, you shouldn't have to find a way out of anything, not in your condition.'

'Wshht!' Mary Jane said impatiently, 'I'm the one who brought all this to your door. I'll be the one to fix it.' Mary Jane ignored the light-headedness, knowing it would soon pass. Poor Molly, she had gone through enough heartache and strain, without her adding to it. 'I'll make us a nice cup of tea. You can solve all of life's problems over a hot cup of tea.'

'You will do no such thing.' Molly's voice was more determined than Mary Jane had ever heard before. 'You will stay put, my girl. I'll make the tea, and we will see this through together.'

Molly's words buoyed her spirits and Mary Jane smiled. As long as they all stuck together, they could win this battle. She was sure.

'You're a good girl Mary Jane,' Molly sniffed, and Mary Jane felt her colour rise. If only Molly knew the truth about her unborn child, she would have nothing to do with her. But that was not the issue right now, she thought, determined to do her best to take that look of desperation from the eyes of her best friend, a woman who had only ever done good things for the people around about. She would get Molly and her children out of this mess if it was the last thing she did.

'I can't give birth in the street, the authorities frown on that kind of thing,' Mary Jane dug deep, to find the humour that saved her many times. 'Maybe I can find a stable going spare – well, it's that time of year. It worked for the Blessed Virgin, Mary.'

She read the address of the landlord's agent and knew she must go and try to make them see sense. She could not have Molly walking the street at Christmas because of her.

'You won't end up on the street, Moll.' Mary Jane wished she felt as positive as her words sounded. However, the look of relief on Molly's face was worth the little white lie. Going into the parlour, she went to the sideboard and took out her rainbow pot, hoping it would not be necessary to offer a financial incentive – or a bribe to turn a blind eye? 'Needs must when the devil rides,' she said.

24

CHRISTMAS EVE

Mary Jane hoped the landlord was a God-fearing man who would not evict a woman with four children for doing a good turn, especially at Christmas. If that was the case, she would do everything she could possibly think of to find out who had been sharing tittle-tattle to the landlord. And when she did, there was no telling what might happen next.

Her eyes swept the address at the top of the letter. The office was in Old Haymarket in the centre of Liverpool and would necessitate a tram ride. After a quick word with Daisy, she made sure her customers did not have to go without their bread and pies on Christmas Eve. When she discovered she had missed a tram, Mary Jane began to walk the length of Great Howard Street alongside the fortified, castellated walls of Stanley Dock, and into the town centre, as the square-faced clock above Martin's Bank told her the tram had been due five minutes ago. She was beginning to panic a little, knowing by the time she got there, walking, the office would have closed for the day.

'Has the tram gone?' she asked a large woman, in a black knitted cloche hat and a fur collared coat, who was standing under the bus sign.

'This tram's never on time, love, so no rush,' she told Mary Jane. 'It'll be here five minutes late as usual, to be sure.'

'Thank you,' said Mary Jane.

'My ankles were just the same over my last one,' the woman said, looking down at Mary Jane's swollen legs. 'Blew up like balloons, they did. You'll have to watch that.'

In flesh-coloured lisle stockings, Mary Jane could clearly see her feet and her ankles were nearly twice their normal size. And the dark blue, kitten-heel shoes were chafing even though she had fastened the instep strap to the last hole.

The lady talked nonstop. At any other time, Mary Jane would have been willing to listen, but today she had other things on her mind. What would she say to the landlord when she saw him? Beg for mercy, perhaps? Or should she go in with all guns blazing, and tell him he had no right to throw a woman and her family onto the street at this time of year? Although, thinking about the situation from the landlord's point of view, he might not take kindly to being told what he could and couldn't do with his own properties.

'When's it due?' the woman asked, shrugging further down her coat, as the cold west wind whipped up from the River Mersey, bringing a light flutter of snow in its wake.

'The end of January' Mary Jane's eyes watered with the ferocity of the incoming gale and the local smells coming up from the docks – fishmeal, tobacco from the British American Tobacco Company, mingling with the sulphurous pong of the gas works. Suddenly she felt nauseous.

'Going shopping?' the lady asked conversationally, and Mary Jane nodded, wishing that's all she had to do. If that was the case, she could turn around and go back home, but, if she did that the Haywoods may have no home. The thought made her determination to sort this matter out even stronger, relieved when the tram rounded the corner. When it stopped, she stepped on to the platform, which still showed some of the bullet hole effects of being in service during the Great War. She hoped the cheerful woman did not sit near her and immediately felt guilty. However, there were only two vacant seats, and they were right next to each other.

'I love these modern styles,' said the woman, who nodded to a stylish young woman in a loose tubular coat, fastened at the hip with a large mother-of-pearl button. Mary Jane, feeling frumpy in her ankle-length skirt and loose-fitting jacket to accommodate her expanding circumference, recalled a time, which seemed so long ago, when she, too, wore a fashionable coat and hat in the most perfect sky blue.

Moments later, the tram began to slow.

'Well, this is us,' the woman said, shuffling to the front of her seat, her shopping basket swinging on her arm. When the tram stopped, she held out her hand and helped Mary Jane ease herself from the seat. Struggling to raise herself, she was sure she could move quicker than this yesterday.

'My last "predicament" did that to me,' she said, 'blew me up like one of those airships, used during the war. Well, I'll love and leave you, ducks, are you sure you can manage now?'

'I'm sure,' Mary Jane answered, grateful for the woman's help, but relieved to see her waddle off towards Lime Street Station, giving her a little time to think without interruption. Checking the address again, Mary Jane realised she did not have far to go when she saw the office above the tobacconist shop across the road.

A small red blotch of heat formed on each of her cheeks as

she waited for somebody to answer the door. Checking her appearance in the brass plate that bore the name of Swanne and Fisher, she was growing hotter even though the weather was bitterly cold. Nerves, she told herself as the scalp-hugging S-shaped finger-waves were already beginning to wilt under her navy-blue cloche hat.

Pressing the bell again, she waited. Maybe they had closed early for Christmas. Moments later, she heard footsteps, and the door was opened by a young clerk, in grey pinstripe, with slicked-down hair parted in the middle. He looked quite important, Mary Jane thought.

'I am Mrs Redfern, here to see Mr Swanne, however—'

'This way,' the clerk threw the words over his shoulder, not waiting for her to finish.

'I do not have an appointment,' Mary Jane said refusing to have her words curtailed. She followed the young man up a flight of marbled stairs. At the top of the second flight, she rested, trying to catch her breath, wondering if she dared ask for a drink of water.

'Wait here,' said the clerk, who, looking no older than a schoolboy at close quarters, waved to a straight-backed wooden bench opposite an opaque window. Then, he disappeared through a semi-glazed door leading to a room filled with shadowy dark-suited men whose heads were bent over their work. Mary Jane felt a flutter in her stomach, which had nothing to do with the child she was carrying, and her legs suddenly had no life in them. The wait seemed interminable, and she wasted time gazing at dust particles dancing in a stream of weak winter sunshine from a small skylight above.

'This way,' the young clerk said abruptly when he opened the door, and if she had been of a more nervous disposition,

Mary Jane was sure she would have been startled by the intrusion into her thoughts. Standing against the door, he watched, uncooperatively, while Mary Jane shuffled a little awkwardly in the seat. With a herculean effort, she managed to get to her feet and felt a surge of indignation. This young man might have position and power, but he certainly had no manners!

'Thank you,' she said as gracefully as she could when he stood aside for her to enter the office.

'Mr Swanne this is Mrs Redfern.' Mary Jane noticed the young man was much more civil to his betters than he had been to her.

'Thank you. Take a seat.' Mr Swanne said without looking up, leaving her sitting there until he had finished writing and she wondered if bad manners were a requisite to working in these stuffy places. It certainly seemed so. Her hackles were up now, all meekness and subservience depleted. 'What can I do for you?' Mr Swanne asked, barely lifting his balding head.

'Good afternoon to you too,' Mary Jane said pointedly. When he did look up, she said, 'I have brought this letter. I need your advice.' She handed over the letter and Mr Swanne's eyes zigzagged through the words.

'What advice do you seek?' He looked up and his stern expression softened, which gave her courage.

'Firstly, I want to know is this legal,' Mary Jane said, pointing to the letter, 'and secondly, who blew Molly up?'

'The first answer is quite straightforward,' Mr Swanne answered. 'Yes, this document is legal – everything we do in this business is kept strictly to the letter of the law.' He paused for a moment, looking puzzled. 'However, I cannot answer your second question, as I do not understand it?'

'You don't understand my question?' Mary Jane felt her

patience wane. For a learned man, he was not paying attention if he could not get the gist of her question. 'It is simple... Who sneaked? Who told tales out of school? Who told those terrible lies about Molly Haywood?'

'Do you mean to tell me that Mrs Haywood is not running a business from her home?'

'No, she is not.' Mary Jane dug the desk with her forefinger, her tone emphatic.

Mr Swanne sat back in his chair, his fingertips forming a steeple. 'So, whomever gave this information is lying?' he said, after some consideration.

'If I got my hands around the neck of whomever, I'll throttle them until their teeth rattle!' Mary Jane was close to exasperation. Some people could be so evil-eyed. 'Can you tell me who told you?'

'I'm afraid, we do not give out such information. Suffice to say, we were informed that the "*disgusting whiff*", their words not mine, "at all hours of the day and night, is upsetting the community."'

'All hours... Chance would be a fine thing!' Mary Jane scoffed. 'I have to sleep sometime!' Although she had to admit, at this stage of her condition, she slept very little, 'I do start work very early, sometimes four o'clock in the morning.'

'So, it is you who is running the business?' Mr. Swanne asked, eyeing her obvious prominence, which could not be hidden by the carpet bag.

'Yes, I am the one making the pies,' Mary Jane said, holding up her hand. 'Here I've brought you some to try.' She took the box, containing four of her best steak and kidney pies in luxurious port wine gravy, and passed it across the desk. She was wide-eyed when he hesitated. They were fresh out of the oven and still warm.

'I must admit they do smell delicious,' he said, drawing in the glorious aroma of the light puff pastry and best beef. The pies were attracting attention, and like the pot-bellied pigs back home, the clerks were curious after spending long hours with their snouts to the desk. Mary Jane could not resist a smile when they had a good sniff.

'Nevertheless employees, and even proprietors of Swanne and Fisher, are not allowed to eat at their desk.' Mr Swanne seemed reluctant to push the pies back across the desk to Mary Jane.

'What a shame,' she said. 'Take them, anyway, for your tea perhaps. I assume Mrs Swanne likes a good, wholesome pie?'

'Indeed, she does.' His stern features softened into a smile. Then he dashed her hopes when he said: 'However, it is neither I, nor my partner who make the rules of the establishments we rent out. We merely enforce them as agents, not landlords.'

'Might I enquire who does make the rules?' Mary Jane said, wondering if she had wasted her time coming here. 'Who owns the house?'

'I should not be telling you this.' Mr. Swanne moved closer to his desk and lowered his voice. 'However, one good turn deserves another.' He looked around the office before saying, 'A Mr Everdine owns most of the properties in Beamer Street some of which he inherited from his father.'

'Mr Ever— Cal Everdine?' His name almost stuck in her throat.

'Yes, do you know him?' Mr Swanne brightened considerably. 'It would be rather helpful for you if you did, but what I have told you should not be repeated.'

'Yes, I know him,' Mary Jane said through clenched teeth. And Mr Swanne whipped the box of pies off the table, secreting them into the drawer of his desk, lest she change her mind about making a gift of them.

'Until we hear otherwise, I am obliged to tell you, if the business of making these delightful pies does not cease, and I certainly hope it does not, I'm afraid Mrs Haywood has to go.'

'But she's not running a business in the house. I have premises.' Mary Jane hooked her feet around the legs of the chair, suddenly feeling light-headed as the room momentarily swam before her eyes. When the room righted itself, Mary Jane took a deep breath.

'In that case, Mrs Redfern, you do not have to cease trading, as you have alternative accommodation to make and sell your pies, so I will let the landlord know and I am sure he will agree that you all can stay living in the house.' His tone brightened as Mary Jane, pushing back her chair, held out her hand to shake his.

'Thank you for all your help,' she said, standing up. The room swam again momentarily, and Mary Jane held onto the desk to steady herself as Mr Swanne had the good grace to offer her a glass of water. The cold liquid refreshed her, and Mary Jane felt a little better. Now she must get back to Molly and tell her all she knew.

'You won't stop baking, I hope?' Mr Swanne said, standing.

'I do hope not, but we will have to wait and see,' Mary Jane answered, preparing to leave.

'Thank you for the pies,' he said, taking her hand again and Mary Jane gave it a hefty shake. 'Mr Swanne junior will show you to the door.'

Mary Jane was surprised to see the door opened for her by the junior clerk. He smiled when Mary Jane thanked him. 'You look much more appealing when you smile,' she said, amused by his look of surprise as she left the stuffy office. She had solved Molly's problem. All she had to do now was go and speak to Mr Everdine and find out what the hell he was playing at!

25

Mary Jane's feet were aching, her head felt as if it was going to burst, and all she wanted to do was quench her thirst with a nice cup of tea and tell Molly all that she had learned. Molly's brows furrowed in confusion when Mary Jane gave her the news she knew who the landlord was. 'Who is *he*?'

'You will never guess in a hundred years,' Mary Jane said, removing her jacket. 'He not only owns this house, but every other house in the street – except her ladyship's next door.' Mary Jane tipped her head to the side of the wall adjoining Cissie Stone's house.

'Never!' Molly's eyes were round and wide. 'Most of these houses were bought by a private landlord years ago when the toffs moved out.'

'I believe so,' Mary Jane nodded.

'And you know who he is?' Molly's voice took on a curious note but noticed Mary Jane looked tired.

'You will never guess,' Mary Jane repeated, wiping the back of her hand across her damp forehead before taking a handkerchief from her pocket and dabbing her top lip. 'Cal Everdine.' Feeling a furnace burning inside her and fanning her face with a newspaper, she pushed back wispy curls that had stuck damply to the side of her peach-bloomed face. 'The very same man who pretended he was just a caretaker of the shop.' The words bounced around Mary Jane's scull like loose ping-pong balls. She could not let Cal get away with threatening to evict her good friend, whose family depended on the roof over their head at Christmas, no matter how befuddled she felt. 'The same one who asked if I wanted a lift when I was dying of the heat outside the town hall, waiting for that two-faced, lying, robbing, no-good Red.'

'Remind me never to ask you for a character reference, Mary Jane,' Molly said, careful to hide the look of concern when she saw Mary Jane's high colour. She had seen something similar in her time and the outcome was never good. 'Here, rest for a while, you look done in.'

'Tell me, Molly,' Mary Jane said, sitting at the table, 'are there any honest, decent men? Because I haven't seen evidence of any. First Red tries to pull the wool over my eyes, and then Mr Everdine pretends he hasn't got two halfpennies to rub together, and he owns half of Liverpool.'

'Cal owns all these houses?' Astonishment laced Molly's words. 'Him who has been so good to you, helping you any way he can?' She rolled the edge of her apron, smoothed it down and began rolling it again.

Mary Jane, silenced by her friend's obvious agitation, eventually spoke in a quiet voice. 'The very same, inherited them from his rich father, apparently. The land agent told me not to repeat the news, so I'll only say it the once... Who'd have thought?'

'He never mixed with anyone in Beamer Street.' Molly said,

'Because he had no cause,' Mary Jane answered, feeling a little better after having a drink as Molly bustled around the kitchen. 'Why would he bother with the likes of us, when he has people doing his dirty work? He has nothing in common with us no matter how much he pretends.' He had more money than any of them ever imagined. 'What would make someone live like a pauper, when they could have anything, their heart desires?' Anger, like sharp barbs, formed Mary Jane's words. 'He had hardly a stick of furniture, nothing of any comfort. I assumed he could not afford chairs and tables and I wondered *how* on earth – or *why* on earth – would he pay me to cook for him when it was cheaper to eat in a workman's canteen. I couldn't fathom it.'

'Now don't go getting yourself into a state.' Molly hurried to her side and put a gentle hand on her shoulder. 'Think of the baby.'

'That's exactly who I am thinking about.' Mary Jane ignored the rising nausea. 'I am going straight over there to have it out with him.'

'Why not have another cup of tea?' Molly said, trying to calm her friend whose face, the colour of a ripe plum, looked like it was about to explode.

Mary Jane paused. That would be the sensible thing to do, but she wasn't feeling sensible, she was feeling angry, and impatient, and she wanted to go over to Mr Everdine and tell him exactly what she thought of his underhand dealings. However, listening to Molly's advice, a nagging doubt formed. Did she have any right to confront Mr Everdine over his deception when she was doing the very same thing?

'Maybe you're right, Molly, if I go across the street in this mood, we'll be evicted today.'

Molly wasn't worrying about her own predicament. She was concerned about Mary Jane's high colour. She would send one of the children to fetch the doctor, knowing whatever happened, she must keep the mother-to-be calm at all costs.

'He puts me in mind of someone,' Molly said, looking out of the window to beckon seven-year-old Freddy, her eyes trailing the street to see Cal Everdine leading his horse through the huge double gates. 'Although, I can't think who.'

Mary Jane was only half-listening, as she bent to remove her shoes, cutting into her swollen feet. And, rising from the chair, she crossed the linoleum-covered floor in lisle-stockings, to fetch her slippers. She waddled out to the back kitchen to get another glass of cold water. She couldn't drink fast enough, as it gushed down her throat like a dashing river, but it did nothing to quench the roaring furnace building up inside her.

'I know who Mr. Everdine reminds me of,' Molly said as she bustled into the scullery and filled the kettle with water from the brass tap. 'Tom Mix! He's a dead ringer.'

'Who's Tom Mix?' Mary Jane's voice echoed in her head as a pulsating throb grew louder.

'Don't tell me you've never heard of Tom Mix?' Molly's eyes widened in surprise. 'He's that handsome American film star. Six feet tall. A cowboy on the pictures.'

'I've never been to the pictures,' Mary Jane's voice was flat and matter of fact. 'There was no picture house in the village where I grew up.'

'In that case you won't have a clue,' Molly said with a sigh, and put the flat of her hand on her heart. 'He's very good-looking – Tom Mix... But never mind all that just now.' She flushed pink to the roots of her salt-and-pepper-coloured hair and quickly changed the subject when she saw Mary Jane was not looking at all well. 'I can't understand what made your husband take off like that, with you in such a delicate condition.' Molly prepared tea, and put the cups and saucers on a tray.

Lifting the tray of tea things, Molly suggested they drink it in the parlour, where she had a good fire going. 'It seems a shame to waste all that lovely heat.' For the moment, Mary Jane could think of nothing more uncomfortable, more inclined to stand outside and let the fierce wind blowing in from the River Mersey cool her down. 'Who'd have thought he owned this street?' Molly said, looking out of the window again to see if she could catch a glimpse of her son. 'If he's got so much money, why does he go out at the crack of dawn and come back late at night,' she wondered aloud, 'unloading all kinds of stuff into that yard, bothering with nobody'

'I know, it is very strange.' Mary Jane was not really interested in what Cal Everdine had in his yard, knowing when she did come face to face with him, she was going to give him a piece of her mind! 'What right has he to evict your family at Christmas?'

'I was shocked to the roots of my hair when you told me,' Molly said, 'because he's always very polite when I speak to him.' She plumped a cushion. 'He never gave any inkling. He smiled and raised his hat when I said good morning, but he doesn't go out of his way to make conversation.'

'You'd think he'd be able to afford a new hat. That one looks like it's been savaged by something feral.' Mary Jane wondered if she should lie down for half an hour, feeling very peculiar indeed. 'If he owns so much, you'd think he could afford a new hat,' she had forgotten she already said this earlier.

'I suppose his kind can wear what they like,' Molly sighed.

It seemed to be a day of sighs, and Mary Jane's repetition raised a warning alarm inside her.

'Can he now?' Mary Jane's reply sounded like a challenge. 'We'll soon see about that.'

'I don't want you to get agitated. The pressure will not do you or the baby any good.' Molly feared the top of Mary Jane's head would blow off.

'You're right, but when I feel less tired, I'm going to have it out with Mr Heartless, Moneybags Everdine.' She was in no humour to start a rebellion against the landlord's rules now. But neither was she going to let the matter slide, and her annoyance rose at the unfairness of the situation. 'He has no right to evict you and your whole family for my offence, and somebody needs to tell him.'

'Don't upset yourself,' Molly placated her, afraid she was going to keel over if she didn't stay calm. 'You'll do yourself a mischief!'

Mary Jane was getting tetchy but knew she shouldn't. 'I'm not an invalid.'

'No, you are not an invalid, but you must take care.'

'I will, Molly,' Mary Jane gave her friend a tired smile. 'And thank you for your concern, I appreciate it.' Not having a mother of her own, Molly was the closest person who cared about her for a long time, and the unfair eviction notice was making Mary Jane angry – no, not angry, she was way past anger, she was feeling more than that. Rage came close. Frustration at not being able to keep Molly and her children safe after all they had done for her. Injustice? Most certainly. The inequality of the haves and the have-nots was the most galling of all. She *was* going to become an independent woman who would battle the odds. But now she was not going to get the chance. To the likes of Cal

Everdine, she was just an ignorant Irishwoman, only fit to cook his meals. Well, Mary Jane thought, she was going to put him straight on that score. The great Cal Everdine, who obviously believed women should know their place, was no better than Red. 'I'll be back in a minute,' she told Molly, 'I need some air.'

26

'Whoa, easy now.' Cal took Mary Jane's elbow and supported her swaying body. 'The cold evening air must have caught you unaware.' He stood rock steady as she leaned against him, and his heart leapt to his throat when her knees buckled. Without a thought, he put his arms around her, supporting her. 'Are you all right, Mary Jane?' Cal asked as she looked at him with large, confused, emerald eyes, and burning red cheeks.

In this theatre of a street, where nothing was private, a crowd of curious children watched Mr Everdine slip his other arm around her. He could smell the clean, lemon fragrance of her that sent his senses into overdrive. Heading back up the steps towards Molly's house, Mary Jane put her hand to the door to push it open, her head bowed. 'I'm fine,' she said, her words thick and groggy, although it was obvious to Cal when Mary Jane stumbled, she was anything but fine. Slipping his arm more securely around her, he felt the faint kick of the child within and immediately tried to push a painful past memory from his mind. The recollection of a woman he could not save, nor the child she had been carrying.

Russet curls sprung loose framing Mary Jane's burning cheeks, and he knew immediately she needed more help than he could offer.

'I've got you,' Cal whispered, his heart beating in his throat. 'You are safe now.' Unlike another woman, who had put her trust in him. He felt remorse course through his veins but knew he had dwelt on the past long enough.

Mary Jane looked confused, as if she had only just noticed he was there. 'Safe, am I?' Mary Jane's low voice indicated her fragility. Nevertheless, there was still a hint of fight in her steady gaze, and for that he was grateful. Maybe if Ellie had been stronger, so pampered she did not know how to take care of herself or their unborn child. If she'd known what it was like to struggle and be one step ahead, she may have been able to save herself and the child.

Mary Jane let out a small whimper, drawing him back. 'I can walk,' she said, moving forward, but the ground began to shift beneath her feet, and Mary Jane knew this was no time to talk. Fighting to overcome an intense weakness seeping into her body, invading her arms, her legs, even her fingers. If Cal had not been there to catch her, she would easily have slid to the ground. Taking a deep breath of cold winter air, Mary Jane tried to clear her head. 'Leave me be, —' She barely managed to get the words out, feeling she was rolling on a rough sea, like she had done when she came over from Ireland. The ground dipping and heaving. Up... Down... Up... She felt herself being lifted off her feet and in moments darkness descended.

'You are not fine,' Cal said, when he felt her go limp in his arms. Fearing he could lose her too, he jolted into action, scooping Mary Jane easily into his arms, he headed through the half-open door, knowing he would never forgive himself if anything happened to her or the child. He had to get her through this. He had to. He must get help, and quickly! When Mary Jane's eyes rolled back and her head flopped to one side, he took immediate action, in a few strides. Molly's eldest lad was right behind them. Home from his day's work, he had seen Mary Jane in trouble. Unlike other workers, Davey did not join his fellow workers in the public bars and music halls to celebrate the Christmas season. He brought his wages home, knowing his mother would be waiting on them to fill the table.

'Davey, fetch the doctor, quickly.' Cal Everdine filled the house with his deep commanding voice, and Davey skidded down the lobby without question, heading towards the front door and the main road.

Molly's footsteps quickened when she heard the commotion, and opening the kitchen door, her hands flew to her lips to restrain the shriek of surging panic.

'I was looking for our Freddy to go and fetch the doctor, but he was nowhere to be found,' Molly knew she should never have let Mary Jane go out when she looked so poorly.

'Davey has gone to fetch Doctor Roberts,' Cal said, knowing there was something not right about Mary Jane's colour. There was too much of it. He had heard of this before in pregnancy – and the consequences were not good. Not good at all.

'I knew it,' Molly cried, 'I just knew something like this would happen. Mary Jane has done too much.' Leading the way into the cosy front room, Molly could not contain her worry. 'Up before the crack of dawn to bake her pastries and bread. Then into town.' Molly, usually so strong and stoic, suddenly burst into tears. 'I blame myself for putting the worry of eviction into her young head. I am such a stupid woman. And her, with only a few weeks to go before she brings a new life into the world,' Molly's panicky tears soaked the handkerchief she had taken from her sleeve, 'I let her go into town to try to plead my case, stop me being evicted. How could I have been so selfish. So stupid. I was the one who should have gone to see the land agent, not Mary Jane!' Her urgent tone broke Cal's gaze from Mary Jane's stricken face.

'Why on earth would you receive an eviction notice?' he asked, confused.

'Because the land agent received an unsigned letter, whoever wrote it didn't have the guts to put their name to it, saying I was running a business and took in lodgers – it's against the rules, as you well know.' Molly could not help her angry outburst, 'On your orders, we were to be out of this house before the new year.'

'I did no such thing.' His jaw tightened as he lay Mary Jane on the highly polished leather sofa. 'I think somebody has overstepped the mark.'

Mary Jane groaned as if in pain and his head turned towards her as fear gripped his heart. This could not happen again. He could not bear it if anything were to happen to Mary Jane because of him. But life was fragile, he knew, having seen too many people perish on Flanders fields. His beloved mother was a long time dead before he even knew she was gone forever, her life snuffed out like a candle's flame in a draught. And the realisation only the toughest survive was starkly, and cruelly, brought home to him that day so long ago when he buried his wife and unborn child. Still the guilt ate away at him, every single day.

27

'I wanted to discuss something with you,' Cal said now just the two of them were alone with Mary Jane

Molly went to the sideboard and took the eviction letter from the drawer where it had been put when Mary Jane returned from the land agent's office. She handed it to him, as they waited for the doctor. Cal read and re-read it. He had never given permission for these rules and had certainly never asked for them to be included before his tenants signed their agreement contract.

'I think I know what you want to say, but this is neither the time nor the place.' Molly said stiffly. She was in no mood to discuss the matter, as they waited, believing he was not the kind-hearted man she thought he was.

'Do you take sugar and milk, Mr Everdine?' Daisy who had come into the room asked politely as Molly hardly took her eyes from Mary Jane in case she stirred.

'No milk or sugar, thank you,' Cal answered before the eldest daughter went off to make tea. These people were salt-of-the-earth, he thought, they didn't have much, but what they did have they shared, and they would give you their last penny without a thought if it helped a poor wretch. Cal lowered his head, silent for a moment as a powerful emotion he had been unable to name overcame him. But he could name it now, it was shame, brought on by guilt. He was not worthy to sit in this warm, devoted household among loving people who cared for each other in a way he could only envy.

'She was gone a long time,' Molly noticed the pained expression on Mr Everdine's face. His rugged complexion was the colour of ashes, and she wondered if she was going too far in her blame, but she could not help herself. 'She was in a right state when she got back, her feet all swollen and her head fit to burst!' Molly saw him wince, as if he had been stabbed in the head by a very sharp pin. 'Then she was about to go over and prepare your evening meal.' Molly omitted to tell him Mary Jane was going over to give him a piece of her mind into the bargain.

Each word was like a stab to his heart, and Cal knew he deserved every one of them. He had been so wrapped up in his own self-imposed misery, he didn't realise that here was a woman much worse off than he was. He had no right to covet this homely, unpretentious way they had with each other. He was an outsider, yet they drew him into their lives with good grace and little sign of blame or censure. He owed Molly an explanation, he owed them all an explanation. Ignorance of the situation was no excuse for the anguish he had caused them all, especially Mary Jane, a woman without a husband by her side, a child on the way and her only means of support her baking skills, which, if she was unwell, would not be in a position to earn.

'I am not a callous man,' he said, wondering how much

lower could he stoop, in their eyes, to equal this shameful state of affairs? Not much, he feared.

Molly's face was drained of colour making her look older than her years. Cal knew she was a good woman. A widow raising a good family in the only way she knew, since her husband had died defending his country. And the shame that had been eating away inside Cal for all these years reared up its ugly head once more. What right had anybody, to whip security from under the feet of diligent people, trying to make ends meet?

'Mary Jane is not one to shirk her duties, Mr Everdine,' Molly said as if hearing his thoughts, before turning to her youngest girl. 'Close that front door, Bridie, I don't want to fill the mouth of her next door with gossip.' Nor did she want the whole street to know what business she had with this quiet man, who moved into Beamer Street after the war. He looked up from the cup and saucer, which Daisy had placed before him, on the small side table. No matter what he said, he could not erase the worry that had caused all this upset. But that didn't mean he couldn't try.

'I would never have endorsed such actions.' Cal's voice was low and contrite. 'What difference does it make to me if she bakes a few loaves and pies? None that I can see.' When he looked over to where she was lying, Mary Jane's now deathly pallor almost stopped his heart beating. From the moment he had set eyes on her, getting off the ferry at the dockside, after that lowlife husband left her alone, he was captivated by her beauty – and her impertinence. She was extraordinary.

Something that had lain dormant for years suddenly stirred within him. He realised he was actually beginning to feel something again. It was raw and it was painful, but he was thankful for it all the same.

'You have no need to fret about being evicted, Mrs Hayward. I will never turn any of you out of this house…'

'I was worried sick, I can't lie,' said Molly in her forthright manner. 'We don't live beyond our means and the rent is always paid on time.'

'I know,' said Cal, shifting uncomfortably in his chair, 'and you have paid every penny you will ever pay.'

'I don't understand,' said Molly, spooning sugar into her cup, not sure if she should sit or stand. What did he mean? Was he saying she did not have to pay rent any more? Such a thing was beyond her wildest dreams – no, surely that was not what he meant at all.

'Where is this doctor?' Cal's tone was impatient as he got up and pulled the cover from the back of the sofa and wrapped it around Mary Jane's limp body.

'She's done too much,' Molly said, trying to quell the panic in her voice. 'She's been running around like a headless chicken, trying to make a go of the pie business so she could put a few coppers aside for when the little'n comes.' Molly was unaware of how much salt her words poured into his wound. 'You know the husband ran off with every penny she earned? Left her with nothing. Not even enough to pay rent to that carousing cow next door.' Molly's words were falling over themselves to be out of her mouth. 'This is the second time in as many months, Mary Jane has been threatened with eviction – I imagine the poor girl was more terrified than I was. She was at her wits' end, worrying where she would bring her child into the world.' Molly was unable to hold her tongue. 'She was on the look-out for a stable, like the Virgin Mary.'

'That would never happen.' Cal understood Molly Hayward's protective nature and her overblown hyperbole.

'What must that fear do to a poor girl,' Molly interrupted,

'left destitute by the man who never even stayed around to see his child born. What good is that?' Cal's breath caught in his throat as Molly continued where she left off, rocking back and forth beside the mantelpiece. 'I don't know what we would do if anything happened to Mary Jane. We'd never get over it, I'm sure.'

'I understand completely,' he said. And for the first time in many years, he began to pray. *Please, Lord, don't do this to me again, let Mary Jane and her unborn child survive.*

Molly felt his expression was one of deep sorrow, his chiselled features creasing the outer edges of his dark blue eyes, which, now barely visible, never left Mary Jane's stricken form. She turned to Daisy, saying quietly, 'Go and fetch me some pillows, we have to raise her feet above her heart.' She had seen this kind of thing before.

'You think it's toxaemia, don't you?' Cal asked, and Molly suddenly stopped what she was doing, and after a moment's pause, she nodded her head.

'How do you know a thing like that?' Molly asked, but he did not answer, so she said, 'There's not much any one can do about it now.'

'The doctor may have to deliver the child to save her life,' Cal said.

'She still has a few weeks to go,' Molly said, recalling her conversation with Mary Jane the night before, but something in Mr Everdine's worldly-wise conviction, stopped her from panicking and she began to see him in a different light. He hadn't headed straight for the door like most men would have done.

'My beloved mother died of toxaemia when I was overseas studying,' he said lowering his head, 'my father did not even write to tell me – when I got back, he had a new wife.'

'Oh my,' Molly gasped. She lifted her cup but did not drink from it, instead she put it back into the saucer. 'Why did nobody write to tell you?'

'I always took mother's side when father had one of his many volatile explosions,' Cal answered. 'That was why he had me sent away to Canada, to continue my studies. I didn't hear from her after that.'

'You must have been devastated,' said Molly, and in his face, she could see the young man he once was and realised he was not as old as she thought he was.

'The doctor will confirm my layman's diagnosis,' Cal said, when he managed to steady his emotions. 'The rest we will leave to him up there.' He raised his eyes heavenwards and felt his heart lurch. And, not for the first time, he prayed his mother did not suffer.

'Will she be all right, Mam?' There was a tremor in Daisy's voice, and Molly shrugged her motherly shoulders, putting her arms around her daughter, watching Mr Everdine gently take another pillow from behind Mary Jane's head to raise her feet even higher.

'Will the boy be much longer? Do you think?' Cal asked, drawing back the newly starched net curtain and peering up the street.

'He'll be back any time,' Molly said. Then to ward off the heavy silence that had invaded the room, 'The doctor lives in one of those big villas in Merton Road.'

'I should have gone,' Cal said, as if talking to himself.

'He runs like the wind, our Dave.' The tension in the room was palpable, and Molly did not know what to say to this quiet man whose emotions, it seemed, ran deeper than the River Mersey.

'She will need round-the-clock care,' he whispered softly. 'I will hire a nurse.'

'If anybody is to look after her, it will be me,' Molly said with such conviction Cal Everdine dared not argue. Nevertheless, when Doctor Roberts arrived a short time later, he confirmed their suspicions. 'Toxaemia? Yes, I'm afraid it is.' He looked grave. 'It is not something I can cure. We have to let nature take its course.' He prodded Mary Jane's swollen hands and feet. Her face so bloated she was almost unrecognisable to the girl who moved into Beamer Street a few months back. When the parlour door opened, Molly scooped her youngest, Bridie, to her bosom. Holding her close, she ushered her into the kitchen with the promise of something nice to eat if she behaved herself and remained quiet while the doctor did what he had to do.

'What does he have to do?' Bridie's questioning eyes were wide.

Molly said she would tell her when she was older. When she returned to the parlour, Mr Everdine looked very repentant. Tears formed in Molly's eyes, and she gripped the doctor's arm, 'Is there nothing you can do?' Molly had never been so terrified. This young, energetic-spirited woman, so determined to succeed, was as helpless as a newborn babe. 'There's got to be something!' Molly cried, and her beseeching tone pricked the compassionate heart that drew Doctor Roberts into medicine in the first place.

'The only option is to bring the child into the world, otherwise we could lose both of them.' Gently shaking his head, he knew these women could be fine and healthy one minute, and the next they were stricken down with something, which modern medicine had not yet been able to find a cure for. 'She doesn't have the luxury of time to go to hospital. I will have to deliver the child here, before the convulsions start. Then all we can do is pray.' He moved quickly when Mary Jane's unseeing eyes fluttered open momentarily. 'There is no time to lose, we have to get her on the table!'

Cal was already moving the vase of flowers, pushing it into Molly's outstretched hands before dragging the heavy table from the window recess and placing it under the gas light in the centre of the room. Molly put the vase on the sideboard. Pulling open the cupboard door and taking out a pristine sheet, she covered the table. They moved quickly, quietly, each one battling their own thoughts.

'We must hurry,' Doctor Roberts broke the silence. 'She could fall into a coma.'

'Holy Mother of God.' Molly made the sign of the cross, managing to bite back the terror rising inside her, to whisper: 'Please spare them both!'

'A strong baby might survive at this stage,' Doctor Roberts said, working quickly to prepare the equipment he was going to need, 'but I have no choice, the placenta is failing and will give the child no more nutrients.'

Molly watched Mr Everdine lift Mary Jane and, as gently as a bouquet of spring flowers, he placed her onto the huge table. Doctor Roberts removed his coat and opened his black bag.

'Mary Jane is strong,' Molly said more in hope than expectation, 'but she's got the fight of her life to come.'

'Get me boiling water and plenty of clean sheets and towels,' Doctor Roberts ordered. When Molly turned to go and do his bidding, he stopped her. Holding her by the elbow, he said quietly, 'Let the girl do it.' He nodded, and Molly knew he wanted Daisy out of the room. 'You stay here and help me.'

'I'll go and help the young one.' Cal Everdine knew he would not be allowed to stay and headed for the door. 'I'll get some more coal for the fire,' Cal told Daisy, 'it's going to be a long night.'

'The coal is in the cellar,' Daisy said, and he picked up the scuttle and headed down the cellar steps. He had to keep busy. He had to stop the thoughts, which he had buried for years. The only way he knew how was to work.

Ripping and twisting pages of the local newspaper, he wove them expertly through cinders that still had some life in them. When he got the fire blazing in the black-leaded range in the kitchen, he continued to fill buckets and basins with water, lifting them onto the hot coals.

'The doctor's utensils must be sterilised, to lessen the threat of infection.' Cal said to Daisy.

Daisy, a sensible girl, nodded and bustled about the scullery, pouring salt into the receptacles, although she did not know why, only that she had seen her mother do it before bathing Davey's leg when he cut it. The water seemed to take forever to boil, and Mr Everdine looked anxious. There was something about him that made her feel sorry for him. He looked as nervous as if it was his own wife lying in the parlour, and not Mary Jane. When the water in the bucket was bubbling hot, Cal took it off the range and silently carried it to the passageway outside the parlour. Then, he knocked on the door with his foot, his hands full. When Molly opened it, he passed her the bucket, his heart thudding, his mouth dry. At thirty-three years old, the pain of losing his beloved mother and then his wife was still as raw as the day it happened.

A while later, they heard the parlour door open, and they looked expectantly towards Molly, who came bustling into the kitchen. Daisy raised quizzical eyebrows and Molly shook her head at the unspoken question. The child was not yet born.

And fetching another bowl of hot water, Molly disappeared back into the parlour.

Cal sat at the table, his head low, deep in thought. He had told Ellie he would do one final job on the mines. It would set them up for life, he had told her...

'I've never known this house so quiet,' Daisy said, pouring boiling water into the teapot. Making more tea. Trying to stay useful. The quiet man nodded, as if coming out of a deep sleep. He looked at the clock. Why did everything take so long?

'Thank you,' he whispered, his eyes dry and stinging when Daisy poured more tea into his cup. He didn't really want it, but good manners did not allow him to refuse her generosity. He ran his tongue across dry lips. He would have preferred something stronger.

Those days are over. The savage voice in his head rasped, knowing when he had left Canada, after the death of his wife and child, he drank his way through every American state into oblivion, until he reached New York City. He woke up one day in a place aptly named Hells Gate. It was as good a point as any to stop a while, having travelled his own personal hell for a few years.

The black filigree fingers on the clock crawled to six, and a bell chimed. Drowning out the incessant tick, tick, tick, which unsettled him. Suddenly, from the other room, they heard the sound of a newborn baby's outraged cry. Daisy and Cal jumped from their chairs and his throat tightened. When the parlour door opened some time later, he watched the young, wide-eyed girl hurry to her mother, who was carrying a bundle, and his heart leapt. A new life! But it wasn't the newborn, Molly had hold of.

'Steep these in boiling water, there's a good girl,' Molly asked, and Daisy took the blood-stained sheets that had earlier been pristine white while Molly placed a newspaper parcel onto the burning coals in the grate and she poked the fire until the flames curled around the afterbirth and devoured it.

Mary Jane had all the help she needed, none better, it seemed. However, her own body could prove to be her worst enemy right now.

'What did she have?' Cal asked.

'A girl,' Molly said proudly, 'safely delivered, she is healthy. Although small, she is quite a handful, and I have a suspicion she is a fighter, like her mother.'

Cal was pleased, although he couldn't think why. Little girls were a mystery with which he rarely had any dealings.

Molly noticed Mr Everdine showed no awkwardness at the remnants of childbirth, which would usually be kept from the men of the house in a situation like this, but not today.

'We've only got a bit of coal left,' Daisy sounded a little awkward, talking like this in front of Mr Everdine.'

'We'll sort something out,' Molly said, giving her daughter a gentle smile that also warned Daisy to say no more on the subject.

'How is Mary Jane?' Cal was desperate to know.

'She's holding her own,' Molly answered, 'but she's not in the clear yet.'

Cal knew without a shadow of doubt he had fallen in love with Mary Jane the moment he set eyes on her. Although this was the first time, he had dared to admit it, if only to himself. There was nothing he could do about his feelings for a married woman, albeit one who had been abandoned

'Let me sort out the coal situation,' Cal said. 'I will get a sack from over the road. We must keep everybody warm, especially the new mother and child.' He headed toward the door and before he left, he said, 'You will never go short again, I will make sure of it.'

He liked this family. Unbeknown to Molly, this was the house his stepmother had lived in before she married his father. He had not stepped inside this house for years and the ambience that had once been so chilly was now warm and welcoming. But was it warm enough for a newborn babe to thrive? He was going to do everything in his power to make sure Mary Jane and the child survived.

* * *

* * *

Molly gently held the precious newborn girl, while the doctor tended Mary Jane. The baby was a good weight and looked healthier than some full-term babes. If the strident cry was anything to go by, she was not only robust, but also hungry and demanding to be fed.

'Daisy,' Molly called from the parlour door, 'bring me Bridie's dolly!'

'What on earth does Mam want this for?' Daisy asked, as she scooped up the rag doll from the sofa Just as Cal Everdine came through the kitchen carrying a hundredweight sack of coal on his back.

'You should have emptied it down the coal hole on the front step,' Daisy said pragmatically, opening the cellar door, before hurrying to the parlour with the doll.

The house was in perpetual motion, Cal thought filling the brass coal scuttle with coal for later. This house needed a family like the Haywoods to bring it alive. Filled with plenty of laughter and chatter and bustle. Unlike times gone by, when, next door, there was hardly any noise beyond the ticking of the mantle clock to break the deep, suffocating silence that may interrupt his father's thoughts. And only when his father's peace was interrupted would there be noise. Angry, unholy noise that sent his mother scurrying to the furthest reaches of the house to hide and pray. That was not the case in this house, he noticed with a sigh of satisfaction. This place was like Lime Street station, someone coming or going, calling out, in one room and answering in another, singing, bickering. It was never still. And it was wonderful.

'Thanks, Daisy, I'll be out soon.' Molly popped her head around the parlour door and took the rag doll, before disappearing inside. Removing the doll's winceyette nighty, which had belonged to Bridie when she was a newborn, Molly was thankful she had washed the garment this morning. She dressed the baby in the nightie and then wrapped her in a shawl and held her expertly close to her own body for warmth.

'This'll do you for the time being,' she said in soothing tones, taking in the baby's flushed, shiny skin, which was made even redder by the forceful yell, so like Mary Jane in temperament. Stroking the baby's velvet cheek, it immediately turned its head, mouth open like a baby bird searching for food.

'I'd say that child needs a damn good feed,' Doctor Roberts said as he finished attending to Mary Jane, 'but I doubt this mother will have the strength to feed it.'

'I agree,' Molly said looking to Mary Jane who had not stirred once as her baby girl was delivered by caesarean section. 'Cry for your mammy.' Molly crooned, walking the length of the room. 'She'll be glad to hear you have a strong lust for life.' Molly prayed to the good Lord, and every saint she could think of to spare this spirited young woman. 'I could try some sugared water from a spoon,' Molly suggested. It had been a few years since she was feeding her youngest, and her own milk had long since dried up.

'She needs more than sugared water, by the sound of it,' said Doctor Roberts. 'We need to find a wet-nurse while this young mother gets plenty of rest and finds the strength in herself to survive.'

'If it is strength she needs, Mary Jane will find it,' Molly told him. Then, a thought struck her. Mary Jane would not be happy when she found out, but her child's only chance of survival was mother's milk. And the one person Molly knew who was capable of giving it was Ina King.

'Mary Jane will go scatty!' Daisy said when Molly told her what she intended to do.

'What choice do I have?' Molly held up her hands. 'I can't do it! That child must be given every chance.'

'Well, let's hope Ina's milk hasn't turned sour, because she would not give Mary Jane the time of day when she first moved into this street.' Daisy's pretty, bright-eyed features altered, and Molly could clearly see the loathing her eldest daughter had for the woman who had turned their back on Mary Jane. 'But you're right, Mam, we have no choice. I'll go and have a word with Ina King,' said Daisy

'Aye, and be quick about it, because this one has my fingertip swollen to twice the size. So, God help her mother.' A moment later, Daisy was knocking on Ina King's door across the cobbled road. When Ina came to the door, she had a couple of children hanging off her skirt and a babe-in-arms. Daisy explained the predicament, and for the first time she saw her neighbour's eyes soften. After rearing eight of her nine children, Ina still had enough milk in those overworked bosoms to feed the street, thought Daisy.

'I'll just put this one down and I'll be right over,' said Ina, already heading up the narrow lobby in her haste to catch up on all the details. The house, surprisingly clean, was swarming with children, Daisy noticed, and she headed back across the road to her own home. Moments later, Ina called up the hallway. 'Cooee, Molly, it's only me, shall I come in?'

'Well, you're not much use standing on the front step,' Molly called back. Ina was surprised to see the towering figure of Mr Everdine coming out. He raised his hat, leaving Ina open-mouthed and wondering what this man was doing in Molly Hayward's kitchen. But there was no use supposing, Molly would never tell.

* * *

'Just like her mother,' Molly's voice was as gentle as a summer breeze watching the child guzzling Ina King's milk 'This little'un knows what she wants.'

'If the agency had not sent that letter, Mary Jane—' Daisy's words were cut short when her mother put a finger to her lips, as the child lay contentedly in her arms. 'She would have had no need to hurry into town, though, Mam.'

The doctor left with the promise to return a little later, and Ina King had been pleasantly surprised when she was given a crisp ten-shilling note for her trouble. Not wasting a minute, to go and tell her brood the good news.

'He's given us the house rent-free,' Molly said in that pragmatic way she had about her, gazing at the sky through the starched net curtains. 'No more rent, Daisy. Can you imagine?'

* * *

Is she going to be all right, Doctor?' Cal asked. 'If she had not gone into town, would this still have happened?'

'I believe it would, old chap,' Doctor Roberts patted his shoulder, 'and you mustn't blame yourself.'

'I do blame myself,' Cal answered. 'She should never have been put in that situation, and even more so at such a time, which, as we know, can prove the most dangerous.' Doctor Roberts had been his mother's physician too.

'These things are more common than you think.' Doctor Roberts, sadly shaking his head, gazed at the ground. Toxaemia did not discriminate.

'I will call back first thing in the morning,' the doctor told Molly as Davey and Cal brought Mary Jane's bed downstairs.

'Try to get as much rest as you all can,' Doctor Roberts said. 'It might be a long haul. We will have to wait and see.'

'She'll have everything she needs, and more.' Molly, gathering a bowl of hot water and some soap, headed to the parlour. Even if Mary Jane were unconscious, she would want to be fresh and clean. Daisy brought in a clean nightdress from the laundry room near the back of the house. Nothing was a trouble to any of this family. The part of the room in which Mary Jane lay had been curtained off, to give her the privacy she needed. While Cal and Davey set up the bed, Daisy held the child.

'Right, give her some privacy while Daisy and I get Mary Jane into her own bed,' Molly said, ushering the two males from the room.

'Looks like we've outlived our usefulness,' Davey said with a grin, and from the other side of the parlour door, his mother answered.

'I heard that. Would you like to hold the child, while we see to her mother?' Molly asked, passing the baby to Cal, who gazed down at the child and felt a surge of something he had not felt before. This situation was beyond his comprehension. Never in his wildest dreams did he think he would be sitting in Molly Hayward's back room with a newborn baby in his arms. His blue eyes, full to overflowing, could not contain his delight when he stroked her velvet cheek, and her tiny hand gripped his little finger. *Is this what it feels like?* he wondered gazing at this little bundle of joy, who snook into his heart and filled his soul.

'This shock of golden hair might explain why she is such a fighter!' Cal Everdine's voice softened as the child nestled in his huge hands like the most precious, delicate flower he had ever seen, reminding him of something he hadn't heard since his mother was alive. 'She's here for the good. Her fight is for the good.'

28

'You have an accent I cannot put my finger on,' Molly said as Cal drank another of Daisy's never-ending cups of tea, reluctant to go back to his own lonely rooms above the empty shop. He made sure the eviction notice was settled and dismissed, never to be mentioned again and although it was getting late Molly invited him to stay for the rest of the evening. After all, it was Christmas Eve. Not the best time to be alone, she thought.

'I must have picked it up when I was in Canada,' Cal said.

'And what is it you do, apart from carting goods along the dock road?'

'I'm a qualified engineer and my last job was working on a new bridge over America's East River.' Cal, sitting around the table after supper, did not say why or how he came to be working on the bridge. The whole family listened attentively. Molly had never seen them so quiet. Even Davey was engrossed in their neighbour's story. 'I would have stayed until the bridge was finished, but war broke out, and I offered my services to my own country,' he told them, opening up about things he had never mentioned to another living soul. It felt good, he realised. 'I returned to Liverpool, signed up and joined the men fighting in Flanders.'

'Is that where you got that limp?' asked Bridie, like her mother, never one to leave a question hanging.

'Bridie!' Daisy was obviously scandalised her young sister was not only curious but had no compunction about asking the question – to which she and everybody else was dying to know the answer.

'Don't mind our Bridie, Mr Everdine?' Molly said with an indulgent smile, and he laughed, shaking his head, wondering why it had taken him so long to get to know this delightful family. As soon as he started to reminisce, it was as if the floodgates opened, and his words fell over each other in an effort to be free. They urged him to divulge the fact that his work touched every technological advance in the campaign, maintaining the railways, roads, water supply, bridges and transport.

'It was a few months short of the end of the war when we were clearing a minefield near no-man's land, my oppo put his best foot forward and was blown to smithereens and I was shot by a sniper, and my femur shattered.' The children's eyes were wide in amazement, as Cal tried not to sound like the war hero he most certainly had been, given a rare, but grateful chance to tell only the sterilised version of what really happened. Nobody needed to know the true details, so he made sure the children were spared the nightmare-triggering truth. 'I spent long months convalescing in London and was then moved to the First Western Hospital in Fazakerley.'

Molly's eyes widened now, too. 'My Albert was in there.' And as usual, when talking about her late husband, she made the sign of the cross and said, 'God rest his saintly soul, he went before I got to him.'

'Albert Haywood...?' Cal asked and Molly nodded, her eyes

full of hope. 'Train driver... Of course!' Cal slapped his forehead with the palm of his huge hand and Molly leaned forward, her eyes alight. He had never met the man, but he had overheard her telling Mary Jane about him, out on the step. Molly sounded so lost when she spoke of her one true love and how they never got to say a final goodbye, but now her eyes were dazzling, eager to know everything, gripping his arm and for a moment, Cal wondered if he had done the right thing?

'You knew him?' Molly asked. 'I missed him by minutes when they told me he was in the hospital. I went straight there, but he had already been taken.'

All the children looked to Cal expectantly. What could he do? He had to make his next words worthwhile. Something they could hold on to for the rest of their lives.

'We travelled in the same ambulance,' Cal fibbed, knowing it was what he called a white lie – one that was told for the good of others. 'He talked about his wonderful wife and family, all the way from France.' Cal wanted to give this deserving family some peace. 'Talking about his family gave him comfort, he said.'

'The family you tried to evict,' Molly, try as she might, could not resist the temptation, and Cal was relieved when he saw her ready smile spread across her motherly face.

'Indeed.' He felt lighter, more at peace with himself than he had done for many a long year. 'I can tell you one thing, though, Albert died a happy man. He knew you were coming to see him, telling me how proud he was to have a wife who was so loving, a wonderful cook, who kept a fine house and gave him four beautiful children.'

'Little Bridie was born two weeks later,' said Molly whose sums were never her strong point. If they had been, she would have realised that Mr Everdine could not possibly have been in the hospital when her husband died. But she was so enraptured by his news that Molly believed every word, and once he started to embroider the truth, Cal could not stop – for the first time in years, he felt he was doing some good.

'He told me what a good homemaker you were, and kind, you would never see anybody go without if you could help. Pride shone like sunshine from his eyes when he talked about you all.'

'He was such a good man, he really was.' Molly had a far-away look in her eyes and all the children nodded.

'He told me you were the only woman he had ever loved.' Cal fed her hungry expectations. 'You were the girl of his dreams, and he was the luckiest man in the world to have you as his wife.' He noticed a tinge of pink on Molly's cheeks.

'He always was a soppy ha'porth,' Molly smiled, as tears glistened in her eyes, lost in her own private thoughts, while Cal suspected she would sleep happy tonight, dreaming of her Albert. 'Mind you, he did have an eye for the ladies,' Molly said, laughing.

'But he picked the best of them, he told me.' Cal felt a warmth seep into his heart that had been long gone. 'When I got out of hospital, I took the rooms I now live in. I only wanted a bed, a yard and a stable to keep my horse. That's all I needed.'

'But how come you own most of Beamer Street?' Molly's words did not sound the least critical. 'You being a rover, I mean.'

'I made a lot of money while I was away in Canada. My father owned most of these properties, and I inherited the houses on this side of the street. When the opportunity arose to buy the housing stock on the other side of the street, it was as good a way as any of using some of the money I earned.'

'None better as far as I can see,' Molly said thoughtfully. 'People always need somewhere to live.'

'I put the properties into the hands of the agents, and then forgot about them,' Cal told Molly, who although keeping a respectable house and family, looked like a woman who was always wondering where the next meal was coming from. Yet she seemed content with her lot, while he was one of the richest men in the north-west and had nobody. Not one person was close enough to share his hopes and dreams. And the one person who had melted his heart over the last months was married to another man, and, as if he were to be dogged by ill-fortune all his days, she, too, had succumbed to near death.

'Did you ever marry, Mr Everdine?' Daisy, the optimistic romantic, knew she was being impertinent, judging by the censorious glimmer in her mother's eye.

'Please excuse our Daisy, Mr Everdine.' Molly said 'She is a good girl, but has a vivid imagination and a runaway tongue in her head.'

'I was married, yes,' Cal said, 'but my wife died.'

'I am so sorry to hear that,' Molly answered. 'I'm sure our Daisy didn't mean to upset you.'

'It was a long time ago, when I was in Canada. Daisy wasn't to know,' Cal said, trying to lighten the heavy atmosphere.

'Excuse us, we have to go and see to Mary Jane,' Molly said, as he and Daisy headed to the parlour.

'You lived in Canada?' Davey was enthralled. He had never been out of Liverpool for one single day in his whole life.

Cal nodded, automatically answering, yet talking as if to himself. 'Silver mining,' he said succinctly, 'it was an adventure and I loved it.'

'What stopped you?' Davey asked before his voice trailed away when Cal, lost in a world of his own, began to explain.

'It was called the Black Bear fire,' Cal told Davey. 'It was one of the most devastating forest fires in the Ontario Northland.' He was silent for a time, and Davey wondered if he had finished.

'The winter that year had been dry, bringing an early spring, which was followed by an abnormally hot, arid spell that lasted well into summer. Ideal conditions for a disaster. Yet, I ignored the small forest fires dotted here and there and insisted on leaving my expectant wife to go prospecting in the silver mines.'

Davey, transfixed by Cal's tale, wanted to ask so many questions, but he had heeded the warning look in his mother's eyes when Daisy was too inquisitive.

'A south-west gale whipped up some small bushfires that gained strength and engulfed the tinder-dry forest, razing everything in its path. Including the village where my young wife was waiting for me to return home.'

'I am sorry to hear that,' Davey's voice was low and respectful. 'I can't imagine anything worse.'

'Living with the guilt comes a close second,' Cal told him. 'I blame myself to this day. I should have been with her. But by the time I got back home, half the town had been destroyed. One hundred and fifty buildings lost. Over three thousand residents homeless.'

'No!' Davey felt heart sorry for the man who lived with his demons on a daily basis.

'I joined the firefighters, a race against time to dynamite buildings, create a firebreak.' But it was way too late for him to save his darling Ellie and their precious child. 'I'm sorry to burden you with this. You have enough to worry about right now.' Cal couldn't dwell on the events of yesteryear at a time like this.

When Molly came into the room, she looked worried, her face pale. 'She's beginning to stir a little, a bit befuddle.'

'Shall I go and fetch the doctor back?' Cal asked and Molly shook her head.

'There's nowt he can do tonight,' Molly answered. 'All we can do is keep an eye on her, and hope the crisis passes. I'll go back in. See if she's up to a cup of—'A low moan clipped the end from Molly's words, and they heard a feeble cry coming from the parlour. Molly rushed from the kitchen.

'Someone. Help me. Please!'

'Oh, please let her live,' Cal only realised he had spoken out loud when he saw Davey's raised eyebrows. He felt an overwhelming surge of protection towards a woman he barely knew. She had to live. She had to. He looked up when Molly entered the room, her whey-coloured pallor telling its own tale.

'Oh, Dear God!' she cried looking directly at Cal, before burying her face in her hands. 'She's gone blind!'

29

Cal Everdine did not sleep a wink all night. Tossing, turning, remembering, worrying. But, for the first time in ten years, he thought of Ellie without hating himself, knowing it had taken too long to realise there was nothing he could have done. Getting up from his bed, he could not spend another moment living in his own head. He waited impatiently until he saw the curtains open in Molly's parlour and could not get over the road fast enough. Desperate to know if Mary Jane was any better. Although, one thing relieved the anxiety he felt. At least the curtains had been opened. That would never have happened if, God forbid, Mary Jane had not survived the night. Knocking on Molly's door, he prayed history would not repeat itself and his bad luck had run out. But he did not believe in luck. Good or bad. He believed in hard work, and the sheer determination to thrive. For what? For whom? Waiting for the door to be answered, Cal prayed Mary Jane was strong enough to recover, knowing she, too, believed in the power to succeed.

'Come in,' Molly said. 'You look a bit rough if you don't mind me speaking plainly.'

'How are they?' Cal asked, his face grave, his voice low, 'Can she see?'

Molly shook her head, in anticipation of more questions she put her finger to her lips, leading the way to the kitchen. 'Aye,' she sighed, eventually, 'the child had a good night, she's thriving, a little fighter like her mother. Although Mary Jane was restless. She must be so worried. Not being able to see her baby. Although she managed with our help to put her to the breast.'

'I've been so worried, Molly,' Cal answered, 'but I didn't want to come over too early and disturb everyone.' She told him the two youngest had been up since the crack of dawn to open their stocking at the end of the bed, and Cal realised it was Christmas Day.

Molly bustled about the kitchen. Scooping a large ladle of porridge into a clean bowl, she put it front of him on the table. 'Add milk and sugar if it's to your taste, you look like you could do with a good start to the day.' She silently urged the youngest two from the table sensing Mr Everdine wanted to talk. 'Go and play with your toy soldiers, Freddy, and you can put that new outfit on your dolly, Bridie.' Not having much money, Molly had knitted a whole wardrobe of clothes for Bridie's rag doll from scraps of wool she managed to glean.

When the kitchen was empty save for the two of them, Molly studied his face closely, he was worldly-wise but as helpless as a newborn foal. If she did not know any better, she would say Mr Everdine had fallen hook, line, and sinker for the new mother.

'Mary Jane will be fine,' Molly assured him as he looked away, uneasy under her piercing scrutiny. 'She's stronger than she looks.'

'She has a child to live for,' Cal agreed as the snow began to fall and the children raced outside to play. Molly wondered if she dare tell him what Ina King had told her last night. Apparently, Red wasn't her husband after all. Mary Jane had never been married. Her husband-to-be had been killed in a terrible accident, that had something to do with Mary Jane's brothers.

30

NEW YEAR'S EVE 1921

'Don't rub them, Mary Jane,' Molly said when she saw her friend massage her eyes with her knuckles.

'I can still smell Christmas,' Mary Jane said, on the eve of 1922, as the delicious smell of oranges and apples filled the parlour with their seasonal scent, she closed her unseeing eyes, taking in the sounds of excited whispers. The Hayward family were busily preparing for tomorrow, the first day of the New Year, in the knowledge that they would always have a roof over their head. 'Did you know you can smell snow?' Mary Jane said as she listened to the sound of busy people around her. A couple of times she imagined she saw shadows, and another time she saw a rainbow of colours over by the window, but maybe it was her imagination playing tricks on her. There were a few things she had come to appreciate that she had never noticed when she could see. She could distinguish who was in the room even when they didn't speak. Their tread on the floor, the way they breathed, their smell. Molly with the smell of talcum powder, Mansion polish and goose grease. Daisy with her lavender water. Even Cal, who had his own individual smell of leather and carbolic soap, and although he didn't always speak, Mary Jane knew the moment he was in the room. Sometimes she could hear him cooing to her beautiful baby daughter who had the most intoxicating smell of all and. Mary Jane could not get enough of it.

Mary Jane thought she was dreaming when that first rainbow of colours filled the room.. Then, slowly, very slowly over the course of the day, the shapes become clearer, she could see the end of the bed and her bedclothes moving when she stretched her legs.

But what filled her with the greatest joy, was the sight of her freshly washed baby girl, hidden under layers of lace covers, sleeping contentedly in a fancy swinging crib beside her bed which at this time she didn't realise had been made by Cal Everdine. Leaning to one side, Mary Jane blinked. This could not be a dream. This was real. She was seeing her daughter for the first time.

'Molly,' Mary Jane whispered as calmly as she could, for fear of her vision disappearing, 'I do like your new apron.'

'Oh, thank you, our Davey bought it me for...' Molly stopped and the silence in the room was almost palpable. '... what colour is it?'

'If I'm not dreaming, it is covered in blue and yellow flowers and has red bias binding around the edges. Am I right?' There was a moment's silence and then pandemonium erupted when Molly called out of the parlour door.

'She can see! Mary Jane can see!'

'Here, let me get her for you,' Molly said, lifting the sleeping child and Mary Jane's heart surged when her eyes took in long dark lashes resting on brand-new, peach perfect, cheeks.

'She's more beautiful than I ever imagined,' Mary Jane

whispered, gently stroking her daughter's face, gazing in wonder at this miracle of human gorgeousness, all soft and warm and smelling of something wonderful.

'That's baby soap and special talcum powder. Mr Everdine brought it over in a fancy box, I've never seen anything like it. He said it will keep her nice and fresh.'

'Did he?' Mary Jane asked, smiling. 'Well, it's not covering up something in her nappy, fancy soaps and powders or no.' Mary Jane marvelled at her daughter's tiny fingers curling around her own. Those teeny fingernails, so flawless, looked like they had been perfectly manicured. The child jumped. Her tiny fingers suddenly outstretched. 'Did I startle you?' Mary Jane whispered, gently brushing her lips against the little girl's velvet complexion. 'I'm so sorry, my darling.' A moment later, the tiny bundle of loveliness opened her navy-blue eyes. Her intense gaze focusing on her mother.

'Look how content she is. She knows you already, Mary Jane.' Molly cooed, knowing this was the moment Mary Jane had been waiting for, to hold her child while seeing her for the first time. 'She knows instinctively, she is in the presence of a mother who will always love her, and care for her, for the rest of her days. If you can bear to let me,' said Molly, 'I'll take her from you and change her.' Molly quickly changed the child and placed her back in her Mary Jane's arms.

'She does know me.' Mary Jane's voice was full of wonder. 'Is it possible I have brought someone so precious into the world?'

'Of course,' Molly said, gazing at the growing bond between mother and child, 'she's been listening to you prattle on for the last nine months.'

'Do I detect a tear in your voice, Molly?' Mary Jane asked, straightening the sheet.

'Only happy ones, Mary Jane.' Molly smiled as a single tear rolled down her cheek.

Mary Jane sighed. 'I'll have to buy her a new layette, some more nappies, vests, nightdresses. She'll need—'

'Nothing,' Molly interrupted, turning now to face Mary Jane. 'She has everything she could possibly want. Every neighbour has brought something; they've been so kind – even Ina King.' Molly opened the dressing-table drawer filled with all manner of baby clothes. 'Even her next door knitted a cardigan – it's got no buttonholes, mind. But we can always add a nice ribbon.'

Mary Jane laughed, she had never felt so happy as she did on this snow-covered morning, knowing she would always associate the fresh fragrance of talcum powder with the day she saw her baby daughter for the first time.

'Oh Molly, the flowers are lovely. They must have cost a fortune at this time of year.' Inhaling deeply, she saw the vase full of roses on the table. 'You shouldn't go spending your money on me.'

'Not me,' Molly smiled and shook her head. Then in a low voice, full of suggestion, she said, 'Mr Everdine brings them every day.' She looked a bit sheepish now. 'And that's not all.' Molly disappeared out to the lobby, and when she returned, proud as you like, she was wheeling a brand-new coach-built perambulator. 'It came this morning by special delivery!'

Mary Jane looked at the maroon and cream-coloured coach-built frame, its swirling embellishments, its high arched silver handle, and its spring-suspension wheels. It was a beauty all right. 'Won't I look the bee's knees,' Mary Jane said, her voice suddenly flat as her flinty emerald eyes took in the baby carriage. 'And won't it make walking the streets a lot easier when *himself* evicts us from this house!'

'Oh Mary Jane, I forgot to tell you, because you were so poorly,' Molly interrupted. 'Mr. Everdine is not evicting us!'

'He's not?' Mary Jane asked, and for the first time since she had collapsed in Cal's arms, she began to think straight.

'Don't excite yourself,' Molly tutted like the good friend she had always been to Mary Jane. 'I don't want you getting sick again.' She went on to tell her the conversation with Cal on the day the baby was born, not leaving out one single detail. Mary Jane was speechless, but very pleased for Molly who would never have to worry about paying rent ever again.

'That must have cost a fortune,' she said, unable to drag her admiring gaze from the pram. 'Top of the range.' She remembered telling him that she only wanted the best for her baby, but she did not expect this from Cal. She did not expect anything from him. 'The shop!' Mary Jane's heart sank as she suddenly remembered the business she had worked so hard to make a success. 'How long have I been ill?'

'Daisy has been keeping it going for you while you were confined to bed. She's done a grand job.' Molly sat on the chair at the foot of Mary Jane's bed, looking as proud as any mother could.

'That is so good of her,' Mary Jane breathed. 'I will make sure she is rewarded for her work.'

'Everybody has pulled together: Daisy has been making bread and pies – although she still has a way to go before, she's as good as you – our Davey has been delivering them and even little Bridie and Freddy have been helping out too.'

'And Mr Everdine?' Mary Jane asked. Surely, he wanted the rent paid on the shop.

'He's been very good.' Molly's voice was tender, like a mother explaining something good to a child, giving Mary Jane cause to wonder if Molly had a motherly soft spot for Cal Everdine. The same man who had almost brought them to the door of penury. She opened her mouth to protest when Molly raised her hand and stopped her. 'Now listen to me, Mary Jane,' Molly said patiently, her pallor returning to its rosy glow, 'we are not being evicted – Mr Everdine said we can stay, and what's more, as I have already told you, for as long as we do stay, we will not have to pay any more rent.'

'Well now, isn't that good of him?' Sarcasm laced Mary Jane's words as she tried desperately to ignore hearing any good of Mr Everdine. Molly and her family could relax, because they did not deserve what they had been put through. Although Mary Jane knew she was desperately trying to deny the truth, even to herself. Molly's burden had been her doing. Not Cal Everdine's. She was the one who should be trying to make amends.

'I'm sorry. I've been the one who caused you so much pain, by cajoling you into letting me bake the pies in the first place, and as soon as I'm on my feet properly, I will be out of your way.' Bringing up a child single-handedly and earning enough money to live on was going to be hard, but she was determined to do it. She could take her daughter into the shop during the day while she worked, but that would not give her much time to look for somewhere to live. So, the sooner she was out of this bed and back on her feet, the better.

'You'll do no such thing,' Molly said. 'You will recover properly now you have a new baby to support.'

'I have to find somewhere for me and the child to live, Molly. I doubt Mr Everdine would allow you to have a lodger.'

'I haven't got a lodger,' Molly said, her brows pleating, 'I have a loving family and we have just had a beautiful addition, in need of love and care from her whole family.'

'Oh, Molly, what would I ever do without you?'

'You could give this beautiful baby girl a name for a start,' Molly said, and Mary Jane gazed at the little bundle in her arms.

'Seeing as she was born at Christmas time, I am going to call her Hollie.'

'Perfect,' said the older woman.

31

LIVERPOOL - FEBRUARY 1922

'Mary Jane, there were men.' The child came running up the street towards her as she came back from the suppliers. 'They broke down Cissie Stone's front door!'

'Hush your tongue, Bridie Haywood,' Molly called as she emerged from the throng of gathered women and pushed her daughter none too gently towards their house. 'They come looking for Red,' Molly told Mary Jane in a low voice, gathering the rest of her brood, and urging them towards their own front door. 'Inside, Bridie, while I have a talk with Mary Jane.' However, her explanation was curtailed when Bridie began to cry.

'Will those men come back and get us, Mam? Will they knock our door down?'

'No, love,' Molly soothed the child. 'They won't be knocking any more doors down. Father Flanagan will see to that.' Everybody in Beamer Street knew the parish priest had as much authority as the local constabulary, and a lot more fearful respect.

Mary Jane knew the street was even more alive than usual with excited chatter, with every housewife discussing the event in great detail, while even Cissie Stone was holding court on her step.

'They must have been eight feet tall!' Cissie told anyone who would listen. 'Built like brick outhouses—'

'Cissie, that's the third time you've told the tale and each time you've added a little more.' Molly interrupted the excitable woman, who was playing to her neighbours, clearly enjoying her moment in the spotlight. 'Gertie,' Molly said, rolling her eyes to a neighbour. 'Will you take her inside and make her a nice cup of hot sweet tea, she's had a terrible shock.'

'I most certainly have,' Cissie said, ignoring Molly's irony, 'because everybody knows you don't have to die to meet the divil. Those fellas had murder in their eyes!'

'Shut your noise, Cissie,' Molly called over her shoulder as she led the way to her own house.

'Me? Shut me noise?' Cissie glared indignantly at Mary Jane. 'I have every reason to shout when it's *herself* they came looking for.'

Every sinew in Mary Jane's body was as taut as piano strings. Surely her brothers hadn't discovered where she lived.

'Take no notice, love,' Molly said, gently edging Mary Jane towards the house.

'I knew they had something to do with her, the minute I set eyes on them,' Cissie sneered. 'It's the colouring, the same dark auburn hair, the flinty look in their eyes.'

'If you've nothing better to do, Cissie Stone,' Molly called, 'go and wash your nets, they're a disgrace.'

Daisy, having witnessed the commotion from Mary Jane's shop, followed them inside, moving her younger sister and brother up the narrow passage by clapping her hands, like she was scattering farmyard chickens.

'There's something I need to ask you.' Molly quietly closed the front door behind her, unheard of around these parts, where people opened their front door as soon as they rose in the morning and didn't shut it again until they were on their way to bed, last thing at night. Leading the way into the parlour, Mary Jane suspected her time in Beamer Street had come to an end. She felt she had outstayed her welcome, having brought nothing but bad luck to Molly and her family; it was time she moved on. She could not expect the neighbours to bear the brunt of her brothers' rage. They must be fighting mad to knock Cissie' Stone's door down. She burned with humiliation, dreading this day since she first came here. Her dirty laundry would be aired for all to judge her. As far as people around here were concerned, she was married to Red.

'I am so sorry, Molly,' Mary Jane could hardly speak the words. So consumed with guilt, she felt ill. Molly sat in the easy chair on the other side of the unlit fireplace, which looked as desolate as Mary Jane felt. When Daisy brought in the tea, Mary Jane doubted she could raise the cup.

'I'll get back to the shop,' Daisy said. 'If people don't get their bread, there'll be skin and hair flying.'

'Thanks, Daisy,' said Mary Jane. When Daisy closed the parlour door behind her, Molly turned to Mary Jane, her usually cheerful expression strained.

'Those men... Are they your brothers?' Molly asked, knowing the girl could do without all this fuss only a couple of months after having her baby and being so unwell. She did not want to sound harsh because there were many out there who would jump at the chance to do the girl down.

Mary Jane nodded; her baby daughter fast asleep in her crib beside the unlit fire.

'I guessed as much,' Molly could see the fear in Mary Jane's eyes and wanted to reassure her.

'Molly, I am sorry. You have been so good to me; you gave me a roof over my head when nobody else would...' her voice began to crack... 'You and your family have become my dearest friends, you are the mother I lost when I was young, and you don't deserve to be put in this position. I don't blame you one jot for wanting me out of here, I've brought you nothing but trouble.'

'Why would I want you out of here?' Molly asked, stirring her tea.

'Those men are my brothers, and they are looking for me.'

'But Cissie said they were asking for Red; they didn't mention you at all.' Molly was quiet for a moment and Mary Jane was puzzled.

'Why would they be looking for Red?'

Guilt flooded her veins and Mary Jane was sure her next words would signal the end of their valuable friendship. She had been happy here. Happier than she had ever been in her life. This was a contented family home and she had brought shame and trouble to the door.

'Red and me...' Mary Jane sat on the edge of the chair, her shoulders hunched, unable to find the words. 'Me and Red, we're...'

'Not married?' Molly said quietly so her voice did not carry beyond the parlour door. She continued: 'Don't you think I know that already? I've known it since I set eyes on you that night, when you were leaning against Cissie's front door.' Molly's words were barely a whisper. 'You were looking for a way out, even then.' Molly didn't tell Mary Jane that Ina knew and would have heard it from Cissie as this wasn't the right time.

'Why did you take me in if you knew?'

'I suspected you had a bit more about you than to take up with the likes of him, out drinking until all hours, playing pitch and toss on the corner of the street.' She sipped her tea. 'I did wonder what the connection was, but it wasn't my place to ask.'

'That's not like you, Moll,' Mary Jane made a stab at humour and gave a tight smile.

'I suppose you're right, girl, but I felt that sorry for you. You looked shell-shocked, reminding me of the look in men's eyes when they came back from the war. Done in. Not much left in the pot to give.'

'And you let me waffle on about Red?' Mary Jane's eyes filled with tears. Not usually one to give in to self-pity, she couldn't help herself. Her throat tightened.

'You never did waffle on about Red – in fact, you rarely mentioned him, leading me to believe my first instincts were true. Even when you had young Hollie, you still didn't talk about him, or wonder what he would think of his beautiful daughter. You didn't even try to get word to him that she had been born.'

'That's the last thing I would do,' Mary Jane said, knowing her beloved daughter would never know Red if she could possibly prevent it.

'I thought you had a bit more nous than to marry an eejit like him, you've got a wise head.'

'Too much to succumb to his shallow charm,' Mary Jane answered. 'Unlike her next door.' Mary Jane's ready smile was strained as she jerked her head to the wall adjoining Cissie Stone's house and Molly laughed.

'She'll have anything in trousers. Even the parish priest looks worried when he calls in to her.'

'I think it's time you heard the whole story.' For the first time since she had left Ireland, Mary Jane felt she could unburden herself. Although, what Molly would think of her after she had told her everything, she had no idea. All she did know was that she could not hold on to her terrible secret any longer. Molly listened while Mary Jane told her the entire sorry tale, which confirmed Molly's suspicions that Red was running away from something and using Mary Jane as a foil for his underhand dealings. Molly knew the news would come as a shock when she told Mary Jane her brothers had informed everybody in Beamer Street, when the authorities caught up with Red, he would hang by the neck until he was dead.

'I don't understand.' Mary Jane was almost too afraid to voice her foolish question. 'Does that mean Red killed his own brother?'

'That's what I took it to mean,' Molly answered. 'They said Red was a murderer and when they got their hands on him, he was going straight to the nearest bridewell – if he survived his injuries.'

'Jesus, Mary and Joseph!' Mary Jane made the sign of the cross, as she always did in times of crisis. 'I can hardly believe it.' Mary Jane was having trouble taking in this latest information. 'Red and Paddy were half of each other, where one went, the other followed. Red was devastated when Paddy was attacked...' However, now she thought about it, Red rarely mentioned his twin brother. In the same way she never mentioned Red. What on earth was Cal going to make of this? He and Molly were Hollie's godparents! Mary Jane was sure, when word got to him, he would never speak to her again. The disturbing notion filled her thoughts more than what her brothers would do when they found out she'd had a child out of wedlock.

32

LIVERPOOL - JUNE 1922

Taking a key from his pocket, Cal slipped it into the lock and opened the door at the top of the stairs. Impatiently, he slammed it with his heel and flung his coat on the hook, glad to be rid of it. His long stride covering the floor in no time, he went to lift up the long sash windows to let some air in the place. When he came back after work, the emptiness of the flat enveloped him as the spring days were quickly rolling into summer. There had been no rain for weeks and even though it had turned seven, the sun was still shining, and the street below was teeming with children. The pram he had bought for Hollie was parked under Molly Hayward's parlour window, the sash pulled up so Mary Jane could lean out and talk to her daughter, who, in her sun bonnet, was sitting up, the hood of the pram well down, enjoying the sight and sounds of street life.

Cal sighed loudly. For the first time in years, he felt restless, and the reason he felt that way was the woman across the cobbled street who was cooing to her daughter. When he heard that Mary Jane was not a married woman, he did not feel disgust for her, nor did he feel the open hostility that some showed. No. He could never feel anything but an unstinting admiration for the way she picked herself up and fought on, as if the very thing that knocked her down had done so to inject even more strength into her. He could not have felt happier, knowing she had no kind of relationship with that reprobate, who, when finally caught, would pay for his wicked deeds.

After his nightly bath, Cal felt cooler but not for long. The air was stifling for want of rainfall. Leaning against the window casement, his arm resting against the wall, he pushed back a mane of thick black hair with slender fingers and smiled when he saw Mary Jane coming out of the house. Pushing the carriage across the bumpy cobbles like Boadicea leading a charge. Her russet hair held in a loose chignon at the nape of her neck. Her head high and proud. Nothing fazed her, he thought. She was magnificent. Fearless and energetic. A balm to his raging self-doubt, if she did but know it.

She positioned the carriage at the double gates below, flicking the brake with the side of her foot before looking up. 'Well then,' she said in that direct way she had about her, 'are you going to let me in, or shall I stand here all night like a mad thing?'

Who would have thought, the day he saw her on the pier, she was going to change his life forever? Her easy-going friendship had woken something inside him he thought long dead, and he could not imagine being unable to see her for just one day. Mary Jane could so easily have died, and the knowledge caused him such pain he winced. Two precious lives at risk. He was never going to make that mistake again.

Mary Jane listened for the familiar tread on the stairs, believing, with a bit of tender care, Mr Everdine could show those handsome features.

'D'you think you're getting slower in your old age, Mr Everdine,' she quipped, as he came out and immediately unclipped the reins that held baby Hollie securely in her pram.

'Come here, you little beauty,' he said, delighted Mary Jane had brought his goddaughter to see him. Something she did regularly. 'Come and see what your uncle Cal has for you?'

'You spoil her,' Mary Jane laughed, enjoying the special bond. Whenever her daughter saw him, her face lit up.

'How many times,' he said with a hint of exasperation. 'I am not spoiling her; I am showing her how much I love her.' His eyes locked into Mary Jane's and for a moment there was nobody else in the world, just them. Beneath that coal-coloured mane, there were a pair of the most exquisite indigo blue eyes, she had ever seen, which spoke volumes even when he said nothing.

'Cal,' she said, drifting towards him like a welcome breeze, her whispered words wrapped in smooth silk. If she asked him for the world, he would give it to her.

'Hmm?' he asked. not daring to speak as the child in his arms wrapped tiny fingers in the small curls hanging around his face.

'There is something I have to do, and I won't take no for an answer.' She nodded to the door and without a word they stepped inside and closed it. Cal led the way, intrigued. He never quite knew what Mary Jane was up to at any one time.

Once upstairs, she took the child from his arms and put her on the new sofa and surrounded her with cushions. Then, she sat him on a straight-backed chair, wrapped an old curtain around his shoulders and took a pair of scissors from her basket. 'Let's see what's under this great mane, shall we.' Mary Jane ignored his feeble attempt to resist her attention and brought out a comb from her bag. 'We might even find your old school cap,' she laughed, and he sat there, silently, while she cut his hair and trimmed his beard.

'I'll look like a mountain goat,' he laughed, enjoying the feel of her fingers as they deftly worked their way around his head and face. When she finished, she nodded to the mirror over the fireplace and he stood up, shook the hair from his shirt and looked in the mirror.

Startled at what she saw, Mary Jane realised that before his hair was shorn, he looked quite handsome, but now, when she could see his face properly, she knew it was a face she wanted to look at for the rest of her days.

'You've done a good job,' he smiled. 'I might have to keep you.'

'You only have to ask,' Mary Jane said, feeling brazen for even thinking such a thing.

Turning to face her, Cal took her in his arms, and he said, 'Mary Jane Starling, will you be my barber forever?'

'I will,' she answered, unable to keep the smile from her face.

'And Mary Jane, will you marry me?'

'Oh no!' she cried, pulling herself from his embrace. 'Hollie's eating your hair!'

Before she could get to her daughter, Cal, scooping her up, ran into the next room and washed her face, her hands and gently wiped them dry.

'You are a natural,' Mary Jane told him, and Cal beamed, she had paid him the ultimate tribute, if she did but know it.

'So,' he asked as they stood in his bathroom and six-month-old Hollie stroked his clean-shaven face, 'do you like your daddy clean-shaven?' He knew his statement would provoke a gasp of surprise from Mary Jane, and he was righ.t

'Of course, I will marry you,' Mary Jane answered, 'but I will not give up the shop.'

'That is good news,' said Cal. 'I worried you might want to become a lady of leisure, which is fine by me, but I am sure there would be a riot if you stopped baking.'

'I'm going to ask Daisy if she would like to become my partner,' Mary Jane said, brushing up the mound of hair while Cal entertained Hollie. 'Molly will look after Hollie for me and—'

'You haven't given it much thought, then?' He interrupted as they both laughed. Mary Jane had never been so happy. However, the laughter died when there was a loud knock on the downstairs door. 'Go away,' Cal said in that lazy drawl that sent her senses reeling. 'I haven't even kissed her yet.' Nevertheless, the knocking continued, and Cal had no choice but to go and answer the door.

Mary Jane hugged her daughter to her and twirled around the room, she had never known happiness like it. But as the door opened, she froze when she saw her three brothers standing in the same room and her blood turned to ice. She knew they were here back in February looking for Red, but they did not mention her.

She asked around to find out where they were staying but when she plucked up the courage to go and see them at their lodgings in Reckoner's Row, they had already caught the boat back home.

'We're not here to cause trouble, Mary Jane,' said Aiden, the eldest, while Bly and Colm looked on, their best hats in their hands. 'We have come to tell you that Redfern got what was coming to him—'

'You didn't!?' Mary Jane could not bring herself to voice the fact her brothers were men who saved lives, not took them. In unison, they shook their heads and Aiden spoke again.

'An accident, but rumour has it Dinny O'Mara did the honours.' He looked down to his highly polished shoes, 'Finding out that Red took his own brother's life was the last straw for Dinny, Paddy's best friend. Red owed Dinny a fortune, on the strength of his brother's friendship, Dinny went to find him. Apparently, Red was already dead when he found him at the foot of Abel Mountain.'

33

LIVERPOOL - JUNE 1923

Mrs Everdine stood next to her husband as the new sign went up over the shop door.

MARY JANE'S KITCHEN
BREAD, PIES, AND CAKES, ENJOYED BY KINGS!

'D'you think Ina King will ever cotton on?' Mary Jane asked Cal, enjoying the feel of his strong hand around her thickening waist, and he laughed, something he did all the time these days.

'Mary Jane you are... what is it Molly calls you – a case! But you are my case, and I adore you.'

'I adore you too, Cal,' she said with a twinkle in her absinthe-coloured eyes that had lured him in the first place. 'And when this little one is born, we may have to think of moving to a bigger house.' She had chosen the furniture and Cal had decorated the flat above the shop, and were so happy there. They had told each other their innermost secrets, leaving nothing out.

'Did you know Cissie Stone's house is up for sale?' Cal asked Mary Jane and she nodded, holding her breath, sure she could imagine what he was about to say. 'I bought it,' he said, 'it is going to be our family home, a happy home full of love, laughter and children who will exorcize the ghosts of the past.'

'How many children?' Mary Jane asked longing to bring the place back to its original grandeur.

'About a dozen.' Cal laughed when he saw the look of mock horror on her beautiful face.

'Really?' Mary Jane asked. 'Do you think I should give birth to this one, before we think of expanding.' She had never known such happiness, celebrating that perfect day when Cal Everdine walked into a Liverpool teashop and bought her a cup of tea... and a custard tart.

ABOUT THE AUTHOR

Sheila Riley wrote four #1 bestselling novels under the pseudonym Annie Groves and is now writing the second of two saga trilogies under her own name. She has set her series around the River Mersey and its docklands near to where she spent her early years.

Visit Sheila's website: http://my-writing-ladder.blogspot.com/

Follow Sheila on social media:

- facebook.com/SheilaRileyAuthor
- twitter.com/1sheilariley
- instagram.com/sheilarileynovelist
- bookbub.com/authors/sheila-riley

ALSO BY SHEILA RILEY

Reckoner's Row Series

The Mersey Orphan

The Mersey Girls

The Mersey Mothers

Beamer Street Series

Finding Friends on Beamer Street

The Dockside Sagas

The Mersey Mistress

The Mersey Angels